Lewis Carroll 著

吳鈞陶 譯

ALICE'S ADVENTURES IN WONDERLAND

愛麗絲夢遊仙境

書　　名：*Alice's Adventures in Wonderland* 愛麗絲夢遊仙境

作　　者：Lewis Carroll

插　　圖：John Tenniel

譯　　者：吳鈞陶

責任編輯：黃家麗　　王朴真

封面設計：張　毅

出　　版：商務印書館 (香港) 有限公司

　　　　　香港筲箕灣耀興道 3 號東滙廣場 8 樓

　　　　　http://www.commercialpress.com.hk

發　　行：香港聯合書刊物流有限公司

　　　　　香港新界大埔汀麗路 36 號中華商務印刷大廈 3 字樓

印　　刷：中華商務彩色印刷有限公司

　　　　　香港新界大埔汀麗路 36 號中華商務印刷大廈

版　　次：2016 年 3 月第 1 版第 2 次印刷

　　　　　© 2013 商務印書館 (香港) 有限公司

　　　　　ISBN 978 962 07 0351 5

　　　　　Printed in Hong Kong

Publisher's Note 出版説明

　　快樂只在於無憂無慮，還是像快樂王子一樣關心他人？夢境與現實縱橫交錯，愛麗絲夢醒之後，仍是天真無邪，卻已有對現實的感悟。童話字字璣珠，更啟發對人生的思考。

　　使用本書時，先閱讀英文原文，如遇到理解障礙，則參照中譯作為輔助。如有餘力，可在閱讀原文部分段落後，查閱相應中譯，觀察同樣詞句在雙語中不同的表達，從而體會如何用優美達意的中文表達英語文學中的深意。

　　文字優美，寓意深刻，啟迪智慧，是為特點，能為初、中級英語程度的讀者提供經典的文學，更帶來對生活的啓發。

商務印書館 (香港) 有限公司

編輯出版部

Contents　目錄

Preface to the Chinese Translation
中文譯本序

三年前從英國回來度假時，給兩歲的姪女小木頭買了五本一套《愛麗絲漫遊仙境》，英國的兒童書出得總是很漂亮，因為是準備着給孩子抓摸撕咬的，所以是厚厚的消毒紙板，每本書沒有幾頁，也沒有多少文字，畫卻很好看。

很久以前，有一個小女孩叫愛麗絲，有一天，她和她的姐姐一起去河邊，躺在草地上，她突然看見一隻兔子走過來，起初她不覺得奇怪，草地上是經常會有兔子的，但奇怪的是那隻兔子掏出懷錶看了看時間，小女孩覺得好奇，便跟着兔子往前走，一頭便掉到兔子洞中去了。

小木頭將信將疑，但還是問，後來呢？

她掉到兔子洞後又發生了許多奇怪的事，碰到許多奇怪的人，最後她在河岸上醒過來，才發現自己是在做夢。

書是英語的，我離開上海回到英國後，家中不再有人讀給她聽。心想這兔子洞的故事，是很容易被她淡忘的。這次回來，看到那本一匣的小書絲毫沒有被打入冷宮的跡象，它們已大大盡了職責，硬紙片的邊角都已很磨損了，圖畫倒仍清晰。

還記得那個掉到兔子洞裏的小女孩嗎？

小孩怎麼會掉到兔子洞裏去？姑媽你還在胡說八道。五歲的小孩，已學會了懷疑一切。你看看，她把最後一本打開，翻到我的鼻子下面，這個小女孩在河邊睡覺，她正在做夢呢。

小木頭說得很自信，都說現在的孩子整天看電視，都被成人文化薰陶得像大人，果不其然。但是慢着，小木頭仍在將着五本小書翻來翻去，並沒有因胡說八道而失去興趣。看着看着，她突然如夢初醒，其實，她還是很危險的，如果她不從夢中醒來，她不就一直呆在兔子洞了麼？

孩子總是孩子，即使是被成人文化培養成了小大人般的孩子，他們總是會出其不意說出些讓你頗能有些咀嚼的孩子話。反過來，也有大人總是像孩子，喜歡與孩子為伴，我們或稱之為老頑童，或稱之為童心未泯。有些童心並不是壞事，老頑童也能很可愛，但如果未泯的童心過濫而變矯情，繼而成為一種工具，對孩子的喜歡變成一種不能割捨的癡迷與迷戀，那就會變得可悲，讓人懷疑這顆未泯的童心不純潔，人們禁不住要發問，為甚麼？

例如，《愛麗絲漫遊仙境》的作者，路易斯‧卡羅爾（Lewis Carroll），便是這樣一位在童心夢中永遠不醒，近來常常讓人有所疑問的人。

卡羅爾向來是個雙重性格的人。據說當年維多利亞女王讀了《愛麗絲》後非常喜歡，立即命令她手下前去搜羅這個故事高手的其他作品，沒想到帶回來的卻是厚厚幾本艱澀難讀的數學著作，署名是道基森（Charles Lutwidge Dodgson）。女王勃然大怒，幾乎將手下斬首，最後才不得不相信，這位著作甚豐的牛津大學數學教授，確實另有名分，也是童話故事高手。

卡羅爾本人對這個故事未予評論，對他來說，數學教授是他冠冕堂皇的正式身份，童話作家是他的愛好，是他的隱私，是他從不願與成人分享的秘密。一八九七年，在他去世的前一年，卡羅爾還是非常堅決地要把他的雙重身份分開。對於那些寫信給道基森詢問卡羅爾作品的人，他準備了一封退信書：

> 許多陌生人毫無道理地認為道基森先生是那些根本沒在他的名下出版的書的作者，他覺得有必要對所有類似的聲稱作個說明。他與任何化名及不在他名下出版的書籍都無關聯，所以他在此沒有必要保留或閱讀你們寄來的任何信函，故而將寫錯地址的尊函原封退還。

卡羅爾的父親是一位牧師，也是一位數學家。他一向希望兒子能步自己後塵，而且卡羅爾自幼也確實在數學上頗有天賦。他尊重父命進入牛津，一方面往數學及教堂方面發展，但終因說話結巴而放棄進入教堂的設想，另一方面，他也始終沒有放棄在文學及藝術上的追求，一八五六年二十五歲的他開始用卡羅爾的名字發表詩作，建立了他的另一個世界。直到他六十六歲時去世，他創作了許多童話。能夠進入這個虛構世界，認識到作為卡羅爾的他的，只有那些可愛的十來歲的小女孩。

愛麗絲的靈感，便來自於這樣一個小女孩，她的名字叫作愛麗絲‧立德爾。卡羅爾第一次講述愛麗絲的故事，是在一八六二年七月四日。若干年後，卡羅爾回憶起那天：

我依然清晰地記得，那天，我絞盡腦汁想講一個新童話給孩子們聽，就這樣把我的女主人公送進了一個兔子洞中，我絲毫不知道下一步會發生甚麼。自那以後，許多年過去了，但那個金色的下午，在我的腦海裏仍如昨天一樣——上是無雲的藍天，下是如鏡的河水，小舟漫自飄浮，來回懶懶盪着的雙槳偶爾濺起幾點水滴，那三張小臉，帶着期待，如飢似渴地注視着那個童話世界中下一步將發生甚麼。

　　卡羅爾與立家相識於一八五六年，立父是卡羅爾執教的學院新來的院長，他們初次見面是在二月，在前往觀看牛津划船比賽的火車上，正式結識是兩個月後，卡羅爾當時剛開始對攝影大感興趣，他與一個朋友拍攝一家教堂，正巧立氏一家在那裏，他邀請愛麗絲三姐妹做他照片中的小模特。這次拍攝並不成功，因為這三個孩子無法安安靜靜聽從安排，但是他與立家孩子的交往卻就此有了基礎。他為他們全家拍照，講故事給孩子們聽聽。但是早在當年秋天，立太太便對卡羅爾與立家孩子的交往抱着謹慎的態度，她覺得照片拍得太多了。"這好像是暗示我我對他們家的侵犯太久了。"卡羅爾在他的日記中這樣一來寫道。幸而在那個冬天，立氏夫婦遠在國外，照顧三個孩子的家庭教師對卡羅爾偏愛有加，她允許卡羅爾自由出入立家大院。立氏夫婦回來後，卡羅爾去他們家的次數減少，但夏日裏仍能一年四五次帶這三個孩子盪舟在牛津附近的泰晤士河上。於是，幾年以後，便有了那個金色的下午，便有了文壇上的這篇不朽之作。

　　第二個夏天，《愛麗絲漫遊仙境》書稿將成，卡羅爾又帶着一群女孩前去遊河，下午三點，其他人都坐馬車上了歸途，卡羅爾帶着立氏三姐妹坐火車回家。卡羅爾在日記中稱此次旅程心情舒暢，特別是旅程的結尾更是十分愉快。第二天，卡羅爾請求立母將三個孩子送去讓他拍照，立母沒有答應，而且至此以後立母便禁止卡羅爾與她的女兒們有任何交往。究竟事出何因，無人知曉。

卡羅爾向來有記日記的習慣，從一八五三年他在牛津的三年級開始，到一八九七年聖誕節他去世前三個星期，卡羅爾從沒間斷過寫日記，總共有十三卷。在他去世後一年，他的姪子根據這些日記出版了第一本《卡羅爾傳》，但是在當時，還沒有人意識到道基森在文學史上的地位有多重要，沒有人再去注意這堆日記，十三本筆記都去向不明。若干年後，人們在一個地窖的硬紙箱中重新見到它們，四本已經丟失，其中兩冊正是他與立德爾一家交往的最關鍵時期。現在的傳記作家做能依據的，只有他第一本傳記中所引用的段落。卡羅爾與立家交往六年，除了丟失的日記之外，最後立母絕交這天的日記也被人撕去，而且此地無銀三百兩，在前一頁的最後，不知是誰的筆跡，寫道日記本此處沒有缺漏。這一撕一辯就造就了文學史上的一個千古疑團。一般最順理成章的猜測便是卡羅爾對立氏三姐妹圖謀不軌，被立母察覺，特別是那個"十分愉快"的旅程的結尾到底發生了甚麼，成了立家與卡羅爾絕交的關鍵。

立家的女孩們自始至終沒有對那天發生的事作過評論或解釋，她們漸漸長大成人，都以她們的美麗及修養而著稱，不再是卡羅爾所喜歡的小女孩們。愛麗絲後與維多利亞的四王子相愛，但終因她出身平民未能成婚。《漫遊仙境》成為經典讀物，她們不再與卡羅爾有任何接觸，這一段公案漸漸被人遺忘，直到近幾年，政治正確的流行讓人們的言談舉止越來越小心翼翼，這段公案才頻頻引起傳記作家的興趣，按照女權童權的諸種觀點，卡羅爾對年幼少女的迷戀非但是極為政治不正確的，簡直就是變態。但在他的有生之年，人們的警惕性及政治正確的覺悟還沒有那麼高，他便也從未缺少過十來歲的小女孩做他的攝影模特和朋友。卡羅爾的世界，是作為作家的他與這些小女孩們共同擁有的世界，這些小女孩，或是他學院同事的孩子，或是許多劇團的小演員們，也有一些，是他自己在火車或沙灘上結識的。這些小女孩雖然沒有任何一個超過愛麗絲三姐妹所給他的靈感，但卻是他整個生活的精神寄託所在，他的無數書信都證明了這一點。

卡羅爾向來愛寫信，從二十九歲到去世，他總共寫了十萬多封信，他曾說，"人是寫信的動物。"在他晚年，他曾發表過一篇關於寫信的短文，論述了他自己寫信的十二條原則。第一條是書寫清晰，最後一條更妙："當你去郵局寄信時，千萬要拿在手中，如果放在口袋裏，根據我的經驗，你會在鄉村道路上來回走，兩次路過郵局，回到家中後才發現信仍然在你的口袋裏。"卡羅爾的信寫給親朋好友，新舊相識，報刊雜誌，更寫給他生活中不能缺少的小朋友們。他寫給成年人的信向來署他的真名，只有在給小女朋友們寫信時，他才署筆名。這兩類信的文體文風也截然不同，前者正式刻板，後者生動活潑，有趣有情。為了讓他的小讀者高興，卡羅爾想辦法變換風格，有的信是圖文並茂，或以圖代文，有的是鏡中之信，文字反寫而成，需從鏡中閱讀才能讀懂，還有些信是他以童話中人物之名義寫成，因為是精靈之信，故而字跡極小，須在放大鏡下才能讀。信的內容往往像講故事，有許多逗趣，調侃，信口開河，胡說八道的成分，其想像力及文風筆調絲毫不遜於他那寫發表了的童話，讓人絕對不能相信寫信的也是個著作甚豐的大學教授。

例如有這樣一封寫給他的小朋友的信：

親愛的孩子：

　　現在天氣太熱了，我虛弱得幾乎無法握住筆，即使我能握住筆，筆中也沒有墨水。墨水都蒸發成了黑色的氣，在屋內亂飛，把牆壁和房頂都染得模模糊糊。今天涼快了一些，有些又變成了黑雪回到墨水瓶中。很快，我就能有足夠的墨水給你寫信，也能預定那些你媽媽想要的照片了。

　　這樣熱的天氣讓我很傷感鬱悶，有時候我真想發脾氣。例如，牛津主教剛剛來看我，他可是一片好心，但我一見他來，怒氣頓發，抓起一本書便向他扔去，而且把他打成重傷。嗯，事實並不是這樣，所以你不要相信我，記住，下一次可不要這麼急急忙忙相信人。為甚麼呢？因為如果你總是相信別人，你腦子中的相信肌肉就會累死了，你也就虛弱得連最簡單的事實都無法相信了。就是在上個星期，我的一個朋友想要相信傑克巨人殺手，他花了好大工夫相信了，但他也累死了。所以，當我告訴他外面正在下雨時，他不相信我。沒有帶雨傘，也沒有戴帽子就衝了出去，有一綹鬈髮過了兩天才恢復到原來的形狀。嗯，對不起，這裏面有一些也不全是真的⋯⋯

有時，他也以真身向他的小朋友們評價自己："我的一個朋友讓我帶信給你，他叫卡羅爾，這個人很奇怪而且太喜歡胡説八道。"許多時候，這種信口開河的胡説八道會在他與小朋友間往返好幾次，漸漸一個故事便舒展開來，人們能在他的書信中看到他童話的影子，例如《鏡中奇遇記》裏的那隻貓：

　　　你又問起那三隻貓，牠們真可愛！自從上次信中告訴你牠們半夜到我這裏，牠們就沒有離開過我！那天我外出散步，牠們把我的書都從書架上取下來，攤在地上，這樣一來我回來時就可以讀了。而且牠們把每本書都翻到第五十頁，牠們覺得從這頁開始讀最合適。不幸的是，牠們把我的一瓶膠水拿出來，把一些畫黏到屋頂上，可能牠們覺得我會很喜歡，但牠們一疏忽，膠水打翻了，都倒在了書上。所以當牠們把書合起來放好時，書頁都黏在一起，我就永遠讀不到第五十頁了。

　　　不管怎樣，牠們的心還是好的，所以我並不生氣，為了獎賞牠們，我送給牠們每隻一勺墨水喝，但牠們好像並不感激我，紛紛做着怪臉，但因為是禮物，牠們也無法拒絕，只得喝了，牠們中有一隻原來是白貓，現在當然變成黑貓了。

卡羅爾的信件大都以取樂他的小朋友為重，雖不乏非正統觀念的內容，例如他在信中多次勸孩子不要輕易相信別人，但總體來説，並沒有甚麼歹念。信中自然也常常有感情的流露，大多數並不過份：

請把我的愛分給你們所碰到的所有孩子，另外我也寄上兩個半吻，由你分給你們四個，注意，可得分得均勻喲！

　　但仍有些信讓人讀來不太舒服，例如一八七七年，四十六歲的他寫過這樣一封信給一位在沙灘上碰到的不知名的小女孩：

　　　　噢，孩子孩子，昨天下午我信守了諾言，來到海邊，這樣一來可以與你一起在岩石間散步，但我卻看到你與另一個男士在一起。我想你可能暫時還不需要我，所以我走開了一會，等我回來時，就再也找不到你了。我在岩石間找啊找的，看到一個穿粉色衣服的孩子特別像你，但我走近之後才知道不是你。可憐的孩子，她不是你，這也不是她的錯呀！我幫她建造沙堡，然後回了家。我一路上都在哭。

　　卡羅爾對小女孩的興趣除了為她們寫信寫故事外，他的另一主要興趣是拍她們的照片，他讓她們穿上各種不同的服飾，扮作吉普賽人、印度人、希臘人、中國人等等，做出許多不同的姿態。他從他的小朋友們中選擇童話中的模特，為她們畫素描，作為童話插圖的底稿，供插圖作家們參考。

　　卡羅爾的夢想也許是這些小朋友們最好都不要長大。一八八零年二月他給另外一個小朋友寫的信中配了一幅畫，畫中的小女孩的腿和頭都已長出了畫面之外，信中說等到下次他們見面時，這個小女孩可能已長得太高，他已無法為她拍出美麗的照片了，"如果你能控制自己的話，求求你不要再長高了。"

然而孩子們總會長大，小女孩都漸漸變成了少女，就像愛麗絲終究會醒來。卡羅爾創作了愛麗絲，他知道離開童話世界不是易事。你們甚麼都不是，只是一幅撲克牌。愛麗絲有勇氣對着耀武揚威的女王及武士們這樣說。

　　整副撲克牌便騰空而起，再紛紛飄落到她身上來。她發出短短一聲尖叫，半是驚恐，半是憤怒，同時試圖把那些撲克牌趕開，卻發現自己正睡在河岸邊，頭正枕在她姐姐的腿上，她姐姐正在把從樹上紛紛飄落的一些枯葉輕輕撣開。

　　看着身邊的小女孩們一個個長大，一個個將她們送離童話故事童話書，又吸引着一個個的新女孩到來，卡羅爾卻一直沒有勇氣告訴他自己童話只是一場夢，總該有夢醒時分。真實生活裏的道基森很快被人遺忘了，那個夢中未醒的卡羅爾卻永遠流傳了下來，無論褒貶，成了永恆。

　　卡羅爾一直未婚。

愷蒂

All in the golden afternoon
    Full leisurely we glide;
For both our oars, with little skill,
    By little arms are plied,
While little hands make vain pretence
    Our wanderings to guide.

Ah, cruel Three! In such an hour,
    Beneath such dreamy weather,
To beg a tale of breath too weak
    To stir the tiniest feather!
Yet what can one poor voice avail
    Against three tongues together?

Imperious Prima flashes forth
    Her edict 'to begin it':
In gentler tones Secunda hopes
    'There will be nonsense in it!'
While Tertia interrupts the tale
    Not *more* than once a minute.

Anon, to sudden silence won,
    In fancy they pursue
The dream-child moving through a land
    Of wonders wild and new,
In friendly chat with bird or beast—
    And half believe it true.

And ever, as the story drained
    The wells of fancy dry,
And faintly strove that weary one
    To put the subject by,
'The rest next time—' 'It *is* next time!'
    The happy voices cry

Thus grew the tale of Wonderland:
    Thus slowly, one by one,
Its quaint events were hammered out—
    And now the tale is done,
And home we steer, a merry crew,
    Beneath the setting sun.

Alice! A childish story take,
    And, with a gentle hand,
Lay it where Childhood's dreams are twined
    In Memory's mystic band,
Like pilgrim's wither'd wreath of flowers
    Pluck'd in a far-off land.

Chapter I

Down the Rabbit-hole

A lice was beginning to get very tired of sitting by her sister on the bank, and of having nothing to do: once or twice she had peeped into the book her sister was reading, but it had no pictures or conversations in it, 'and what is the use of a book,' thought Alice, 'without pictures or conversations?'

So she was considering, in her own mind (as well as she could, for the hot day made her feel very sleepy and stupid), whether the pleasure of making a daisy-chain would be worth the trouble of getting up and picking the daisies, when suddenly a White Rabbit with pink eyes ran close by her.

There was nothing so very remarkable in that; nor did Alice think it so very much out of the way to hear the Rabbit say to itself 'Oh dear! Oh dear! I shall be too late!' (when she thought it over afterwards, it occurred to her that she ought to have wondered at this, but at the time it all seemed quite natural); but, when the Rabbit actually *took a watch out of its waistcoat-pocket*, and looked at it, and then hurried on, Alice started to her feet, for it flashed across her mind that she had never before seen a rabbit with either a waistcoat-pocket, or a watch to take out of it, and, burning with curiosity; she ran across the field after it, and was just in time to see it pop down a large rabbit-hole under the hedge.

In another moment down went Alice after it, never once considering how in the world she was to get out again.

The rabbit-hole went straight on like a tunnel for some way, and then dipped suddenly down, so suddenly that Alice had not a moment to think about stopping herself before she found herself falling down what seemed to be a very deep well.

Either the well was very deep, or she fell very slowly, for she had plenty of time as she went down to look about her, and to wonder what was going to happen next. First, she tried to look down and make out what she was coming to, but it was too dark to see anything: then she looked at the sides of the well, and noticed that they were filled with cupboards and bookshelves: here and there she saw maps and pictures hung upon pegs. She took down a jar from one of the shelves as she passed: it was labeled 'ORANGE MARMALADE,' but to her great disappointment it was empty: she did not like to drop the jar, for fear of killing somebody underneath, so managed to put it into one of the cupboards as she fell past it.

'Well!' thought Alice to herself. 'After such a fall as this, I shall think nothing of tumbling downstairs! How brave they'll all think me at home! Why, I wouldn't say anything about it, even if I fell off the top of the house!' (Which was very likely true.)

Down, down, down. Would the fall *never* come to an end? 'I wonder how many miles I've fallen by this time?' she said aloud. 'I must be getting somewhere near the centre of the earth. Let me see: that would be four thousand miles down, I think—' (for, you see, Alice had learnt several things of this sort in her lessons in the school-room, and though this was not a very good opportunity for showing off her knowledge, as there was no one to listen to her, still it was good practice to say it over) '—yes, that's about the right distance—but then I wonder what Latitude or Longitude I've got to?' (Alice had not the slightest idea what Latitude was, or Longitude either, but she thought they were nice grand words to say.)

Presently she began again. 'I wonder if I shall fall right *through* the earth! How funny it'll seem to come out among the people that walk with their heads downwards! The antipathies, I think—' (she was rather glad there was no one listening, this time, as it didn't sound at all the right word) '—but I shall have to ask them what the name of the country is, you know. Please, Ma'am, is this New Zealand? Or Australia?' (and she tried to curtsey as she spoke— fancy, *curtseying* as you're falling through the air! Do you think you could manage it?) 'And what an ignorant little girl she'll think me for asking! No, it'll never do to ask: perhaps I shall see it written up somewhere.'

Down, down, down. There was nothing else to do, so Alice soon began talking again. 'Dinah'll miss me very much tonight, I should think!' (Dinah was the cat.) 'I hope they'll remember her saucer of milk at tea-time. Dinah, my dear! I wish you were down here with me! There are no mice in the air, I'm afraid, but you might catch a bat, and that's very like a mouse, you know But do cats eat bats, I wonder?' And here Alice began to get rather sleepy, and went on saying to herself, in a dreamy sort of way, 'Do cats eat bats? Do cats eat bats?' and sometimes 'Do bats eat cats?', for, you see, as she couldn't answer either question, it didn't much matter which way she put it. She felt that she was dozing off, and had just begun to dream that she was walking hand in hand with Dinah, and was saying to her, very earnestly, 'Now, Dinah, tell me the truth: did you ever eat a bat?', when suddenly, thump! thump! down she came upon a heap of sticks and dry leaves, and the fall was over.

Alice was not a bit hurt, and she jumped up on to her feet in a moment: she looked up, but it was all dark overhead: before her was another long passage, and the White Rabbit was still in sight, hurrying down it. There was not a moment to be lost: away went Alice like the wind, and was just in time to hear it say, as it turned a corner, 'Oh my ears and whiskers, how late it's getting!' She was close behind it when she turned the corner, but the Rabbit was no longer to be seen: she found herself in a long, low hall, which was lit up by a row of lamps hanging from the roof.

There were doors all round the hall, but they were all locked; and when Alice had been all the way down one side and up the other, trying every door, she walked sadly down the middle, wondering how she was ever to get out again.

Suddenly she came upon a little three-legged table, all made of solid glass: there was nothing on it but a tiny golden key, and Alice's first idea was that this might belong to one of the doors of the hall; but, alas! either the locks were too large, or the key was too small, but at any rate it would not open any of them. However, on the second time round, she came upon a low curtain she had not noticed before, and behind it was a little door about fifteen inches high: she tried the little golden key in the lock, and to her great delight it fitted!

Alice opened the door and found that it led into a small passage, not much larger than a rat-hole: she knelt down and looked along the passage into the loveliest garden you ever saw. How she longed to get out of that dark hall, and wander about among those beds of bright flowers and those cool fountains, but she could not even get her head through the doorway; 'and even if my head *would* go through,' thought poor Alice, 'it would be of very little use without my shoulders. Oh, how I wish I could shut up like a telescope! I think I could, if I only knew how to begin.' For, you see, so many out-of-the-way things had happened lately, that Alice had begun to think that very few things indeed were really impossible.

There seemed to be no use in waiting by the little door, so she went back to the table, half hoping she might find another key on it, or at any rate a book of rules for shutting people up like telescopes: this time she found a little bottle on it ('which certainly was not here before,' said Alice), and tied round the neck of the bottle was a paper label, with the words 'DRINK ME' beautifully printed on it in large letters.

It was all very well to say 'Drink me,' but the wise little Alice was not going to do *that* in a hurry. 'No, I'll look first,' she said, 'and see whether it's marked "*poison*" or not'; for she had read several nice little stories about children who had got burnt, and eaten up by wild beasts, and other unpleasant things, all because they *would* not remember the simple rules their friends had taught them: such as, that a red-hot poker will burn you if you hold it too long; and that, if you cut your finger very deeply with a knife, it usually bleeds; and she had never forgotten that, if you drink much from a bottle marked 'poison,' it is almost certain to disagree with you, sooner or later.

However, this bottle was *not* marked 'poison,' so Alice ventured to taste it, and, finding it very nice (it had, in fact, a sort of mixed flavour of cherry-tart, custard, pineapple, roast turkey, toffy, and hot buttered toast), she very soon finished it off.

'What a curious feeling!' said Alice. 'I must be shutting up like a telescope.'

And so it was indeed: she was now only ten inches high, and her face brightened up at the thought that she was now the right size for going through the little door into that lovely garden. First, however, she waited for a few minutes to see if she was going to shrink any further: she felt a little nervous about this; 'for it might end, you know,' said Alice to herself, 'in my going out altogether, like a candle. I wonder what I should be like then?' And she tried to fancy what the flame of a candle looks like after the candle is blown out, for she could not remember ever having seen such a thing.

After a while, finding that nothing more happened, she decided on going into the garden at once; but, alas for poor Alice! when she got to the door, she found she had forgotten the little golden key, and when she went back to the table for it, she found she could not possibly reach it: she could see it quite plainly through the glass, and she tried her best to climb up one of the legs of the table, but it was too slippery; and when she had tired herself out with trying, the poor little thing sat down and cried.

'Come, there's no use in crying like that!' said Alice to herself rather sharply. 'I advise you to leave off this minute!' She generally gave herself very good advice (though she very seldom followed it), and sometimes she scolded herself so severely as to bring tears into her eyes; and once she remembered trying to box her own ears for having cheated herself in a game of croquet she was playing against herself, for this curious child was very fond of pretending to be two people. 'But it's no use now,' thought poor Alice, 'to pretend to be two people! Why, there's hardly enough of me left to make *one* respectable person!'

Soon her eye fell on a little glass box that was lying under the table: she opened it, and found in it a very small cake, on which the words 'EAT ME' were beautifully marked in currants. 'Well, I'll eat it,' said Alice, 'and if it makes me grow larger, I can reach the key; and if it makes me grow smaller, I can creep under the door: so either way I'll get into the garden, and I don't care which happens!'

She ate a little bit, and said anxiously to herself 'Which way? Which way?', holding her hand on the top of her head to feel which way it was growing; and she was quite surprised to find that she remained the same size. To be sure, this is what generally happens when one eats cake; but Alice had got so much into the way of expecting nothing but out-of-the-way things to happen, that it seemed quite dull and stupid for life to go on in the common way.

So she set to work, and very soon finished off the cake.

Chapter II

The Pool of Tears

'Curiouser and curiouser!'
cried Alice (she was so much
surprised, that for the moment
she quite forgot how to speak
good English). 'Now I'm opening
out like the largest telescope that
ever was! Goodbye, feet!' (for
when she looked down at her feet,
they seemed to be almost out of
sight, they were getting so far off).
'Oh, my poor little feet, I wonder
who will put on your shoes and
stockings for you now, dears? I'm
sure I shan't be able! I shall be a
great deal too far off to trouble
myself about you: you must
manage the best way you can—but
I must be kind to them,' thought

Alice, 'or perhaps they won't walk the way I want to go! Let me see. I'll give them a new pair of boots every Christmas.'

And she went on planning to herself how she would manage it. 'They must go by the carrier,' she thought; 'and how funny it'll seem, sending presents to one's own feet! And how odd the directions will look!

> *Alice's Right Foot, Esq.*
> *Hearthrug,*
> > *near the Fender*
> > *(with Alice's love).*

Oh dear, what nonsense I'm talking!'

Just at this moment her head struck against the roof of the hall: in fact she was now rather more than nine feet high, and she at once took up the little golden key and hurried off to the garden door.

Poor Alice! It was as much as she could do, lying down on one side, to look through into the garden with one eye; but to get through was more hopeless than ever: she sat down and began to cry again.

'You ought to be ashamed of yourself,' said Alice, 'a great girl like you,' (she might well say this), 'to go on crying in this way! Stop this moment, I tell you!' But she went on all the same, shedding gallons of tears, until there was a large pool all round her, about four inches deep, and reaching half down the hall.

After a time she heard a little pattering of feet in the distance, and she hastily dried her eyes to see what was coming. It was the White Rabbit returning, splendidly dressed, with a pair of white kid-gloves in one hand and a large fan in the other: he came trotting along in a great hurry, muttering to himself, as he came, 'Oh! The Duchess, the Duchess! Oh! *Won't* she be savage if I've kept her waiting!' Alice felt so desperate that she was ready to ask help of any one: so, when the Rabbit came near her, she began, in a low, timid voice, 'If you please, Sir—' The Rabbit started violently, dropped the white kid-gloves and the fan, and skurried away into the darkness as hard as he could go.

Alice took up the fan and gloves, and, as the hall was very hot, she kept fanning herself all the time she went on talking. 'Dear,

dear! How queer everything is today! And yesterday things went on just as usual. I wonder if I've been changed in the night? Let me think: was I the same when I got up this morning? I almost think I can remember feeling a little different. But if I'm not the same, the next question is 'Who in the world am I?' Ah, *that's* the great puzzle!' And she began thinking over all the children she knew that were of the same age as herself, to see if she could have been changed for any of them.

'I'm sure I'm not Ada,' she said, 'for her hair goes in such long ringlets, and mine doesn't go in ringlets at all; and I'm sure I can't be Mabel, for I know all sorts of things, and she, oh, she knows such a very little! Besides, she's she, and I'm I, and—oh dear, how puzzling it all is! I'll try if I know all the things I used to know. Let me see: four times five is twelve, and four times six is thirteen, and four times seven is—oh dear! I shall never get to twenty at that rate! However, the Multiplication-Table doesn't signify: let's try Geography. London is the capital of Paris, and Paris is the capital of Rome, and Rome—no, that's all wrong, I'm certain! I must have been changed for Mabel! I'll try and say "How doth the little—",' and she crossed her hands on her lap, as if she were saying lessons, and began to repeat it, but her voice sounded hoarse and strange, and the words did not come the same as they used to do:—

> 'How doth the little crocodile
> Improve his shining tail,
> And pour the waters of the Nile
> On every golden scale!'

'How cheerfully he seems to grin,
How neatly spreads his claws,
And welcomes little fishes in,
With gently smiling jaws!'

'I'm sure those are not the right words,' said poor Alice, and her eyes filled with tears again as she went on, 'I must be Mabel after all, and I shall have to go and live in that poky little house, and have next to no toys to play with, and oh, ever so many lessons to learn! No, I've made up my mind about it: if I'm Mabel, I'll stay down here! It'll be no use their putting their heads down and saying 'Come up again, dear!' I shall only look up and say 'Who am I, then? Tell me that first, and then, if I like being that person, I'll come up: if not, I'll stay down here till I'm somebody else'—but, oh dear!' cried Alice, with a sudden burst of tears, 'I do wish they *would* put their heads down! I am so very tired of being all alone here!'

As she said this she looked down at her hands, and was surprised to see that she had put on one of the Rabbit's little white kid-gloves while she was talking. 'How can I have done that?' she thought. 'I must be growing small again.' She got up and went to the table to measure herself by it, and found that, as nearly as she could guess, she was now about two feet high, and was going on shrinking rapidly: she soon found out that the cause of this was the fan she was holding, and she dropped it hastily, just in time to save herself from shrinking away altogether.

'That *was* a narrow escape!' said Alice, a good deal frightened at the sudden change, but very glad to find herself still in existence. 'And now for the garden!' And she ran with all speed back to the

little door; but, alas! the little door was shut again, and the little golden key was lying on the glass table as before, 'and things are worse than ever,' thought the poor child, 'for I never was so small as this before, never! And I declare it's too bad, that it is!'

As she said these words her foot slipped, and in another moment, splash! she was up to her chin in salt-water. Her first idea was that she had somehow fallen into the sea, 'and in that case I can go back by railway,' she said to herself. (Alice had been to the seaside once in her life, and had come to the general conclusion that, wherever you go to on the English coast, you find a number of bathing-machines in the sea, some children digging in the sand with wooden spades, then a row of lodging-houses, and behind them a railway-station.) However, she soon made out that she was in the pool of tears which she had wept when she was nine feet high.

'I wish I hadn't cried so much!' said Alice, as she swam about, trying to find her way out. 'I shall be punished for it now, I suppose, by being drowned in my own tears! That will be a queer thing, to be sure! However, everything is queer today.'

Just then she heard something splashing about in the pool a little way off, and she swam nearer to make out what it was: at first she thought it must be a walrus or hippopotamus, but then she remembered how small she was now, and she soon made out that it was only a mouse, that had slipped in like herself.

'Would it be of any use, now,' thought Alice, 'to speak to this mouse? Everything is so out-of-the-way down here, that I should think very likely it can talk: at any rate, there's no harm in trying.' So she began: 'O Mouse, do you know the way out of this pool? I am very tired of swimming about here, O Mouse!' (Alice thought this must be the right way of speaking to a mouse: she had never done such a thing before, but she remembered having seen, in her brother's Latin Grammar, 'A mouse—of a mouse—to a mouse— a mouse—O mouse!) The mouse looked at her rather inquisitively, and seemed to her to wink with one of its little eyes, but it said nothing.

'Perhaps it doesn't understand English,' thought Alice. 'I daresay it's a French mouse, come over with William the Conqueror.' (For, with all her knowledge of history, Alice had no very clear notion how long ago anything had happened.) So she began again: 'Où est ma chatte?', which was the first sentence in her French lesson-book. The Mouse gave a sudden leap out of the water, and seemed to quiver all over with fright. 'Oh, I beg your pardon!' cried Alice hastily, afraid that she had hurt the poor animal's feelings. 'I quite forgot you didn't like cats.'

'Not like cats!' cried the Mouse in a shrill, passionate voice.

'Would you like cats, if you were me?'

'Well, perhaps not,' said Alice in a soothing tone: 'don't be angry about it. And yet I wish I could show you our cat Dinah. I think you'd take a fancy to cats, if you could only see her. She is such a dear quiet thing,' Alice went on, half to herself, as she swam lazily about in the pool, 'and she sits purring so nicely by the fire, licking her paws and washing her face—and she is such a nice soft thing to nurse—and she's such a capital one for catching mice—oh, I beg your pardon!' cried Alice again, for this time the Mouse was bristling all over, and she felt certain it must be really offended. 'We won't talk about her any more, if you'd rather not.'

'We, indeed!' cried the Mouse, who was trembling down to the end of its tail. 'As if I would talk on such a subject! Our family always *hated* cats: nasty, low, vulgar things! Don't let me hear the name again!'

'I won't indeed!' said Alice, in a great hurry to change the subject of conversation. 'Are you—are you fond—of—of dogs?' The Mouse did not answer, so Alice went on eagerly: 'There is such a nice little dog, near our house, I should like to show you! A little bright-eyed terrier, you know, with oh, such long curly brown hair! And it'll fetch things when you throw them, and it'll sit up and beg for its dinner, and all sorts of things—I can't remember half of them—and it belongs to a farmer, you know, and he says it's so useful, it's worth a hundred pounds! He says it kills all the rats and—oh dear!' cried Alice in a sorrowful tone. 'I'm afraid I've offended it again!' For the Mouse was swimming away from her as hard as it could go, and making quite a commotion in the pool as it went.

So she called softly after it, 'Mouse dear! Do come back again, and we won't talk about cats, or dogs either, if you don't like them!' When the Mouse heard this, it turned round and swam slowly back to her: its face was quite pale (with passion, Alice thought), and it said, in a low trembling voice, 'Let us get to the shore, and then I'll tell you my history, and you'll understand why it is I hate cats and dogs.'

It was high time to go, for the pool was getting quite crowded with the birds and animals that had fallen into it: there was a Duck and a Dodo, a Lory and an Eaglet, and several other curious creatures. Alice led the way, and the whole party swam to the shore.

Chapter III

A Caucus-race and a Long Tale

They were indeed a queer-looking party that assembled on the bank—the birds with draggled feathers, the animals with their fur clinging close to them, and all dripping wet, cross, and uncomfortable.

The first question of course was, how to get dry again: they had a consultation about this, and after a few minutes it seemed quite natural to Alice to find herself talking familiarly with them, as if she had known them all her life. Indeed, she had quite a long argument with the Lory, who at last turned sulky, and would only say 'I'm older than you, and must know better.' And this Alice would not allow, without knowing how old it was, and, as the Lory positively refused to tell its age, there was no more to be said.

At last the Mouse, who seemed to be a person of some authority among them, called out 'Sit down, all of you, and listen to me! I'll soon make you dry enough!' They all sat down at once, in a large ring, with the Mouse in the middle. Alice kept her eyes anxiously fixed on it, for she felt sure she would catch a bad cold if she did not get dry very soon.

'Ahem!' said the Mouse with an important air. 'Are you all ready? This is the driest thing I know. Silence all round, if you please! "William the Conqueror, whose cause was favoured by the pope, was soon submitted to by the English, who wanted leaders, and had been of late much accustomed to usurpation and conquest. Edwin and Morcar, the earls of Mercia and Northumbria—"'

'Ugh!' said the Lory, with a shiver.

'I beg your pardon!' said the Mouse, frowning, but very politely. 'Did you speak?'

'Not I!' said the Lory, hastily.

'I thought you did,' said the Mouse. 'I proceed. "Edwin and Morcar, the earls of Mercia and Northumbria, declared for him; and even Stigand, the patriotic archbishop of Canterbury found it advisable—"'

'Found what?' said the Duck.

'Found it,' the Mouse replied rather crossly: 'of course you know what "it" means.'

'I know what "it" means well enough, when I find a thing,' said the Duck: 'it's generally a frog, or a worm. The question is, what did the archbishop find?'

The Mouse did not notice this question, but hurriedly went on, '"—found it advisable to go with Edgar Atheling to meet William and offer him the crown. William's conduct at first was moderate. But the insolence of his Normans—" How are you getting on now, my dear?' it continued, turning to Alice as it spoke.

'As wet as ever,' said Alice in a melancholy tone: 'it doesn't seem to dry me at all.'

'In that case,' said the Dodo solemnly, rising to its feet, 'I move that the meeting adjourn, for the immediate adoption of more energetic remedies—'

'Speak English!' said the Eaglet. 'I don't know the meaning of half those long words, and, what's more, I don't believe you do either!' And the Eaglet bent down its head to hide a smile: some of the other birds tittered audibly.

'What I was going to say,' said the Dodo in an offended tone, 'was, that the best thing to get us dry would be a Caucus-race.'

'What is a Caucus-race?' said Alice; not that she much wanted to know, but the Dodo had paused as if it thought that somebody ought to speak, and no one else seemed inclined to say anything. 'Why,' said the Dodo, 'the best way to explain it is to do it.' (And, as you might like to try the thing yourself, some winter-day, I will tell you how the Dodo managed it.)

First it marked out a racecourse, in a sort of circle, ('the exact shape doesn't matter,' it said,) and then all the party were placed along the course, here and there. There was no 'One, two, three, and away!', but they began running when they liked, and left off when they liked, so that it was not easy to know when the race was over. However, when they had been running half an hour or so, and were quite dry again, the Dodo suddenly called out 'The race is over!', and they all crowded round it, panting, and asking 'But who has won?'

This question the Dodo could not answer without a great deal of thought, and it stood for a long time with one finger pressed upon its forehead (the position in which you usually see Shakespeare, in the pictures of him), while the rest waited in silence. At last the Dodo said '*Everybody* has won, and *all* must have prizes.'

'But who is to give the prizes?' quite a chorus of voices asked.

'Why, *she*, of course,' said the Dodo, pointing to Alice with one finger; and the whole party at once crowded round her, calling out, in a confused way, 'Prizes! Prizes!'

Alice had no idea what to do, and in despair she put her hand in her pocket, and pulled out a box of comfits (luckily the salt water had not got into it), and handed them round as prizes. There was exactly one a-piece, all round.

'But she must have a prize herself, you know;' said the Mouse.

'Of course,' the Dodo replied very gravely. 'What else have you got in your pocket?' it went on, turning to Alice.

'Only a thimble,' said Alice sadly.

'Hand it over here,' said the Dodo.

Then they all crowded round her once more, while the Dodo solemnly presented the thimble, saying 'We beg your acceptance of this elegant thimble'; and, when it had finished this short speech, they all cheered.

Alice thought the whole thing very absurd, but they all looked so grave that she did not dare to laugh; and, as she could not think of anything to say, she simply bowed, and took the thimble, looking as solemn as she could.

The next thing was to eat the comfits: this caused some noise and confusion, as the large birds complained that they could not taste theirs, and the small ones choked and had to be patted on the back. However, it was over at last, and they sat down again in a ring, and begged the Mouse to tell them something more.

'You promised to tell me your history you know,' said Alice, 'and why it is you hate—C and D,' she added in a whisper, half afraid that it would be offended again.

'Mine is a long and a sad tale!' said the Mouse, turning to Alice, and sighing.

'It is a long tail, certainly' said Alice, looking down with wonder at the Mouse's tail: 'but why do you call it sad?' And she kept on puzzling about it while the Mouse was speaking, so that her idea of the tale was something like this:—

'Fury said to
a mouse, That
he met in the
house, "Let
us both go
to law: *I*
will prose-
cute you.—
Come, I'll
take no de-
nial: We
must have
the trial;
For really
this morn-
ing I've
nothing
to do."
Said the
mouse to
the cur,
"Such a
trial, dear
sir, With
no jury
or judge,
would
be wast-
ing our
breath."
"I'll be
judge,
I'll be
jury,"
said
cun-
ning
old
Fury:
"I'll
try
the
whole
cause,
and
con-
demn
you to
death".'

'You are not attending!' said the Mouse to Alice, severely. 'What are you thinking of?'

'I beg your pardon,' said Alice very humbly: 'you had got to the fifth bend, I think?'

'I had *not*!' cried the Mouse, sharply and very angrily.

'A knot!' said Alice, always ready to make herself useful, and looking anxiously about her. 'Oh, do let me help to undo it!'

'I shall do nothing of the sort,' said the Mouse, getting up and walking away. 'You insult me by talking such nonsense!'

'I didn't mean it!' pleaded poor Alice. 'But you're so easily offended, you know!'

The Mouse only growled in reply.

'Please come back, and finish your story!' Alice called after it. And the others all joined in chorus 'Yes, please do!' But the Mouse only shook its head impatiently, and walked a little quicker.

'What a pity it wouldn't stay!' sighed the Lory, as soon as it was quite out of sight. And an old Crab took the opportunity of saying to her daughter 'Ah, my dear! Let this be a lesson to you never to lose *your* temper!'

'Hold your tongue, Ma!' said the young Crab, a little snappishly. 'You're enough to try the patience of an oyster!'

'I wish I had our Dinah here, I know I do!' said Alice aloud, addressing nobody in particular. '*She'd* soon fetch it back!'

'And who is Dinah, if! might venture to ask the question?' said the Lory.

Alice replied eagerly, for she was always ready to talk about her pet: 'Dinah's our cat. And she's such a capital one for catching mice, you can't think! And oh, I wish you could see her after the birds! Why, she'll eat a little bird as soon as look at it!'

This speech caused a remarkable sensation among the party. Some of the birds hurried off at once: one old Magpie began wrapping itself up very carefully, remarking 'I really must be getting home: the night-air doesn't suit my throat!' And a Canary called out in a trembling voice, to its children, 'Come away, my dears! It's high time you were all in bed!' On various pretexts they all moved off, and Alice was soon left alone.

'I wish I hadn't mentioned Dinah!' she said to herself in a melancholy tone. 'Nobody seems to like her, down here, and I'm sure she's the best cat in the world! Oh, my dear Dinah! I wonder if I shall ever see you any more!' And here poor Alice began to cry again, for she felt very lonely and low-spirited. In a little while, however, she again heard a little pattering of footsteps in the distance, and she looked up eagerly, half hoping that the Mouse had changed his mind, and was coming back to finish his story.

Chapter IV

The Rabbit Sends in a Little Bill

It was the White Rabbit, trotting slowly back again, and looking anxiously about as it went, as if it had lost something; and she heard it muttering to itself, 'The Duchess! The Duchess! Oh my dear paws! Oh my fur and whiskers! She'll get me executed, as sure as ferrets are ferrets! Where can I have dropped them, I wonder?' Alice guessed in a moment that it was looking for the fan and the pair of white kid-gloves, and she very good-naturedly began hunting about for them, but they were nowhere to be seen—everything seemed to have changed since her swim in the pool; and the great hall, with the glass table and the little door, had vanished completely.

Very soon the Rabbit noticed Alice, as she went hunting about, and called out to her, in an angry tone, 'Why, Mary Ann, what are you doing out here? Run home this moment, and fetch me a pair of gloves and a fan! Quick, now!' And Alice was so much frightened that she ran off at once in the direction it pointed to, without trying to explain the mistake that it had made.

'He took me for his housemaid,' she said to herself as she ran.

'How surprised he'll be when he finds out who I am! But I'd better take him his fan and gloves—that is, if I can find them.' As she said this, she came upon a neat little house, on the door of which was a bright brass plate with the name 'W. RABBIT' engraved upon it. She went in without knocking, and hurried upstairs, in great fear lest she should meet the real Mary Ann, and be turned out of the house before she had found the fan and gloves.

'How queer it seems,' Alice said to herself, 'to be going messages for a rabbit! I suppose Dinah'll be sending me on messages next!' And she began fancying the sort of thing that would happen:' '—Miss Alice! Come here directly, and get ready for your walk!' 'Coming in a minute, nurse! But I've got to watch this mouse-hole till Dinah comes back, and see that the mouse doesn't get out.' Only I don't think,' Alice went on, 'that they'd let Dinah stop in the house if it began ordering people about like that!'

By this time she had found her way into a tidy little room with a table in the window, and on it (as she had hoped) a fan and two or three pairs of tiny white kid-gloves: she took up the fan and a pair of the gloves, and was just going to leave the room, when her eye fell upon a little bottle that stood near the looking-glass. There was no label this time with the words 'DRINK ME,' but nevertheless she uncorked it and put it to her lips. 'I know *something* interesting is sure to happen,' she said to herself, 'whenever I eat or drink anything: so I'll just see what this bottle does. I do hope it'll make me grow large again, for really I'm quite tired of being such a tiny little thing!'

It did so indeed, and much sooner than she had expected: before she had drunk half the bottle, she found her head pressing against the ceiling, and had to stoop to save her neck from being broken. She hastily put down the bottle, saying to herself 'That's quite enough—I hope I shan't grow any more—As it is, I can't get out at the door—I do wish I hadn't drunk quite so much!'

Alas! It was too late to wish that! She went on growing, and growing, and very soon had to kneel down on the floor: in another minute there was not even room for this, and she tried the effect of lying down with one elbow against the door, and the other arm curled round her head. Still she went on growing, and, as a last resource, she put one arm out of the window, and one foot up the chimney, and said to herself 'Now I can do no more, whatever happens. What *will* become of me?'

Luckily for Alice, the little magic bottle had now had its full effect, and she grew no larger: still it was very uncomfortable, and, as there seemed to be no sort of chance of her ever getting out of the room again, no wonder she felt unhappy.

'It was much pleasanter at home,' thought poor Alice, 'when one wasn't always growing larger and smaller, and being ordered about by mice and rabbits. I almost wish I hadn't gone down that rabbit-hole—and yet—and yet—it's rather curious, you know, this sort of life! I do wonder what *can* have happened to me! When I used to read fairy tales, I fancied that kind of thing never happened, and now here I am in the middle of one! There ought to be a book written about me, that there ought! And when I grow up, I'll write one—but I'm grown up now,' she added in a sorrowful tone: 'at least there's no room to grow up any more *here*.'

'But then,' thought Alice, 'shall I *never* get any older than I am now? That'll be a comfort, one way—never to be an old woman—but then—always to have lessons to learn! Oh, I shouldn't like *that*!'

'Oh, you foolish Alice!' she answered herself. 'How can you learn lessons in here? Why, there's hardly room for *you*, and no room at all for any lesson-books!'

And so she went on, taking first one side and then the other, and making quite a conversation of it altogether; but after a few minutes she heard a voice outside, and stopped to listen.

'Mary Ann! Mary Ann!' said the voice. 'Fetch me my gloves this moment!' Then came a little pattering of feet on the stairs. Alice knew it was the Rabbit coming to look for her, and she trembled till she shook the house, quite forgetting that she was now about a thousand times as large as the Rabbit, and had no reason to be afraid of it.

Presently the Rabbit came up to the door, and tried to open it; but, as the door opened inwards, and Alice's elbow was pressed hard against it, that attempt proved a failure. Alice heard it say to itself 'Then I'll go round and get in at the window.'

'*That* you won't!' thought Alice, and, after waiting till she fancied she heard the Rabbit just under the window, she suddenly spread out her hand, and made a snatch in the air. She did not get hold of anything, but she heard a little shriek and a fall, and a crash of broken glass, from which she concluded that it was just possible it had fallen into a cucumber-frame, or something of the sort.

Next came an angry voice—the Rabbit's—'Pat! Pat! Where are you?' And then a voice she had never heard before, 'Sure then I'm here! Digging for apples, yer honour!'

'Digging for apples, indeed!' said the Rabbit angrily. 'Here! Come and help me out of *this*!' (Sounds of more broken glass.)

'Now tell me, Pat, what's that in the window?'

'Sure, it's an arm, yer honour!' (He pronounced it 'arrum.')

'An arm, you goose! Who ever saw one that size? Why, it fills the whole window!'

'Sure, it does, yer honour: but it's an arm for all that.'

'Well, it's got no business there, at any rate: go and take it away!'

There was a long silence after this, and Alice could only hear whispers now and then; such as 'Sure, I don't like it, yer honour, at all, at all!' 'Do as I tell you, you coward!', and at last she spread out her hand again, and made another snatch in the air. This time there were *two* little shrieks, and more sounds of broken glass. 'What a number of cucumber-frames there must be!' thought Alice. 'I wonder what they'll do next! As for pulling me out of the window, I only wish they *could*! I'm sure *I* don't want to stay in here any longer!'

She waited for some time without hearing anything more: at last came a rumbling of little cart-wheels, and the sound of a good many voices all talking together: she made out the words: 'Where's the other ladder?—Why, I hadn't to bring but one. Bill's got the other—Bill! Fetch it here, lad!—Here, put 'em up at this corner—No, tie 'em together first—they don't reach half high enough yet—Oh, they'll do well enough. Don't be particular—Here, Bill! Catch hold of this rope—Will the roof bear?—Mind that loose slate—Oh, it's coming down! Heads below!' (a loud crash)—'Now, who did that?—It was Bill, I fancy—Who's to go down the chimney?—Nay, *I* shan't! You do it!—*That* I won't, then!—Bill's got to go down—Here, Bill! The master says you've got to go down the chimney!'

'Oh! So Bill's got to come down the chimney, has he?' said Alice to herself. 'Why, they seem to put everything upon Bill! I wouldn't be in Bill's place for a good deal: this fireplace is narrow, to be sure; but I *think* I can kick a little!'

She drew her foot as far down the chimney as she could, and waited till she heard a little animal (she couldn't guess of what sort it was) scratching and scrambling about in the chimney close above her: then, saying to herself 'This is Bill', she gave one sharp kick, and waited to see what would happen next.

The first thing she heard was a general chorus of 'There goes Bill!' then the Rabbit's voice alone—'Catch him, you by the hedge!' then silence, and then another confusion of voices—'Hold up his head—Brandy now—Don't choke him—How was it, old fellow? What happened to you? Tell us all about it!'

Last came a little feeble, squeaking voice ('That's Bill,' thought Alice), 'Well, I hardly know—No more, thank ye; I'm better now—but I'm a deal too flustered to tell you—all I know is, something comes at me like a Jack-in-the-box, and up I goes like a sky-rocket!'

'So you did, old fellow!' said the others.

'We must burn the house down!' said the Rabbit's voice. And Alice called out, as loud as she could, 'If you do, I'll set Dinah at you!'

There was a dead silence instantly, and Alice thought to herself 'I wonder what they *will* do next! If they had any sense, they'd take the roof off.' After a minute or two, they began moving about again, and Alice heard the Rabbit say 'A barrowful will do, to begin with.'

'A barrowful of *what*?' thought Alice. But she had not long to doubt, for the next moment a shower of little pebbles came rattling in at the window, and some of them hit her in the face. 'I'll put a stop to this,' she said to herself, and shouted out 'You'd better not do that again!', which produced another dead silence.

Alice noticed, with some surprise, that the pebbles were all turning into little cakes as they lay on the floor, and a bright idea came into her head. 'If I eat one of these cakes,' she thought, 'it's sure to make *some* change in my size; and, as it can't possibly make me larger, it must make me smaller, I suppose.'

So she swallowed one of the cakes, and was delighted to find that she began shrinking directly. As soon as she was small enough to get through the door, she ran out of the house, and found quite a crowd of little animals and birds waiting outside. The poor little Lizard, Bill, was in the middle, being held up by two guinea pigs, who were giving it something out of a bottle. They all made a rush at Alice the moment she appeared; but she ran off as hard as she could, and soon found herself safe in a thick wood.

'The first thing I've got to do,' said Alice to herself; as she wandered about in the wood, 'is to grow to my right size again; and the second thing is to find my way into that lovely garden. I think that will be the best plan.'

It sounded an excellent plan, no doubt, and very neatly and simply arranged: the only difficulty was, that she had not the smallest idea how to set about it; and while she was peering about anxiously among the trees, a little sharp bark just over her head made her look up in a great hurry.

An enormous puppy was looking down at her with large round eyes, and feebly stretching out one paw, trying to touch her. 'Poor little thing!' said Alice, in a coaxing tone, and she tried hard to whistle to it; but she was terribly frightened all the time at the thought that it might be hungry, in which case it would be very likely to eat her up in spite of all her coaxing.

Hardly knowing what she did, she picked up a little bit of stick, and held it out to the puppy: whereupon the puppy jumped into the air off all its feet at once, with a yelp of delight, and rushed at the stick, and made believe to worry it: then Alice dodged behind a great thistle, to keep herself from being run over; and, the moment she appeared on the other side, the puppy made another rush at the stick, and tumbled head over heels in its hurry to get hold of it: then Alice, thinking it was very like having a game of play with a cart-horse, and expecting every moment to be trampled under its feet, ran round the thistle again: then the puppy began a series of short charges at the stick, running a very little way forwards each time and a long way back, and barking hoarsely all the while, till at last it sat down a good way off, panting, with its tongue hanging out of its mouth, and its great eyes half shut.

This seemed to Alice a good opportunity for making her escape: so she set off at once, and ran till she was quite tired and out of breath, and till the puppy's bark sounded quite faint in the distance.

'And yet what a dear little puppy it was!' said Alice, as she leant against a buttercup to rest herself, and fanned herself with one of the leaves. 'I should have liked teaching it tricks very much, if—if I'd only been the right size to do it! Oh dear! I'd nearly forgotten that I've got to grow up again! Let me see—how *is* it to be managed? I suppose I ought to eat or drink something or other; but the great question is "What?'"

The great question certainly was 'What?'. Alice looked all round her at the flowers and the blades of grass, but she could not see anything that looked like the right thing to eat or drink under the circumstances. There was a large mushroom growing near her, about the same height as herself; and, when she had looked under it, and on both sides of it, and behind it, it occurred to her that she might as well look and see what was on the top of it.

She stretched herself up on tiptoe, and peeped over the edge of the mushroom, and her eyes immediately met those of a large blue caterpillar, that was sitting on the top, with its arms folded, quietly smoking a long hookah, and taking not the smallest notice of her or of anything else.

Chapter V

Advice from a Caterpillar

The Caterpillar and Alice looked at each other for some time in silence: at last the Caterpillar took the hookah out of its mouth, and addressed her in a languid, sleepy voice.

'Who are *you*?' said the Caterpillar.

This was not an encouraging opening for a conversation. Alice replied, rather shyly, 'I—I hardly know, Sir, just at present—at least I know who I was when I got up this morning, but I think I must have been changed several times since then.'

'What do you mean by that?' said the Caterpillar, sternly. 'Explain yourself!'

'I can't explain *myself*, I'm afraid, Sir,' said Alice, 'because I'm not myself, you see.'

'I don't see,' said the Caterpillar.

'I'm afraid I can't put it more clearly,' Alice replied, very politely, 'for I can't understand it myself, to begin with; and being so many different sizes in a day is very confusing.'

'It isn't,' said the Caterpillar.

'Well, perhaps you haven't found it so yet,' said Alice; 'but when you have to turn into a chrysalis—you will some day, you know—and then after that into a butterfly, I should think you'll feel it a little queer, won't you?'

'Not a bit,' said the Caterpillar.

'Well, perhaps *your* feelings may be different,' said Alice: 'all I know is, it would feel very queer to *me*.'

'You!' said the Caterpillar contemptuously. 'Who are *you*?'

Which brought them back again to the beginning of the conversation. Alice felt a little irritated at the Caterpillar's making such very short remarks, and she drew herself up and said, *very* gravely, 'I think you ought to tell me who *you* are, first.'

'Why?' said the Caterpillar.

Here was another puzzling question; and, as Alice could not think of any good reason, and the Caterpillar seemed to be in a very unpleasant state of mind, she turned away.

'Come back!' the Caterpillar called after her. 'I've something important to say!'

This sounded promising, certainly. Alice turned and came back again.

'Keep your temper,' said the Caterpillar.

'Is that all?' said Alice, swallowing down her anger as well as she could.

'No,' said the Caterpillar.

Alice thought she might as well wait, as she had nothing else to do, and perhaps after all it might tell her something worth hearing. For some minutes it puffed away without speaking; but at last it unfolded its arms, took the hookah out of its mouth again, and said 'So you think you're changed, do you?'

'I'm afraid I am, Sir,' said Alice. 'I can't remember things as I used—and I don't keep the same size for ten minutes together!'

'Can't remember *what* things?' said the Caterpillar.

'Well, I've tried to say "*How doth the little busy bee*," but it all came different!' Alice replied in a very melancholy voice.

'Repeat "*You are old, Father William*,"' said the Caterpillar.

Alice folded her hands, and began:—

'*You are old, Father William,' the young man said,*
    '*And your hair has become very white;*
And yet you incessantly stand on your head–
    Do you think, at your age, it is right?'

'*In my youth,' Father William replied to his son,*
    '*I feared it might injure the brain;*
But, now that I'm perfectly sure I have none,
    Why, I do it again and again.'

'You are old,' said the youth, 'as I mentioned before,
    And have grown most uncommonly fat;
Yet you turned a back-somersault in at the door—
    Pray, what is the reason of that?'

'In my youth,' said the sage, as he shook his grey locks,
    'I kept all my limbs very supple
By the use of this ointment—one shilling the box—
    Allow me to sell you a couple?'

'You are old,' said the youth, 'and your jaws are too weak
    For anything tougher than suet;
Yet you finished the goose, with the bones and the beak—
    Pray, how did you manage to do it?'

'In my youth,' said his father, 'I took to the law,
    And argued each case with my wife;
And the muscular strength, which it gave to my jaw
    Has lasted the rest of my life.'

'You are old,' said the youth, 'one would hardly suppose
    That your eye was as steady as ever;
Yet you balanced an eel on the end of your nose—
    What made you so awfully clever?'

'I have answered three questions, and that is enough,'
    Said his father: 'Don't give yourself airs!
Do you think I can listen all day to such stuff?
    Be off, or I'll kick you downstairs!'

'That is not said right,' said the Caterpillar.

'Not *quite* right, I'm afraid,' said Alice, timidly: 'some of the words have got altered.'

'It is wrong from beginning to end,' said the Caterpillar, decidedly; and there was silence for some minutes.

The Caterpillar was the first to speak.

'What size do you want to be?' it asked.

'Oh, I'm not particular as to size,' Alice hastily replied; 'only one doesn't like changing so often, you know'

'I *don't* know,' said the Caterpillar.

Alice said nothing: she had never been so much contradicted in all her life before, and she felt that she was losing her temper.

'Are you content now?' said the Caterpillar.

'Well, I should like to be a *little* larger, Sir, if you wouldn't mind,' said Alice: 'three inches is such a wretched height to be.'

'It is a very good height indeed!' said the Caterpillar angrily, rearing itself upright as it spoke (it was exactly three inches high).

'But I'm not used to it!' pleaded poor Alice in a piteous tone. And she thought to herself 'I wish the creatures wouldn't be so easily offended!'

'You'll get used to it in time,' said the Caterpillar; and it put the hookah into its mouth, and began smoking again.

This time Alice waited patiently until it chose to speak again. In a minute or two the Caterpillar took the hookah out of its mouth, and yawned once or twice, and shook itself Then it got down off the mushroom, and crawled away into the grass, merely remarking, as it went, 'One side will make you grow taller, and the other side will make you grow shorter.'

'One side of *what*? The other side of *what*?' thought Alice to herself.

'Of the mushroom,' said the Caterpillar, just as if she had asked it aloud; and in another moment it was out of sight.

Alice remained looking thoughtfully at the mushroom for a minute, trying to make out which were the two sides of it; and, as it was perfectly round, she found this a very difficult question. However, at last she stretched her arms round it as far as they would go, and broke off a bit of the edge with each hand.

'And now which is which?' she said to herself, and nibbled a little of the right-hand bit to try the effect. The next moment she felt a violent blow underneath her chin: it had struck her foot!

She was a good deal frightened by this very sudden change, but she felt that there was no time to be lost, as she was shrinking rapidly: so she set to work at once to eat some of the other bit. Her chin was pressed so closely against her foot, that there was hardly room to open her mouth; but she did it at last, and managed to swallow a morsel of the left-hand bit.

'Come, my head's free at last!' said Alice in a tone of delight, which changed into alarm in another moment, when she found that her shoulders were nowhere to be found: all she could see, when she looked down, was an immense length of neck, which seemed to rise like a stalk out of a sea of green leaves that lay far below her.

'What can all that green stuff be?' said Alice. 'And where have my shoulders got to? And oh, my poor hands, how is it I can't see you?' She was moving them about, as she spoke, but no result seemed to follow, except a little shaking among the distant green leaves.

As there seemed to be no chance of getting her hands up to her head, she tried to get her head down to them, and was delighted to find that her neck would bend about easily in any direction, like a serpent. She had just succeeded in curving it down into a graceful zigzag, and was going to dive in among the leaves, which she found to be nothing but the tops of the trees under which she had been wandering, when a sharp hiss made her draw back in a hurry: a large pigeon had flown into her face, and was beating her violently with its wings.

'Serpent!' screamed the Pigeon.

'I'm not a serpent!' said Alice indignantly. 'Let me alone!'

'Serpent, I say again!' repeated the Pigeon, but in a more subdued tone, and added, with a kind of sob, 'I've tried every way, but nothing seems to suit them!'

'I haven't the least idea what you're talking about,' said Alice.

'I've tried the roots of trees, and I've tried banks, and I've tried hedges,' the Pigeon went on, without attending to her; 'but those serpents! There's no pleasing them!'

Alice was more and more puzzled, but she thought there was no use in saying anything more till the Pigeon had finished.

'As if it wasn't trouble enough hatching the eggs,' said the Pigeon; 'but I must be on the look-out for serpents, night and day! Why, I haven't had a wink of sleep these three weeks!'

'I'm very sorry you've been annoyed,' said Alice, who was beginning to see its meaning.

'And just as I'd taken the highest tree in the wood,' continued the Pigeon, raising its voice to a shriek, 'and just as I was thinking I should be free of them at last, they must needs come wriggling down from the sky! Ugh, Serpent!'

'But I'm *not* a serpent, I tell you!' said Alice. 'I'm a—I'm a—'

'Well! *What* are you?' said the Pigeon. 'I can see you're trying to invent something!'

'I—I'm a little girl,' said Alice, rather doubtfully, as she remembered the number of changes she had gone through, that day.

'A likely story indeed!' said the Pigeon, in a tone of the deepest contempt. 'I've seen a good many little girls in my time, but never *one* with such a neck as that! No, no! You're a serpent; and there's no use denying it. I suppose you'll be telling me next that you never tasted an egg!'

'I *have* tasted eggs, certainly' said Alice, who was a very truthful child; 'but little girls eat eggs quite as much as serpents do, you know'

'I don't believe it,' said the Pigeon; 'but if they do, why, then they're a kind of serpent: that's all I can say.'

This was such a new idea to Alice, that she was quite silent for a minute or two, which gave the Pigeon the opportunity of adding 'You're looking for eggs, I know that well enough; and what does it matter to me whether you're a little girl or a serpent?'

'It matters a good deal to *me*,' said Alice hastily; 'but I'm not looking for eggs, as it happens; and, if I was, I shouldn't want *yours*: I don't like them raw'

'Well, be off, then!' said the Pigeon in a sulky tone, as it settled down again into its nest. Alice crouched down among the trees as well as she could, for her neck kept getting entangled among the branches, and every now and then she had to stop and untwist it. After a while she remembered that she still held the pieces of mushroom in her hands, and she set to work very carefully, nibbling first at one and then at the other, and growing sometimes taller, and sometimes shorter, until she had succeeded in bringing herself down to her usual height.

It was so long since she had been anything near the right size, that it felt quite strange at first; but she got used to it in a few minutes, and began talking to herself, as usual, 'Come, there's half my plan done now! How puzzling all these changes are! I'm never sure what I'm going to be, from one minute to another! However, I've got back to my right size: the next thing is, to get into that beautiful garden—how is that to be done, I wonder?' As she said this, she came suddenly upon an open place, with a little house in it about four feet high. 'Whoever lives there,' thought Alice, 'it'll never do to come upon them this size: why, I should frighten them out of their wits!' So she began nibbling at the right-hand bit again, and did not venture to go near the house till she had brought herself down to nine inches high.

Chapter VI

Pig and Pepper

For a minute or two she stood looking at the house, and wondering what to do next, when suddenly a footman in livery came running out of the wood—(she considered him to be a footman because he was in livery: otherwise, judging by his face only, she would have called him a fish)—and rapped loudly at the door with his knuckles. It was opened by another footman in livery with a round face, and large eyes like a frog; and both footmen, Alice noticed, had powdered hair that curled all over their heads. She felt very curious to know what it was all about, and crept a little way out of the wood to listen.

The Fish-Footman began by producing from under his arm a great letter, nearly as large as himself, and this he handed over to the other, saying, in a solemn tone, 'For the Duchess. An invitation from the Queen to play croquet.' The Frog-Footman repeated, in the same solemn tone, only changing the order of the words a little, 'From the Queen. An invitation for the Duchess to play croquet.'

Then they both bowed low, and their curls got entangled together.

Alice laughed so much at this, that she had to run back into the wood for fear of their hearing her; and, when she next peeped out, the Fish-Footman was gone, and the other was sitting on the ground near the door, staring stupidly up into the sky.

Alice went timidly up to the door, and knocked.

'There's no sort of use in knocking,' said the Footman, 'and that for two reasons. First, because I'm on the same side of the door as you are: secondly, because they're making such a noise inside, no one could possibly hear you.' And certainly there was a most extraordinary noise going on within—a constant howling and sneezing, and every now and then a great crash, as if a dish or kettle had been broken to pieces.

'Please, then,' said Alice, 'how am I to get in?'

'There might be some sense in your knocking,' the Footman went on, without attending to her, 'if we had the door between us. For instance, if you were *inside*, you might knock, and I could let you out, you know.' He was looking up into the sky all the time he was speaking, and this Alice thought decidedly uncivil. 'But perhaps he can't help it,' she said to herself; 'his eyes are so *very* nearly at the top of his head. But at any rate he might answer questions.—How am I to get in?' she repeated, aloud.

'I shall sit here,' the Footman remarked, 'till tomorrow—'

At this moment the door of the house opened, and a large plate came skimming out, straight at the Footman's head: it just grazed his nose, and broke to pieces against one of the trees behind him.

'—or next day, maybe,' the Footman continued in the same tone, exactly as if nothing had happened.

'How am I to get in?' asked Alice again, in a louder tone.

'*Are* you to get in at all?' said the Footman. 'That's the first question, you know.'

It was, no doubt: only Alice did not like to be told so. 'It's really dreadful,' she muttered to herself, 'the way all the creatures argue. It's enough to drive one crazy!'

The Footman seemed to think this a good opportunity for repeating his remark, with variations. 'I shall sit here,' he said, 'on and off, for days and days.'

'But what am *I* to do?' said Alice.

'Anything you like,' said the Footman, and began whistling.

'Oh, there's no use in talking to him,' said Alice desperately: 'he's perfectly idiotic!' And she opened the door and went in.

The door led right into a large kitchen, which was full of

smoke from one end to the other: the Duchess was sitting on a three-legged stool in the middle, nursing a baby: the cook was leaning over the fire, stirring a large cauldron which seemed to be full of soup.

'There's certainly too much pepper in that soup!' Alice said to herself, as well as she could for sneezing.

There was certainly too much of it in the *air*. Even the Duchess sneezed occasionally; and as for the baby, it was sneezing and howling alternately without a moment's pause. The only two creatures in the kitchen, that did *not* sneeze, were the cook, and a large cat, which was lying on the hearth and grinning from ear to ear.

'Please would you tell me,' said Alice, a little timidly, for she was not quite sure whether it was good manners for her to speak first, 'why your cat grins like that?'

'It's a Cheshire-Cat,' said the Duchess, 'and that's why. Pig!'

She said the last word with such sudden violence that Alice quite jumped; but she saw in another moment that it was addressed to the baby, and not to her, so she took courage, and went on again:—

'I didn't know that Cheshire-Cats always grinned; in fact, I didn't know that cats *could* grin.'

'They all can,' said the Duchess; 'and most of 'em do.'

'I don't know of any that do,' Alice said very politely, feeling quite pleased to have got into a conversation.

'You don't know much,' said the Duchess; 'and that's a fact.'

Alice did not at all like the tone of this remark, and thought it would be as well to introduce some other subject of conversation. While she was trying to fix on one, the cook took the cauldron of soup off the fire, and at once set to work throwing everything within her reach at the Duchess and the baby—the fire-irons came first; then followed a shower of saucepans, plates, and dishes. The Duchess took no notice of them even when they hit her; and the baby was howling so much already, that it was quite impossible to say whether the blows hurt it or not.

'Oh, *please* mind what you're doing!' cried Alice, jumping up and down in an agony of terror. 'Oh, there goes his *precious* nose, as an unusually large saucepan flew close by it, and very nearly carried it off.

'If everybody minded their own business,' the Duchess said, in a hoarse growl, 'the world would go round a deal faster than it does.'

'Which would *not* be an advantage,' said Alice, who felt very glad to get an opportunity of showing off a little of her knowledge.

'Just think what work it would make with the day and night! You see the earth takes twenty-four hours to turn round on its axis—'

'Talking of axes,' said the Duchess, 'chop off her head!'

Alice glanced rather anxiously at the cook, to see if she meant to take the hint; but the cook was busily stirring the soup, and seemed not to be listening, so she went on again: 'Twenty-four hours, I *think*; or is it twelve? I—'

'Oh, don't bother *me*!' said the Duchess. 'I never could abide figures!' And with that she began nursing her child again, singing a sort of lullaby to it as she did so, and giving it a violent shake at the end of every line:—

> *'Speak roughly to your little boy,*
> *And beat him when he sneezes:*
> *He only does it to annoy,*
> *Because he knows it teases.'*

CHORUS
(in which the cook and the baby joined):—
'Wow! wow! wow!'

While the Duchess sang the second verse of the song, she kept tossing the baby violently up and down, and the poor little thing howled so, that Alice could hardly hear the words:—

> *'I speak severely to my boy,*
> *I beat him when he sneezes;*
> *For he can thoroughly enjoy*
> *The pepper when he pleases!'*

CHORUS

'Wow! wow! wow!'

'Here! You may nurse it a bit, if you like!' the Duchess said to Alice, flinging the baby at her as she spoke. 'I must go and get ready to play croquet with the Queen,' and she hurried out of the room. The cook threw a frying-pan after her as she went, but it just missed her.

Alice caught the baby with some difficulty, as it was a queer-shaped little creature, and held out its arms and legs in all directions, 'just like a star-fish,' thought Alice. The poor little thing was snorting like a steam-engine when she caught it, and kept doubling itself up and straightening itself out again, so that altogether, for the first minute or two, it was as much as she could do to hold it. As soon as she had made out the proper way of nursing it (which was to twist it up into a sort of knot, and then keep tight hold of its right ear and left foot, so as to prevent its undoing itself), she carried it out into the open air. 'If I don't take this child away with me,' thought Alice, 'they're sure to kill it in a day or two. Wouldn't it be murder to leave it behind?' She said the last words out loud, and the little thing grunted in reply (it had left off sneezing by this time). 'Don't grunt,' said Alice; 'that's not at all a proper way of expressing yourself.'

The baby grunted again, and Alice looked very anxiously into its face to see what was the matter with it. There could be no doubt that it had a *very* turn-up nose, much more like a snout than a real nose: also its eyes were getting extremely small for a baby: altogether Alice did not like the look of the thing at all. 'But perhaps it was only sobbing,' she thought, and looked into its eyes

again, to see if there were any tears.

No, there were no tears. 'If you're going to turn into a pig, my dear,' said Alice, seriously, 'I'll have nothing more to do with you. Mind now!' The poor little thing sobbed again (or grunted, it was impossible to say which), and they went on for some while in silence.

Alice was just beginning to think to herself, 'Now, what am I to do with this creature, when I get it home?' when it grunted again, so violently, that she looked down into its face in some alarm. This time there could be no mistake about it: it was neither more nor less than a pig, and she felt that it would be quite absurd for her to carry it any further.

So she set the little creature down, and felt quite relieved to see it trot away quietly into the wood. 'If it had grown up,' she said to herself, 'it would have made a dreadfully ugly child: but it makes rather a handsome pig, I think.' And she began thinking over other children she knew, who might do very well as pigs, and was just saying to herself 'if one only knew the right way to change them—' when she was a little startled by seeing the Cheshire-Cat sitting on a bough of a tree a few yards off.

The Cat only grinned when it saw Alice. It looked good-natured, she thought: still it had very long claws and a great many teeth, so she felt that it ought to be treated with respect.

'Cheshire-Puss,' she began, rather timidly, as she did not at all know whether it would like the name: however, it only grinned a little wider. 'Come, it's pleased so far,' thought Alice, and she went on. 'Would you tell me, please, which way I ought to go from here?'

'That depends a good deal on where you want to get to,' said the Cat.

'I don't much care where—' said Alice.

'Then it doesn't matter which way you go,' said the Cat.

'—so long as I get *somewhere*,' Alice added as an explanation.

'Oh, you're sure to do that,' said the Cat, 'if only you walk long enough.'

Alice felt that this could not be denied, so she tried another question. 'What sort of people live about here?'

'In *that* direction,' the Cat said, waving its right paw round, 'lives a Hatter: and in *that* direction,' waving the other paw, 'lives a March Hare. Visit either you like: they're both mad.'

'But I don't want to go among mad people,' Alice remarked.

'Oh, you can't help that,' said the Cat: 'we're all mad here. I'm mad. You're mad.'

'How do you know I'm mad?' said Alice.

'You must be,' said the Cat, 'or you wouldn't have come here.'

Alice didn't think that proved it at all: however, she went on: 'And how do you know that you're mad?'

'To begin with,' said the Cat, 'a dog's not mad. You grant that?'

'I suppose so,' said Alice. 'Well, then,' the Cat went on, 'you see a dog growls when it's angry and wags its tail when it's pleased. Now I growl when I'm pleased, and wag my tail when I'm angry Therefore I'm mad.'

'*I* call it purring, not growling,' said Alice.

'Call it what you like,' said the Cat. 'Do you play croquet with the Queen today?'

'I should like it very much,' said Alice, 'but I haven't been invited yet.'

'You'll see me there,' said the Cat, and vanished.

Alice was not much surprised at this, she was getting so well used to queer things happening. While she was still looking at the place where it had been, it suddenly appeared again.

'By-the-bye, what became of the baby?' said the Cat. 'I'd nearly forgotten to ask.'

'It turned into a pig,' Alice answered very quietly, just as if the Cat had come back in a natural way.

'I thought it would,' said the Cat, and vanished again.

Alice waited a little, half expecting to see it again, but it did not appear, and after a minute or two she walked on in the direction in which the March Hare was said to live. 'I've seen hatters before,' she said to herself: 'the March Hare will be much the most interesting, and perhaps, as this is May, it won't be raving mad— at least not so mad as it was in March.' As she said this, she looked up, and there was the Cat again, sitting on a branch of a tree.

'Did you say 'pig', or 'fig'?' said the Cat.

'I said "pig",' replied Alice; 'and I wish you wouldn't keep appearing and vanishing so suddenly: you make one quite giddy!'

'All right,' said the Cat; and this time it vanished quite slowly, beginning with the end of the tail, and ending with the grin, which remained some time after the rest of it had gone.

'Well! I've often seen a cat without a grin,' thought Alice; 'but a grin without a cat! It's the most curious thing I ever saw in all my life!'

She had not gone much farther before she came in sight of the house of the March Hare: she thought it must be the right house, because the chimneys were shaped like ears and the roof was thatched with fur. It was so large a house, that she did not like to go nearer till she had nibbled some more of the left-hand bit of mushroom, and raised herself to about two feet high: even then she walked up towards it rather timidly, saying to herself 'Suppose it should be raving mad after all! I almost wish I'd gone to see the Hatter instead!'

Chapter VII

A Mad Tea-party

There was a table set out under a tree in front of the house, and the March Hare and the Hatter were having tea at it: a Dormouse was sitting between them, fast asleep, and the other two were using it as a cushion, resting their elbows on it, and talking over its head. 'Very uncomfortable for the Dormouse,' thought Alice; 'only as it's asleep, I suppose it doesn't mind.'

The table was a large one, but the three were all crowded together at one corner of it. 'No room! No room!' they cried out when they saw Alice coming. 'There's *plenty* of room!' said Alice indignantly, and she sat down in a large armchair at one end of the table.

'Have some wine,' the March Hare said in an encouraging tone.

Alice looked all round the table, but there was nothing on it but tea. 'I don't see any wine,' she remarked.

'There isn't any,' said the March Hare.

'Then it wasn't very civil of you to offer it,' said Alice angrily.

'It wasn't very civil of you to sit down without being invited,' said the March Hare.

'I didn't know it was *your* table,' said Alice: 'it's laid for a great many more than three.'

'Your hair wants cutting,' said the Hatter. He had been looking at Alice for some time with great curiosity, and this was his first speech.

'You should learn not to make personal remarks,' Alice said with some severity: 'it's very rude.'

The Hatter opened his eyes very wide on hearing this; but all he *said* was 'Why is a raven like a writing-desk?'

'Come, we shall have some fun now!' thought Alice. 'I'm glad they've begun asking riddles—I believe I can guess that,' she added aloud.

'Do you mean that you think you can find out the answer to it?' said the March Hare.

'Exactly so,' said Alice.

'Then you should say what you mean,' the March Hare went on.

'I do,' Alice hastily replied; 'at least—at least I mean what I say—that's the same thing, you know'

'Not the same thing a bit!' said the Hatter. 'Why, you might just as well say that "I see what I eat" is the same thing as "I eat what I see"!'

'You might just as well say' added the March Hare, 'that "I like what I get" is the same thing as "I get what I like"!'

'You might just as well say' added the Dormouse, which seemed to be talking in its sleep, 'that "I breathe when I sleep" is the same thing as "I sleep when I breathe"!'

'It is the same thing with you,' said the Hatter, and here the conversation dropped, and the party sat silent for a minute, while

Alice thought over all she could remember about ravens and writing-desks, which wasn't much.

The Hatter was the first to break the silence. 'What day of the month is it?' he said, turning to Alice: he had taken his watch out of his pocket, and was looking at it uneasily, shaking it every now and then, and holding it to his ear.

Alice considered a little, and then said 'The fourth.'

'Two days wrong!' sighed the Hatter. 'I told you butter wouldn't suit the works!' he added, looking angrily at the March Hare.

'It was the *best* butter,' the March Hare meekly replied.

'Yes, but some crumbs must have got in as well,' the Hatter grumbled: 'you shouldn't have put it in with the bread-knife.'

The March Hare took the watch and looked at it gloomily: then he dipped it into his cup of tea, and looked at it again: but he could think of nothing better to say than his first remark, 'It was the *best* butter, you know.'

Alice had been looking over his shoulder with some curiosity. 'What a funny watch!' she remarked. 'It tells the day of the month, and doesn't tell what o'clock it is!'

'Why should it?' muttered the Hatter. 'Does *your* watch tell you what year it is?'

'Of course not,' Alice replied very readily: 'but that's because it stays the same year for such a long time together.'

'Which is just the case with *mine*,' said the Hatter.

Alice felt dreadfully puzzled. The Hatter's remark seemed to her to have no sort of meaning in it, and yet it was certainly English. 'I don't quite understand you,' she said, as politely as she could.

'The Dormouse is asleep again,' said the Hatter, and he poured a little hot tea upon its nose.

The Dormouse shook its head impatiently, and said, without opening its eyes, 'Of course, of course: just what I was going to remark myself.'

'Have you guessed the riddle yet?' the Hatter said, turning to Alice again.

'No, I give it up,' Alice replied. 'What's the answer?'

'I haven't the slightest idea,' said the Hatter.

'Nor I,' said the March Hare.

Alice sighed wearily. 'I think you might do something better with the time,' she said, 'than wasting it in asking riddles that have no answers.'

'If you knew Time as well as I do,' said the Hatter, 'you wouldn't talk about wasting *it*. It's him.'

'I don't know what you mean,' said Alice.

'Of course you don't!' the Hatter said, tossing his head contemptuously. 'I dare say you never even spoke to Time!'

'Perhaps not,' Alice cautiously replied; 'but I know I have to beat time when I learn music.'

'Ah! That accounts for it,' said the Hatter. 'He won't stand beating. Now, if you only kept on good terms with him, he'd do almost anything you liked with the clock. For instance, suppose it were nine o'clock in the morning, just time to begin lessons: you'd only have to whisper a hint to Time, and round goes the clock in a twinkling! Half-past one, time for dinner!'

('I only wish it was,' the March Hare said to itself in a whisper.)

'That would be grand, certainly,' said Alice thoughtfully; 'but then—I shouldn't be hungry for it, you know.'

'Not at first, perhaps,' said the Hatter: 'but you could keep it to half-past one as long as you liked.'

'Is that the way *you* manage?' Alice asked.

The Hatter shook his head mournfully. 'Not I!' he replied. 'We quarreled last March—just before *he* went mad, you know—' (pointing with his teaspoon at the March Hare,) '—it was at the great concert given by the Queen of Hearts, and I had to sing

> *"Twinkle, twinkle, little bat!*
> *How I wonder what you're at!"*

You know the song, perhaps?'

'I've heard something like it,' said Alice.

'It goes on, you know' the Hatter continued, 'in this way:—

> *"Up above the world you fly,*
> *Like a tea-tray in the sky.*
> *Twinkle, twinkle—"*

Here the Dormouse shook itself, and began singing in its sleep 'Twinkle, twinkle, twinkle, twinkle—' and went on so long that they had to pinch it to make it stop.

'Well, I'd hardly finished the first verse,' said the Hatter, 'when the Queen bawled out "He's murdering the time! Off with his head!"'

'How dreadfully savage!' exclaimed Alice.

'And ever since that,' the Hatter went on in a mournful tone, 'he won't do a thing I ask! It's always six o'clock now.'

A bright idea came into Alice's head, 'Is that the reason so many tea-things are put out here?' she asked.

'Yes, that's it,' said the Hatter with a sigh: 'it's always tea-time, and we've no time to wash the things between whiles.'

'Then you keep moving round, I suppose?' said Alice.

'Exactly so,' said the Hatter: 'as the things get used up.'

'But what happens when you come to the beginning again?' Alice ventured to ask.

'Suppose we change the subject,' the March Hare interrupted, yawning. 'I'm getting tired of this. I vote the young lady tells us a story.'

'I'm afraid I don't know one,' said Alice, rather alarmed at the proposal.

'Then the Dormouse shall!' they both cried. 'Wake up, Dormouse!' And they pinched it on both sides at once.

The Dormouse slowly opened its eyes. 'I wasn't asleep,' it said in a hoarse, feeble voice, 'I heard every word you fellows were saying.'

'Tell us a story!' said the March Hare.

'Yes, please do!' pleaded Alice.

'And be quick about it,' added the Hatter, 'or you'll be asleep again before it's done.'

'Once upon a time there were three little sisters,' the Dormouse began in a great hurry: 'and their names were Elsie, Lade, and Tillie; and they lived at the bottom of a well—'

'What did they live on?' said Alice, who always took a great interest in questions of eating and drinking.

'They lived on treacle,' said the Dormouse, after thinking a minute or two.

'They couldn't have done that, you know,' Alice gently remarked. 'They'd have been ill.'

'So they were,' said the Dormouse; '*very* ill.'

Alice tried a little to fancy to herself what such an extraordinary way of living would be like, but it puzzled her too much: so she went on: 'But why did they live at the bottom of a well?'

'Take some more tea,' the March Hare said to Alice, very earnestly.

'I've had nothing yet,' Alice replied in an offended tone: 'so I can't take more.'

'You mean you can't take *less*,' said the Hatter: 'it's very easy to take *more* than nothing.'

'Nobody asked *your* opinion,' said Alice.

'Who's making personal remarks now?' the Hatter asked triumphantly.

Alice did not quite know what to say to this: so she helped herself to some tea and bread-and-butter, and then turned to the Dormouse, and repeated her question. 'Why did they live at the bottom of a well?'

The Dormouse again took a minute or two to think about it,

and then said 'It was a treacle-well.'

'There's no such thing!' Alice was beginning very angrily, but the Hatter and the March Hare went 'Sh! Sh!' and the Dormouse sulkily remarked 'If you can't be civil, you'd better finish the story for yourself.'

'No, please go on!' Alice said very humbly. 'I won't interrupt you again. I dare say there may be *one*.'

'One, indeed!' said the Dormouse indignantly. However, he consented to go on. 'And so these three little sisters—they were learning to draw, you know—'

'What did they draw?' said Alice, quite forgetting her promise.

'Treacle,' said the Dormouse, without considering at all, this time.

'I want a clean cup,' interrupted the Hatter: 'let's all move one place on.'

He moved on as he spoke, and the Dormouse followed him: the March Hare moved into the Dormouse's place, and Alice rather unwillingly took the place of the March Hare. The Hatter was the only one who got any advantage from the change; and Alice was a good deal worse off than before, as the March Hare had just upset the milk-jug into his plate.

Alice did not wish to offend the Dormouse again, so she began very cautiously: 'But I don't understand. Where did they draw the treacle from?'

'You can draw water out of a water-well,' said the Hatter; 'so I should think you could draw treacle out of a treacle-well—eh, stupid?'

'But they were *in* the well,' Alice said to the Dormouse, not choosing to notice this last remark.

'Of course they were,' said the Dormouse: 'well in.'

This answer so confused poor Alice, that she let the Dormouse go on for some time without interrupting it.

'They were learning to draw,' the Dormouse went on, yawning and rubbing its eyes, for it was getting very sleepy; 'and they drew all manner of things—everything that begins with an M—'

'Why with an M?' said Alice.

'Why not?' said the March Hare.

Alice was silent.

The Dormouse had closed its eyes by this time, and was going off into a doze; but, on being pinched by the Hatter, it woke up again with a little shriek, and went on: '—that begins with an M, such as mouse-traps, and the moon, and memory and muchness—you know you say things are 'much of a muchness'—did you ever see such a thing as a drawing of a muchness!'

'Really, now you ask me,' said Alice, very much confused, 'I don't think—'

'Then you shouldn't talk,' said the Hatter.

This piece of rudeness was more than Alice could bear: she got up in great disgust, and walked off: the Dormouse fell asleep instantly, and neither of the others took the least notice of her going, though she looked back once or twice, half hoping that they would call after her: the last time she saw them, they were trying to put the Dormouse into the teapot.

'At any rate I'll never go *there* again!' said Alice, as she picked her way through the wood. 'It's the stupidest tea-party I ever was at in all my life!'

Just as she said this, she noticed that one of the trees had a door leading right into it. 'That's very curious!' she thought. 'But everything's curious today. I think I may as well go in at once.' And in she went.

Once more she found herself in the long hall, and close to the little glass table. 'Now, I'll manage better this time,' she said to herself, and began by taking the little golden key, and unlocking the door that led into the garden. Then she set to work nibbling at the mushroom (she had kept a piece of it in her pocket) till she was about a foot high: then she walked down the little passage: and *then*—she found herself at last in the beautiful garden, among the bright flower-beds and the cool fountains.

Chapter VIII

The Queen's Croquet-ground

A large rose-tree stood near the entrance of the garden: the roses growing on it were white, but there were three gardeners at it, busily painting them red. Alice thought this a very curious thing, and she went nearer to watch them, and, just as she came up to them, she heard one of them say 'Look out now, Five! Don't go splashing paint over me like that!'

'I couldn't help it,' said Five, in a sulky tone. 'Seven jogged my elbow.'

On which Seven looked up and said 'That's right, Five! Always lay the blame on others!'

'*You'd* better not talk!' said Five. 'I heard the Queen say only yesterday you deserved to be beheaded.'

'What for?' said the one who had spoken first.

'That's none of *your* business, Two!' said Seven.

'Yes, it is his business!' said Five. 'And I'll tell him—it was for bringing the cook tulip-roots instead of onions.

Seven flung down his brush, and had just begun 'Well, of all the unjust things—' when his eye chanced to fall upon Alice, as she stood watching them, and he checked himself suddenly: the others looked round also, and all of them bowed low.

'Would you tell me, please,' said Alice, a little timidly, 'why you are painting those roses?'

Five and Seven said nothing, but looked at Two. Two began, in a low voice, 'Why, the fact is, you see, Miss, this here ought to have been a *red* rose-tree, and we put a white one in by mistake; and, if the Queen was to find it out, we should all have our heads cut off, you know. So you see, Miss, we're doing our best, afore she comes, to—' At this moment, Five, who had been anxiously looking across the garden, called out 'The Queen! The Queen!', and the three gardeners instantly threw themselves flat upon their faces. There was a sound of many footsteps, and Alice looked round, eager to see the Queen.

First came ten soldiers carrying clubs: these were all shaped like the three gardeners, oblong and flat, with their hands and feet at the corners: next the ten courtiers: these were ornamented all over with diamonds, and walked two and two, as the soldiers did. After these came the royal children: there were ten of them, and the little dears came jumping merrily along, hand in hand, in couples: they were all ornamented with hearts. Next came the guests, mostly Kings and Queens, and among them Alice recognised the White Rabbit: it was talking in a hurried nervous manner, smiling at everything that was said, and went by without noticing her. Then followed the Knave of Hearts, carrying the King's crown on a crimson velvet cushion; and, last of all this grand procession, came THE KING AND THE QUEEN OF HEARTS.

Alice was rather doubtful whether she ought not to lie down on her face like the three gardeners, but she could not remember ever having heard of such a rule at processions; 'and besides, what would be the use of a procession,' thought she, 'if people had all to lie down on their faces, so that they couldn't see it?' So she stood where she was, and waited.

When the procession came opposite to Alice, they all stopped and looked at her, and the Queen said, severely, 'Who is this?'. She said it to the Knave of Hearts, who only bowed and smiled in reply.

'Idiot!' said the Queen, tossing her head impatiently; and, turning to Alice, she went on: 'What's your name, child?'

'My name is Alice, so please your Majesty,' said Alice very politely; but she added, to herself, 'Why, they're only a pack of cards, after all. I needn't be afraid of them!'

'And who are *these*?' said the Queen, pointing to the three gardeners who were lying round the rose-tree; for, you see, as they were lying on their faces, and the pattern on their backs was the same as the rest of the pack, she could not tell whether they were gardeners, or soldiers, or courtiers, or three of her own children.

'How should I know?' said Alice, surprised at her own courage. 'It's no business of *mine*.'

The Queen turned crimson with fury, and, after glaring at her for a moment like a wild beast, began screaming 'Off with her head! Off with— '

'Nonsense!' said Alice, very loudly and decidedly, and the Queen was silent.

The King laid his hand upon her arm, and timidly said 'Consider, my dear: she is only a child!'

The Queen turned angrily away from him, and said to the Knave 'Turn them over!'

The Knave did so, very carefully, with one foot.

'Get up!' said the Queen in a shrill, loud voice, and the three gardeners instantly jumped up, and began bowing to the King, the Queen, the royal children, and everybody else.

'Leave off that!' screamed the Queen. 'You make me giddy.' And then, turning to the rose-tree, she went on 'What have you been doing here?'

'May it please your Majesty,' said Two, in a very humble tone, going down on one knee as he spoke, 'we were trying—'

'I see!' said the Queen, who had meanwhile been examining the roses. 'Off with their heads!' and the procession moved on, three of the soldiers remaining behind to execute the unfortunate gardeners, who ran to Alice for protection.

'You shan't be beheaded!' said Alice, and she put them into a large flower-pot that stood near. The three soldiers wandered about for a minute or two, looking for them, and then quietly marched off after the others.

'Are their heads off?' shouted the Queen.

'Their heads are gone, if it please your Majesty!' the soldiers shouted in reply.

'That's right!' shouted the Queen. 'Can you play croquet?'

The soldiers were silent, and looked at Alice, as the question was evidently meant for her.

'Yes!' shouted Alice.

'Come on, then!' roared the Queen, and Alice joined the procession, wondering very much what would happen next.

'It's—it's a very fine day!' said a timid voice at her side. She was walking by the White Rabbit, who was peeping anxiously into her face.

'Very,' said Alice. 'Where's the Duchess?'

'Hush! Hush!' said the Rabbit in a low hurried tone. He looked anxiously over his shoulder as he spoke, and then raised himself upon tiptoe, put his mouth close to her ear, and whispered 'She's under sentence of execution.'

'What for?' said Alice.

'Did you say "What a pity!"?' the Rabbit asked.

'No, I didn't,' said Alice. 'I don't think it's at all a pity. I said "What for?"'

'She boxed the Queen's ears—' the Rabbit began. Alice gave a little scream of laughter. 'Oh, hush!' the Rabbit whispered in a frightened tone. 'The Queen will hear you! You see she came rather late, and the Queen said—'

'Get to your places!' shouted the Queen in a voice of thunder, and people began running about in all directions, tumbling up against each other: however, they got settled down in a minute or two, and the game began.

Alice thought she had never seen such a curious croquet-ground in her life: it was all ridges and furrows: the croquet balls were live hedgehogs, and the mallets live flamingoes, and the soldiers had to double themselves up and stand on their hands and feet, to make the arches.

The chief difficulty Alice found at first was in managing her flamingo: she succeeded in getting its body tucked away, comfortably enough, under her arm, with its legs hanging down, but generally, just as she had got its neck nicely straightened out, and was going to give the hedgehog a blow with its head, it *would* twist itself round and look up in her face, with such a puzzled

expression that she could not help bursting out laughing; and, when she had got its head down, and was going to begin again, it was very provoking to find that the hedgehog had unrolled itself, and was in the act of crawling away: besides all this, there was generally a ridge or a furrow in the way wherever she wanted to send the hedgehog to, and, as the doubled-up soldiers were always getting up and walking off to other parts of the ground, Alice soon came to the conclusion that it was a very difficult game indeed.

The players all played at once, without waiting for turns, quarreling all the while, and fighting for the hedgehogs; and in a very short time the Queen was in a furious passion, and went stamping about, and shouting 'Off with his head!' or 'Off with her head!' about once in a minute.

Alice began to feel very uneasy: to be sure, she had not as yet had any dispute with the Queen, but she knew that it might happen any minute, 'and then,' thought she, 'what would become of me? They're dreadfully fond of beheading people here: the great wonder is, that there's anyone left alive!'

She was looking about for some way of escape, and wondering whether she could get away without being seen, when she noticed a curious appearance in the air: it puzzled her very much at first, but after watching it a minute or two she made it out to be a grin, and she said to herself 'It's the Cheshire-Cat: now I shall have somebody to talk to.'

'How are you getting on?' said the Cat, as soon as there was mouth enough for it to speak with.

Alice waited till the eyes appeared, and then nodded. 'It's no use speaking to it,' she thought, 'till its ears have come, or at least one of them.' In another minute the whole head appeared, and then Alice put down her flamingo, and began an account of the game, feeling very glad she had some one to listen to her. The Cat seemed to think that there was enough of it now in sight, and no more of it appeared.

'I don't think they play at all fairly,' Alice began, in rather a complaining tone, 'and they all quarrel so dreadfully one can't hear oneself speak—and they don't seem to have any rules in particular: at least, if there are, nobody attends to them—and you've no idea how confusing it is all the things being alive: for instance, there's the arch I've got to go through next walking about at the other end of the ground—and I should have croqueted the Queen's hedgehog just now, only it ran away when it saw mine coming!'

'How do you like the Queen?' said the Cat in a low voice.

'Not at all,' said Alice: 'she's so extremely—' Just then she noticed that the Queen was close behind her, listening: so she went on '—likely to win, that it's hardly worth while finishing the game.'

The Queen smiled and passed on.

'Who *are* you talking to?' said the King, coming up to Alice, and looking at the Cat's head with great curiosity.

'It's a friend of mine—a Cheshire-Cat,' said Alice: 'allow me to introduce it.'

'I don't like the look of it at all,' said the King: 'however, it may kiss my hand, if it likes.'

'I'd rather not,' the Cat remarked.

'Don't be impertinent,' said the King, 'and don't look at me like that!' He got behind Alice as he spoke.

'A cat may look at a king,' said Alice. 'I've read that in some book, but I don't remember where.'

'Well, it must be removed,' said the King very decidedly; and he called to the Queen, who was passing at the moment, 'My dear! I wish you would have this cat removed!'

The Queen had only one way of settling all difficulties, great or small. 'Off with his head!' she said without even looking round.

'I'll fetch the executioner myself,' said the King eagerly, and he hurried off.

Alice thought she might as well go back and see how the game was going on, as she heard the Queen's voice in the distance, screaming with passion. She had already heard her sentence three of the players to be executed for having missed their turns, and she did not like the look of things at all, as the game was in such confusion that she never knew whether it was her turn or not. So she went off in search of her hedgehog.

The hedgehog was engaged in a fight with another hedgehog, which seemed to Alice an excellent opportunity for croqueting one of them with the other: the only difficulty was, that her flamingo was gone across to the other side of the garden, where Alice could see it trying in a helpless sort of way to fly up into a tree.

By the time she had caught the flamingo and brought it back, the fight was over, and both the hedgehogs were out of sight: 'but it doesn't matter much,' thought Alice, 'as all the arches are gone from this side of the ground.' So she tucked it away under her arm, that it might not escape again, and went back to have a little more conversation with her friend.

When she got back to the Cheshire-Cat, she was surprised to find quite a large crowd collected round it: there was a dispute going on between the executioner, the King, and the Queen, who were all talking at once, while all the rest were quite silent, and looked very uncomfortable.

The moment Alice appeared, she was appealed to by all three to settle the question, and they repeated their arguments to her, though, as they all spoke at once, she found it very hard to make out exactly what they said.

The executioner's argument was, that you couldn't cut off a head unless there was a body to cut it off from: that he had never had to do such a thing before, and he wasn't going to begin at his time of life.

The King's argument was that anything that had a head could be beheaded, and that you weren't to talk nonsense.

The Queen's argument was that, if something wasn't done about it in less than no time, she'd have everybody executed, all round. (It was this last remark that had made the whole party look so grave and anxious.)

Alice could think of nothing else to say but 'It belongs to the Duchess: you'd better ask her about it.'

'She's in prison,' the Queen said to the executioner: 'fetch her here.' And the executioner went off like an arrow.

The Cat's head began fading away the moment he was gone, and, by the time he had come back with the Duchess, it had entirely disappeared: so the King and the executioner ran wildly up and down, looking for it, while the rest of the party went back to the game.

Chapter IX

The Mock Turtle's Story

'You can't think how glad I am to see you again, you dear old thing!' said the Duchess, as she tucked her arm affectionately into Alice's, and they walked off together.

Alice was very glad to find her in such a pleasant temper, and thought to herself that perhaps it was only the pepper that had made her so savage when they met in the kitchen.

'When I'm a Duchess,' she said to herself (not in a very hopeful tone, though), 'I won't have any pepper in my kitchen *at all*. Soup does very well without—Maybe it's always pepper that makes people hot-tempered,' she went on, very much pleased at having found out a new kind of rule, 'and vinegar that makes them sour—and camomile that makes them bitter—and—and barley-sugar and such things that make children sweet-tempered. I only wish people knew that: then they wouldn't be so stingy about it, you know—'

She had quite forgotten the Duchess by this time, and was a little startled when she heard her voice close to her ear. 'You're thinking about something, my dear, and that makes you forget to talk. I can't tell you just now what the moral of that is, but I shall remember it in a bit.'

'Perhaps it hasn't one,' Alice ventured to remark.

'Tut, tut, child!' said the Duchess. 'Every thing's got a moral, if only you can find it.' And she squeezed herself up closer to Alice's side as she spoke.

Alice did not much like her keeping so close to her: first, because the Duchess was *very* ugly; and secondly, because she was exactly the right height to rest her chin on Alice's shoulder, and it was an uncomfortably sharp chin. However, she did not like to be rude: so she bore it as well as she could.

'The game's going on rather better now,' she said, by way of keeping up the conversation a little.

''Tis so,' said the Duchess: 'and the moral of that is—"Oh, 'tis love, 'tis love, that makes the world go round!"'

'Somebody said,' Alice whispered, 'that it's done by everybody minding their own business!'

'Ah, well! It means much the same thing,' said the Duchess, digging her sharp little chin into Alice's shoulder as she added 'and the moral of *that* is—"Take care of the sense, and the sounds will take care of themselves."'

'How fond she is of finding morals in things!' Alice thought to herself

'I dare say you're wondering why I don't put my arm round your waist,' the Duchess said, after a pause: 'the reason is, that I'm doubtful about the temper of your flamingo. Shall I try the experiment?'

'He might bite,' Alice cautiously replied, not feeling at all anxious to have the experiment tried.

'Very true,' said the Duchess: 'flamingoes and mustard both bite. And the moral of that is—"Birds of a feather flock together."'

'Only mustard isn't a bird,' Alice remarked.

'Right, as usual,' said the Duchess: 'what a clear way you have of putting things!'

'It's a mineral, I *think*,' said Alice.

'Of course it is,' said the Duchess, who seemed ready to agree to everything that Alice said: 'there's a large mustard-mine near here. And the moral of that is—"The more there is of mine, the less there is of yours."'

'Oh, I know!' exclaimed Alice, who had not attended to this last remark. 'It's a vegetable. It doesn't look like one, but it is.'

'I quite agree with you,' said the Duchess; 'and the moral of that is—"Be what you would seem to be"—or, if you'd like it put more simply—"Never imagine yourself not to be otherwise than what it might appear to others that what you were or might have been was not otherwise than what you had been would have appeared to them to be otherwise.'"

'I think I should understand that better,' Alice said very politely, 'if I had it written down: but I can't quite follow it as you say it.'

'That's nothing to what I could say if I chose,' the Duchess replied, in a pleased tone.

'Pray don't trouble yourself to say it any longer than that,' said Alice.

'Oh, don't talk about trouble!' said the Duchess. 'I make you a present of everything I've said as yet.'

'A cheap sort of present!' thought Alice. 'I'm glad people don't give birthday-presents like that!' But she did not venture to say it out loud.

'Thinking again?' the Duchess asked, with another dig of her sharp little chin.

'I've a right to think,' said Alice sharply, for she was beginning to feel a little worried.

'Just about as much right,' said the Duchess, 'as pigs have to fly; and the m—'

But here, to Alice's great surprise, the Duchess's voice died away, even in the middle of her favourite word 'moral,' and the arm that was linked into hers began to tremble. Alice looked up, and there stood the Queen in front of them, with her arms folded, frowning like a thunderstorm.

'A fine day, your Majesty!' the Duchess began in a low, weak voice.

'Now, I give you fair warning,' shouted the Queen, stamping on the ground as she spoke; 'either you or your head must be off, and that in about half no time! Take your choice!'

The Duchess took her choice, and was gone in a moment.

'Let's go on with the game,' the Queen said to Alice; and Alice was too much frightened to say a word, but slowly followed her back to the croquet-ground.

The other guests had taken advantage of the Queen's absence, and were resting in the shade: however, the moment they saw her, they hurried back to the game, the Queen merely remarking that a moment's delay would cost them their lives.

All the time they were playing the Queen never left off quarreling with the other players, and shouting 'Off with his head!' or 'Off with her head!' Those whom she sentenced were taken into custody by the soldiers, who of course had to leave off being arches to do this, so that, by the end of half an hour or so, there were no arches left, and all the players, except the King, the Queen, and Alice, were in custody and under sentence of execution.

Then the Queen left off, quite out of breath, and said to Alice 'Have you seen the Mock Turtle yet?'

'No,' said Alice. 'I don't even know what a Mock Turtle is.'

'It's the thing Mock Turtle Soup is made from,' said the Queen.

'I never saw one, or heard of one,' said Alice.

'Come on, then,' said the Queen, 'and he shall tell you his history'

As they walked off together, Alice heard the King say in a low voice, to the company generally, 'You are all pardoned.' 'Come, *that's* a good thing!' she said to herself, for she had felt quite unhappy at the number of executions the Queen had ordered.

They very soon came upon a Gryphon, lying fast asleep in the sun. (If you don't know what a Gryphon is, look at the picture.) 'Up, lazy thing!' said the Queen, 'and take this young lady to see the Mock Turtle, and to hear his history. I must go back and see after some executions I have ordered;' and she walked off, leaving Alice alone with the Gryphon. Alice did not quite like the look of the creature, but on the whole she thought it would be quite as safe to stay with it as to go after that savage Queen: so she waited.

The Gryphon sat up and rubbed its eyes: then it watched the Queen till she was out of sight: then it chuckled. 'What fun!' said the Gryphon, half to itself, half to Alice.

'What is the fun?' said Alice

'Why, *she*,' said the Gryphon. 'It's all her fancy, that: they never executes nobody, you know. Come on!'

'Everybody says 'come on!' here,' thought Alice, as she went slowly after it: 'I never was so ordered about before, in all my life, never!'

They had not gone far before they saw the Mock Turtle in the distance, sitting sad and lonely on a little ledge of rock, and,

as they came nearer, Alice could hear him sighing as if his heart would break. She pitied him deeply. 'What is his sorrow?' she asked the Gryphon. And the Gryphon answered, very nearly in the same words as before, 'It's all his fancy, that: he hasn't got no sorrow, you know. Come on!'

So they went up to the Mock Turtle, who looked at them with large eyes full of tears, but said nothing.

'This here young lady,' said the Gryphon, 'she wants for to know your history; she do.'

'I'll tell it to her,' said the Mock Turtle in a deep, hollow tone. 'Sit down, both of you, and don't speak a word till I've finished.'

So they sat down, and nobody spoke for some minutes. Alice thought to herself 'I don't see how he can ever finish, if he doesn't begin.' But she waited patiently.

'Once,' said the Mock Turtle at last, with a deep sigh, 'I was a real Turtle.'

These words were followed by a very long silence, broken only by an occasional exclamation of 'Hjckrrh!' from the Gryphon, and the constant heavy sobbing of the Mock Turtle. Alice was very nearly getting up and saying 'Thank you, Sir, for your interesting story,' but she could not help thinking there must be more to come, so she sat still and said nothing.

'When we were little,' the Mock Turtle went on at last, more calmly, though still sobbing a little now and then, 'we went to school in the sea. The master was an old Turtle—we used to call him Tortoise—'

'Why did you call him Tortoise, if he wasn't one?' Alice asked.

'We called him Tortoise because he taught us,' said the Mock Turtle angrily. 'Really you are very dull!'

'You ought to be ashamed of yourself for asking such a simple question,' added the Gryphon; and then they both sat silent and looked at poor Alice, who felt ready to sink into the earth. At last the Gryphon said to the Mock Turtle 'Drive on, old fellow! Don't be all day about it', and he went on in these words:—

'Yes, we went to school in the sea, though you mayn't believe it—'

'I never said I didn't!' interrupted Alice.

'You did,' said the Mock Turtle.

'Hold your tongue!' added the Gryphon, before Alice could speak again. The Mock Turtle went on.

'We had the best of educations—in fact, we went to school every day—'

'*I've* been to a day-school, too,' said Alice. 'You needn't be so proud as all that.'

'With extras?' asked the Mock Turtle, a little anxiously.

'Yes,' said Alice: 'we learned French and music.'

'And washing?' said the Mock Turtle.

'Certainly not!' said Alice indignantly.

'Ah! Then yours wasn't a really good school,' said the Mock Turtle in a tone of great relief. 'Now, at *ours*, they had, at the end of the bill, "French, music, *and washing*—extra."'

'You couldn't have wanted it much,' said Alice; 'living at the bottom of the sea.'

'I couldn't afford to learn it,' said the Mock Turtle with a sigh. 'I only took the regular course.'

'What was that?' inquired Alice.

'Reeling and Writhing, of course, to begin with,' the Mock Turtle replied; 'and then the different branches of Arithmetic—

Ambition, Distraction, Uglification, and Derision.'

'I never heard of "Uglification,"' Alice ventured to say. 'What is it?'

The Gryphon lifted up both its paws in surprise. 'Never heard of uglifying!' it exclaimed. 'You know what to beautify is, I suppose?'

'Yes,' said Alice doubtfully: 'it means—to—make—anything—prettier.'

'Well, then,' the Gryphon went on, 'if you don't know what to uglify is, you *are* a simpleton.'

Alice did not feel encouraged to ask any more questions about it: so she turned to the Mock Turtle, and said 'What else had you to learn?'

'Well, there was Mystery,' the Mock Turtle replied, counting off the subjects on his flappers,—'Mystery, ancient and modern, with Seaography: then Drawling—the Drawling-master was an old conger-eel, that used to come once a week: *he* taught us Drawling, Stretching, and Fainting in Coils.'

'What was *that* like?' asked Alice.

'Well, I can't show it you, myself,' the Mock Turtle said: 'I'm too stiff. And the Gryphon never learnt it.'

'Hadn't time,' said the Gryphon. 'I went to the Classical master, though. He was an old crab, *he* was.'

'I never went to him,' the Mock Turtle said with a sigh. 'He taught Laughing and Grief, they used to say'

'So he did, so he did,' said the Gryphon, sighing in his turn; and both creatures hid their faces in their paws.

'And how many hours a day did you do lessons?' said Alice, in a hurry to change the subject.

'Ten hours the first day,' said the Mock Turtle: 'nine the next, and so on.'

'What a curious plan!' exclaimed Alice.

'That's the reason they're called lessons,' the Gryphon remarked: 'because they lessen from day to day.'

This was quite a new idea to Alice, and she thought it over a little before she made her next remark. 'Then the eleventh day must have been a holiday?'

'Of course it was,' said the Mock Turtle.

'And how did you manage on the twelfth?' Alice went on eagerly.

'That's enough about lessons,' the Gryphon interrupted in a very decided tone. 'Tell her something about the games now.'

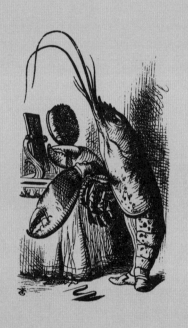

Chapter X

The Lobster-quadrille

The Mock Turtle sighed deeply, and drew the back of one flapper across his eyes. He looked at Alice and tried to speak, but, for a minute or two, sobs choked his voice. 'Same as if he had a bone in his throat,' said the Gryphon; and it set to work shaking him and punching him in the back. At last the Mock Turtle recovered his voice, and, with tears running down his cheeks, he went on again:—

'You may not have lived much under the sea—' ('I haven't,' said Alice)—'and perhaps you were never even introduced to a lobster—' (Alice began to say 'I once tasted—' but checked herself hastily, and said 'No, never') '—so you can have no idea what a delightful thing a Lobster-Quadrille is!'

'No, indeed,' said Alice. 'What sort of a dance is it?'

'Why' said the Gryphon, 'you first form into a line along the seashore—'

'Two lines!' cried the Mock Turtle. 'Seals, turtles, salmon, and so on: then, when you've cleared all the jellyfish out of the way—'

'*That* generally takes some time,' interrupted the Gryphon.

'—you advance twice—'

'Each with a lobster as a partner!' cried the Gryphon.

'Of course,' the Mock Turtle said: 'advance twice, set to partners—'

'—change lobsters, and retire in same order,' continued the Gryphon.

'Then, you know,' the Mock Turtle went on, 'you throw the—'

'The lobsters!' shouted the Gryphon, with a bound into the air.

'—as far out to sea as you can—'

'Swim after them!' screamed the Gryphon.

'Turn a somersault in the sear!' cried the Mock Turtle, capering wildly about.

'Change lobsters again!' yelled the Gryphon at the top of its voice.

'Back to land again, and—that's all the first figure,' said the Mock Turtle, suddenly dropping his voice; and the two creatures, who had been jumping about like mad things all this time, sat down again very sadly and quietly and looked at Alice.

'It must be a very pretty dance,' said Alice timidly.

'Would you like to see a little of it?' said the Mock Turtle.

'Very much indeed,' said Alice.

'Come, let's try the first figure!' said the Mock Turtle to the Gryphon. 'We can do it without lobsters, you know Which shall sing?'

'Oh, *you* sing,' said the Gryphon. 'I've forgotten the words.'

So they began solemnly dancing round and round Alice, every now and then treading on her toes when they passed too close, and waving their fore-paws to mark the time, while the Mock Turtle sang this, very slowly and sadly:—

'Will you walk a little faster?' said a whiting to a snail,
'There's a porpoise close behind us, and he's treading on my tail.
See how eagerly the lobsters and the turtles all advance!
They are waiting on the shingle—will you come and join
    the dance?
  Will you, won't you, will you, won't you, will you join
    the dance?
  Will you, won't you, will you, won't you, won't you join
    the dance?

'You can really have no notion how delightful it will be

When they take us up and throw us, with the lobsters, out to sea!'
But the snail replied 'Too far, too far!', and gave a look
askance—
Said he thanked the whiting kindly, but he would not join
the dance.
Would not, could not, would not, could not, would not join
the dance.
Would not, could not, would not, could not, could not join
the dance.

'What matters it how far we go?' his scaly friend replied.
'There is another shore, you know, upon the other side.
The further off from England the nearer is to France—
Then turn not pale, beloved snail, but come and join
the dance.
Will you, won't you, will you, won't you, will you join
the dance?
Will you, won't you, will you, won't you, won't you join
the dance?'

'Thank you, it's a very interesting dance to watch,' said Alice, feeling very glad that it was over at last: 'and I do so like that curious song about the whiting!'

'Oh, as to the whiting,' said the Mock Turtle, 'they—you've seen them, of course?'

'Yes,' said Alice, 'I've often seen them at dinn—' she checked herself hastily.

'I don't know where Dinn may be,' said the Mock Turtle; 'but, if you've seen them so often, of course you know what they're like?'

'I believe so,' Alice replied thoughtfully. 'They have their tails in their mouths—and they're all over crumbs.'

'You're wrong about the crumbs,' said the Mock Turtle: 'crumbs would all wash off in the sea. But they *have* their tails in their mouths; and the reason is—' here the Mock Turtle yawned and shut his eyes. 'Tell her about the reason and all that,' he said to the Gryphon.

'The reason is,' said the Gryphon, 'that they *would* go with the lobsters to the dance. So they got thrown out to sea. So they had to fall a long way. So they got their tails fast in their mouths. So they couldn't get them out again. That's all.'

'Thank you,' said Alice, 'it's very interesting. I never knew so much about a whiting before.'

'I can tell you more than that, if you like,' said the Gryphon. 'Do you know why it's called a whiting?'

'I never thought about it,' said Alice. 'Why?'

'It does the *boots and shoes*,' the Gryphon replied very solemnly.

Alice was thoroughly puzzled. 'Does the boots and shoes!' she repeated in a wondering tone.

'Why, what are *your* shoes done with?' said the Gryphon. 'I mean, what makes them so shiny?'

Alice looked down at them, and considered a little before she gave her answer. 'They're done with blacking, I believe.'

'Boots and shoes under the sea,' the Gryphon went on in a deep voice, 'are done with whiting. Now you know.'

'And what are they made of?' Alice asked in a tone of great curiosity.

'Soles and eels, of course,' the Gryphon replied, rather

impatiently: 'any shrimp could have told you that.'

'If I'd been the whiting,' said Alice, whose thoughts were still running on the song, 'I'd have said to the porpoise 'Keep back, please! We don't want *you* with us!''

'They were obliged to have him with them,' the Mock Turtle said. 'No wise fish would go anywhere without a porpoise.'

'Wouldn't it, really?' said Alice, in a tone of great surprise.

'Of course not,' said the Mock Turtle. 'Why, if a fish came to *me*, and told me he was going a journey, I should say 'With what porpoise?''

'Don't you mean "purpose?"' said Alice.

'I mean what I say,' the Mock Turtle replied, in an offended tone. And the Gryphon added 'Come, let's hear some of *your* adventures.'

'I could tell you my adventures—beginning from this morning,' said Alice a little timidly; 'but it's no use going back to yesterday, because I was a different person then.'

'Explain all that,' said the Mock Turtle.

'No, no! The adventures first,' said the Gryphon in an impatient tone: 'explanations take such a dreadful time.'

So Alice began telling them her adventures from the time when she first saw the White Rabbit. She was a little nervous about it, just at first, the two creatures got so close to her, one on each side, and opened their eyes and mouths so very wide; but she gained courage as she went on. Her listeners were perfectly quiet till she got to the part about her repeating 'You are old, Father William,' to the Caterpillar, and the words all coming different, and then the Mock Turtle drew a long breath, and said 'That's very curious!'

'It's all about as curious as it can be,' said the Gryphon.

'It all came different!' the Mock Turtle repeated thoughtfully. 'I should like to hear her try and repeat something now. Tell her to begin.' He looked at the Gryphon as if he thought it had some kind of authority over Alice.

'Stand up and repeat "*'Tis the voice of the sluggard*"', said the Gryphon.

'How the creatures order one about, and make one repeat lessons!' thought Alice. 'I might just as well be at school at once.' However, she got up, and began to repeat it, but her head was so full of the Lobster-Quadrille, that she hardly knew what she was saying; and the words came very queer indeed:—

' 'Tis the voice of the Lobster: I heard him declare
'You have baked me too brown, I must sugar my hair.'
As a duck with its eyelids, so he with his nose
Trims his belt and his buttons, and turns out his toes.

When the sands are all dry, he is gay as a lark,
And will talk in contemptuous tones of the Shark:
But, when the tide rises and sharks are around,
His voice has a timid and tremulous sound.'

'That's different from what I used to say when I was a child,' said the Gryphon.

'Well, I never heard it before,' said the Mock Turtle; 'but it sounds uncommon nonsense.'

Alice said nothing: she had sat down with her face in her hands, wondering if anything would *ever* happen in a natural way again.

'I should like to have it explained,' said the Mock Turtle.

'She can't explain it,' said the Gryphon hastily. 'Go on with the next verse.'

'But about his toes?' the Mock Turtle persisted. 'How *could* he turn them out with his nose, you know?'

'It's the first position in dancing,' Alice said; but she was dreadfully puzzled by the whole thing, and longed to change the subject.

'Go on with the next verse,' the Gryphon repeated: 'it begins "*I passed by his garden.*"'

Alice did not dare to disobey, though she felt sure it would all come wrong, and she went on in a trembling voice: —

> '*I passed by his garden, and marked, with one eye,*
> *How the Owl and the Panther were sharing a pie:*
> *The Panther took pie-crust, and gravy, and meat,*
> *While the Owl had the dish as its share of the treat.*
> *When the pie was all finished, the Owl, as a boon,*
> *Was kindly permitted to pocket the spoon:*
> *While the Panther received knife and fork with a growl,*
> *And concluded the banquet by—*'

'What is the use of repeating all that stuff?' the Mock Turtle interrupted, 'if you don't explain it as you go on? It's by far the most confusing thing *I* ever heard!'

'Yes, I think you'd better leave off,' said the Gryphon, and Alice was only too glad to do so.

'Shall we try another figure of the Lobster-Quadrille?' the Gryphon went on. 'Or would you like the Mock Turtle to sing you another song?'

'Oh, a song, please, if the Mock Turtle would be so kind,' Alice replied, so eagerly that the Gryphon said, in a rather offended tone, 'Hm! No accounting for tastes! Sing her 'Turtle Soup,' will you, old fellow?'

The Mock Turtle sighed deeply, and began, in a voice choked with sobs, to sing this:—

'Beautiful Soup, so rich and green,
Waiting in a hot tureen!
Who for such dainties would not stoop?
Soup of the evening, beautiful Soup!
Soup of the evening, beautiful Soup!
    Beau—ootiful Soo—oop!
    Beau—ootiful Soo—oop!
Soo—oop of the e—e—evening,
    Beautiful, beautiful Soup!

'Beautiful Soup! Who cares for fish,
Game, or any other dish?
Who would not give all else for two
Pennyworth only of beautiful Soup?
Pennyworth only of beautiful soup?
    Beau—ootiful Soo—oop!
    Beau—ootiful Soo—oop!
Soo—oop of the e—e—evening,
    Beautifitl, beauti—FUL SOUP!'

'Chorus again!' cried the Gryphon, and the Mock Turtle had just begun to repeat it, when a cry of 'The trial's beginning!' was heard in the distance.

'Come on!' cried the Gryphon, and, taking Alice by the hand, it hurried off, without waiting for the end of the song.

'What trial is it?' Alice panted as she ran; but the Gryphon only answered 'Come on!' and ran the faster, while more and more faintly came, carried on the breeze that followed them, the melancholy words:—

> 'Soo—oop of the e—e—evening,
> Beautiful, beautiful Soup!'

Chapter XI

Who Stole the Tarts?

The King and Queen of Hearts were seated on their throne when they arrived, with a great crowd assembled about them—all sorts of little birds and beasts, as well as the whole pack of cards: the Knave was standing before them, in chains, with a soldier on each side to guard him; and near the King was the White Rabbit, with a trumpet in one hand, and a scroll of parchment in the other. In the very middle of the court was a table, with a large dish of tarts upon it: they looked so good, that it made Alice quite hungry to look at them—'I wish they'd get the trial done,' she thought, 'and hand round the refreshments!' But there seemed to be no chance of this; so she began looking at everything about her to pass away the time.

Alice had never been in a court of justice before, but she had read about them in books, and she was quite pleased to find that she knew the name of nearly everything there. 'That's the judge,' she said to herself, 'because of his great wig.'

The judge, by the way, was the King; and, as he wore his crown over the wig (look at the frontispiece if you want to see how he did it), he did not look at all comfortable, and it was certainly not becoming.

'And that's the jury-box,' thought Alice; 'and those twelve creatures,' (she was obliged to say 'creatures,' you see, because some of them were animals, and some were birds,) 'I suppose they are the jurors.' She said this last word two or three times over to herself, being rather proud of it: for she thought, and rightly too, that very few little girls of her age knew the meaning of it at all. However, 'jurymen' would have done just as well.

The twelve jurors were all writing very busily on slates. 'What are they doing?' Alice whispered to the Gryphon. 'They can't have anything to put down yet, before the trial's begun.'

'They're putting down their names,' the Gryphon whispered in reply, 'for fear they should forget them before the end of the trial.'

'Stupid things!' Alice began in a loud indignant voice; but she stopped herself hastily, for the White Rabbit cried out 'Silence in the court!', and the King put on his spectacles and looked anxiously round, to make out who was talking.

Alice could see, as well as if she were looking over their shoulders, that all the jurors were writing down 'Stupid things!' on their slates, and she could even make out that one of them didn't know how to spell 'stupid,' and that he had to ask his neighbour to tell him. 'A nice muddle their slates'll be in, before the trial's over!' thought Alice.

One of the jurors had a pencil that squeaked. This, of course, Alice could *not* stand, and she went round the court and got behind him, and very soon found an opportunity of taking it away. She did it so quickly that the poor little juror (it was Bill, the Lizard) could not make out at all what had become of it; so, after hunting all about for it, he was obliged to write with one finger for the rest of the day; and this was of very little use, as it left no mark on the slate.

'Herald, read the accusation!' said the King.

On this the White Rabbit blew three blasts on the trumpet, and then unrolled the parchment-scroll, and read as follows:—

'The Queen of Hearts, she made some tarts,
    All on a summer day:
The Knave of Hearts, he stole those tarts
    And took them quite away!'

'Consider your verdict,' the King said to the jury.

'Not yet, not yet!' the Rabbit hastily interrupted. 'There's a great deal to come before that!'

'Call the first witness,' said the King; and the White Rabbit blew three blasts on the trumpet, and called out 'First witness!'

The first witness was the Hatter. He came in with a teacup in one hand and a piece of bread-and-butter in the other. 'I beg pardon, your Majesty,' he began, 'for bringing these in; but I hadn't quite finished my tea when I was sent for.'

'You ought to have finished,' said the King. 'When did you begin?'

The Hatter looked at the March Hare, who had followed him into the court, arm-in-arm with the Dormouse. 'Fourteenth of March, I *think* it was,' he said.

'Fifteenth,' said the March Hare.

'Sixteenth,' said the Dormouse.

'Write that down,' the King said to the jury; and the jury eagerly wrote down all three dates on their slates, and then added them up, and reduced the answer to shillings and pence.

'Take off your hat,' the King said to the Hatter.

'It isn't mine,' said the Hatter.

'*Stolen!*' the King exclaimed, turning to the jury, who instantly made a memorandum of the fact.

'I keep them to sell,' the Hatter added as an explanation. 'I've none of my own. I'm a hatter.'

Here the Queen put on her spectacles, and began staring hard at the Hatter, who turned pale and fidgeted.

'Give your evidence,' said the King; 'and don't be nervous, or I'll have you executed on the spot.'

This did not seem to encourage the witness at all: he kept

shifting from one foot to the other, looking uneasily at the Queen, and in his confusion he bit a large piece out of his teacup instead of the bread-and-butter.

Just at this moment Alice felt a very curious sensation, which puzzled her a good deal until she made out what it was: she was beginning to grow larger again, and she thought at first she would get up and leave the court; but on second thoughts she decided to remain where she was as long as there was room for her.

'I wish you wouldn't squeeze so,' said the Dormouse, who was sitting next to her. 'I can hardly breathe.'

'I can't help it,' said Alice very meekly: 'I'm growing.'

'You've no right to grow *here*,' said the Dormouse.

'Don't talk nonsense,' said Alice more boldly: 'you know you're growing too.'

'Yes, but *I* grow at a reasonable pace,' said the Dormouse: 'not in that ridiculous fashion.' And he got up very sulkily and crossed over to the other side of the court.

All this time the Queen had never left off staring at the Hatter, and, just as the Dormouse crossed the court, she said, to one of the officers of the court, 'Bring me the list of the singers in the last concert!' on which the wretched Hatter trembled so, that he shook off both his shoes.

'Give your evidence,' the King repeated angrily, 'or I'll have you executed, whether you're nervous or not.

'I'm a poor man, your Majesty,' the Hatter began, in a trembling voice, 'and I hadn't begun my tea—not above a week or so—and what with the bread-and-butter getting so thin—and the twinkling of the tea—'

'The twinkling of *what*?' said the King.

'It *began* with the tea,' the Hatter replied.

'Of course twinkling *begins* with a T!' said the King sharply. 'Do you take me for a dunce? Go on!'

'I'm a poor man,' the Hatter went on, 'and most things twinkled after that—only the March Hare said—'

'I didn't!' the March Hare interrupted in a great hurry.

'You did!' said the Hatter.

'I deny it!' said the March Hare.

'He denies it,' said the King: 'leave out that part.'

'Well, at any rate, the Dormouse said—' the Harter went on, looking anxiously round to see if he would deny it too; but the Dormouse denied nothing, being fast asleep.

'After that,' continued the Hatter, 'I cut some more bread-and-butter—'

'But what did the Dormouse say?' one of the jury asked.

'That I can't remember,' said the Hatter.

'You *must* remember,' remarked the King, 'or I'll have you executed.'

The miserable Hatter dropped his teacup and bread-and-butter; and went down on one knee. 'I'm a poor man, your Majesty;' he began.

'You're a *very* poor *speaker*,' said the King.

Here one of the guinea pigs cheered, and was immediately suppressed by the officers of the court. (As that is rather a hard word, I will just explain to you how it was done. They had a large canvas bag, which tied up at the mouth with strings: into this they slipped the guinea-pig head first, and then sat upon it.)

'I'm glad I've seen that done,' thought Alice. 'I've so often read in the newspapers, at the end of trials, 'There was some attempt at applause, which was immediately suppressed by the officers of the court,' and I never understood what it meant till now.'

'If that's all you know about it, you may stand down,' continued the King.

'I can't go no lower,' said the Hatter: 'I'm on the floor, as it is.'

'Then you may *sit* down,' the King replied.

Here the other guinea pig cheered, and was suppressed.

'Come, that finishes the guinea pigs!' thought Alice. 'Now we shall get on better.'

'I'd rather finish my tea,' said the Hatter, with an anxious look at the Queen, who was reading the list of singers.

'You may go,' said the King, and the Hatter hurriedly left the court, without even waiting to put his shoes on.

'—and just take his head off outside,' the Queen added to one of the officers; but the Hatter was out of sight before the officer

could get to the door.

'Call the next witness!' said the King.

The next witness was the Duchess's cook. She carried the pepper-box in her hand, and Alice guessed who it was, even before she got into the court, by the way the people near the door began sneezing all at once.

'Give your evidence,' said the King.

'Shan't,' said the cook.

The King looked anxiously at the White Rabbit, who said, in a low voice, 'Your Majesty must cross-examine *this* witness.'

'Well, if I must, I must,' the King said with a melancholy air, and, after folding his arms and frowning at the cook till his eyes were nearly out of sight, he said, in a deep voice, 'What are tarts made of?'

'Pepper, mostly,' said the cook.

'Treacle,' said a sleepy voice behind her.

'Collar that Dormouse!' the Queen shrieked out. 'Behead that Dormouse! Turn that Dormouse out of court! Suppress him! Pinch him! Off with his whiskers!'

For some minutes the whole court was in confusion, getting the Dormouse turned out, and, by the time they had settled down again, the cook had disappeared.

'Never mind!' said the King, with an air of great relief. 'Call the next witness.' And, he added, in an under-tone to the Queen, 'Really, my dear, you must cross-examine the next witness. It quite makes my forehead ache!'

Alice watched the White Rabbit as he fumbled over the list, feeling very curious to see what the next witness would be like, '—for they haven't got much evidence *yet*,' she said to herself.

Imagine her surprise, when the White Rabbit read out, at the top of his shrill little voice, the name 'Alice!'

Chapter XII

Alice's Evidence

'Here!' cried Alice, quite forgetting in the flurry of the moment how large she had grown in the last few minutes, and she jumped up in such a hurry that she tipped over the jury-box with the edge of her skirt, upsetting all the jurymen on to the heads of the crowd below; and there they lay sprawling about, reminding her very much of a globe of goldfish she had accidentally upset the week before.

'Oh, I *beg* your pardon!' she exclaimed in a tone of great dismay, and began picking them up again as quickly as she could, for the accident of the goldfish kept running in her head, and she had a vague sort of idea that they must be collected at once and put back into the jury-box, or they would die.

'The trial cannot proceed,' said the King, in a very grave voice, 'until all the jurymen are back in their proper places—*all*,' he repeated with great emphasis, looking hard at Alice as he said so.

Alice looked at the jury-box, and saw that, in her haste, she had put the Lizard in head downwards, and the poor little thing was waving its tail about in a melancholy way, being quite unable to move. She soon got it out again, and put it right; 'not that it signifies much,' she said to herself; 'I should think it would be *quite* as much use in the trial one way up as the other.'

As soon as the jury had a little recovered from the shock of being upset, and their slates and pencils had been found and handed back to them, they set to work very diligently to write out a history of the accident, all except the Lizard, who seemed too much overcome to do anything but sit with its mouth open, gazing up into the roof of the court.

'What do you know about this business?' the King said to Alice.

'Nothing,' said Alice.

'Nothing *whatever*?' persisted the King.

'Nothing whatever,' said Alice.

'That's very important,' the King said, turning to the jury. They were just beginning to write this down on their slates, when the White Rabbit interrupted: '*Un*important, your Majesty means, of course,' he said, in a very respectful tone, but frowning and making faces at him as he spoke.

'*Un*important, of course, I meant,' the King hastily said, and went on to himself in an undertone, 'important—unimportant— unimportant—important—' as if he were trying which word sounded best.

Some of the jury wrote it down 'important,' and some 'unimportant.' Alice could see this, as she was near enough to look over their slates; 'but it doesn't matter a bit,' she thought to herself.

At this moment the King, who had been for some time busily writing in his notebook, called out 'Silence!', and read out from his book, 'Rule Forty-two. *All persons more than a mile high to leave the court.*'

Everybody looked at Alice.

'*I'm* not a mile high,' said Alice.

'You are,' said the King.

'Nearly two miles high,' added the Queen.

'Well, I shan't go, at any rate,' said Alice: 'besides, that's not a regular rule: you invented it just now.'

'It's the oldest rule in the book,' said the King.

'Then it ought to be Number One,' said Alice.

The King turned pale, and shut his notebook hastily. 'Consider your verdict,' he said to the jury in a low trembling voice.

'There's more evidence to come yet, please your Majesty,' said the White Rabbit, jumping up in a great hurry: 'this paper has just been picked up.'

'What's in it?' said the Queen.

'I haven't opened it yet,' said the White Rabbit; 'but it seems to be a letter, written by the prisoner to—to somebody.'

'It must have been that,' said the King, 'unless it was written to nobody, which isn't usual, you know.'

'Who is it directed to?' said one of the jurymen.

'It isn't directed at all,' said the White Rabbit: 'in fact, there's nothing written on the *outside*.' He unfolded the paper as he spoke, and added 'It isn't a letter, after all: it's a set of verses.'

'Are they in the prisoner's handwriting?' asked another of the jurymen.

'No, they're not,' said the White Rabbit, 'and that's the queerest thing about it.' (The jury all looked puzzled.)

'He must have imitated somebody else's hand,' said the King. (The jury all brightened up again.)

'Please your Majesty' said the Knave, 'I didn't write it, and they can't prove that I did: there's no name signed at the end.'

'If you didn't sign it,' said the King, 'that only makes the matter worse. You *must* have meant some mischief, or else you'd have signed your name like an honest man.'

There was a general clapping of hands at this: it was the first really clever thing the King had said that day.

'That *proves* his guilt, of course,' said the Queen: 'so, off with—'

'It doesn't prove anything of the sort!' said Alice. 'Why, you don't even know what they're about!'

'Read them,' said the King.

The White Rabbit put on his spectacles. 'Where shall I begin, please your Majesty?' he asked.

'Begin at the beginning,' the King said, very gravely, 'and go on till you come to the end: then stop.'

There was dead silence in the court, whilst the White Rabbit read out these verses:—

'They told me you had been to her,
  And mentioned me to him:
She gave me a good character,
  But said I could not swim.

He sent them word I had not gone
  (We know it to be true):
If she should push the matter on,
  What would become of you?

I gave her one, they gave him two,

You gave us three or more;
They all returned from him to you,
Though they were mine before.

If I or she should chance to be
Involved in this affair,
He trusts to you to set them free,
Exactly as we were.

My notion was that you had been
(Before she had this fit)
An obstacle that came between
Him, and ourselves, and it.

Don't let him know she liked them best,
For this must ever be
A secret, kept from all the rest,
Between yourself and me.'

'That's the most important piece of evidence we've heard yet,' said the King, rubbing his hands; 'so now let the jury—'

'If any one of them can explain it,' said Alice, (she had grown so large in the last few minutes that she wasn't a bit afraid of interrupting him,) 'I'll give him sixpence. I don't believe there's an atom of meaning in it.'

The jury all wrote down, on their slates, '*She* doesn't believe there's an atom of meaning in it,' but none of them attempted to explain the paper.

'If there's no meaning in it,' said the King, 'that saves a world of trouble, you know, as we needn't try to find any. And yet I don't know,' he went on, spreading out the verses on his knee, and looking at them with one eye; 'I seem to see some meaning in them, after all. '—*said I could not swim*—' you can't swim, can you?' he added, turning to the Knave.

The Knave shook his head sadly. 'Do I look like it?' he said. (Which he certainly did *not*, being made entirely of cardboard.)

'All right, so far,' said the King; and he went on muttering over the verses to himself: '"*We know it to be true*"—that's the jury of course—"*If she should push the matter on*"—that must be the Queen—"*What would become of you?*" —What, indeed!—"*I gave her one, they gave him two*"—why, that must be what he did with the tarts, you know—'

'But it goes on "*they all returned from him to you*,"' said Alice.

'Why, there they are?' said the King triumphantly, pointing to the tarts on the table. 'Nothing can be clearer than that. Then again—"*before site had this fit*"— you never had fits, my dear, I think?' he said to the Queen.

'Never!' said the Queen, furiously, throwing an inkstand at the Lizard as she spoke. (The unfortunate little Bill had left off writing on his slate with one finger, as he found it made no mark; but he now hastily began again, using the ink, that was trickling down his face, as long as it lasted.)

'Then the words don't *fit* you,' said the King, looking round the court with a smile. There was a dead silence.

'It's a pun!' the King added in an angry tone, and everybody laughed. 'Let the jury consider their verdict,' the King said, for about the twentieth time that day.

'No, no!' said the Queen. 'Sentence first—verdict afterwards.'

'Stuff and nonsense!' said Alice loudly. 'The idea of having the sentence first!'

'Hold your tongue!' said the Queen, turning purple.

'I won't!' said Alice.

'Off with her head!' the Queen shouted at the top of her voice. Nobody moved.

'Who cares for *you*?' said Alice (she had grown to her full size by this time). 'You're nothing but a pack of cards!'

At this the whole pack rose up into the air, and came flying down upon her; she gave a little scream, half of fright and half of anger, and tried to beat them off, and found herself lying on the bank, with her head in the lap of her sister, who was gently brushing away some dead leaves that had fluttered down from the trees upon her face.

'Wake up, Alice dear!' said her sister. 'Why, what a long sleep you've had!'

'Oh, I've had such a curious dream!' said Alice. And she told her sister, as well as she could remember them, all these strange Adventures of hers that you have just been reading about; and, when she had finished, her sister kissed her, and said 'It *was* a curious dream, dear, certainly; but now run in to your tea: it's getting late.' So Alice got up and ran off, thinking while she ran, as well she might, what a wonderful dream it had been.

But her sister sat still just as she left her, leaning her head on her hand, watching the setting sun, and thinking of little Alice and all her wonderful Adventures, till she too began dreaming after a fashion, and this was her dream:—

First, she dreamed about little Alice herself: once again the tiny hands were clasped upon her knee, and the bright eager eyes were looking up into hers—she could hear the very tones of her voice, and see that queer little toss of her head to keep back the wandering hair that would always get into her eyes—and still as she listened, or seemed to listen, the whole place around her became alive with the strange creatures of her little sister's dream.

The long grass rustled at her feet as the White Rabbit hurried by—the frightened Mouse splashed his way through the neighbouring pool—she could hear the rattle of the teacups as the March Hare and his friends shared their never-ending meal, and the shrill voice of the Queen ordering off her unfortunate guests to execution—once more the pig-baby was sneezing on the Duchess's knee, while plates and dishes crashed around it—once more the shriek of the Gryphon, the squeaking of the Lizard's slate-pencil, and the choking of the suppressed guinea pigs, filled the air, mixed up with the distant sob of the miserable Mock Turtle.

So she sat on, with closed eyes, and half believed herself in Wonderland, though she knew she had but to open them again, and all would change to dull reality—the grass would be only rustling in the wind, and the pool rippling to the waving of the reeds—the rattling teacups would change to tinkling sheep-bells, and the Queen's shrill cries to the voice of the shepherd-boy—and the sneeze of the baby, the shriek of the Gryphon, and all the other queer noises, would change (she knew) to the confused clamour of the busy farmyard—while the lowing of the cattle in the distance would take the place of the Mock Turtle's heavy sobs.

Lastly, she pictured to herself how this same little sister of hers would, in the after-time, be herself a grown woman; and how she would keep, through all her riper years, the simple and loving heart of her childhood; and how she would gather about her other little children, and make their eyes bright and eager with many a strange tale, perhaps even with the dream of Wonderland of long ago; and how she would feel with all their simple sorrows, and find a pleasure in all their simple joys, remembering her own child-life, and the happy summer days.

THE END

正是在下午，金光燦爛，
　　我們悠閒自在地盪船。
划起雙槳，划得不在行，
　　用力揮動小小的臂膀，
小小的手假裝識途，卻枉然，
　　指點我們漂航的方向。

啊，狠心的你們仨！在此時，
　　如此令人陶醉的天氣，
竟要求講一個輕鬆的故事，
　　輕鬆得連羽毛都不會動一絲！
可歎這貧口薄舌如何能
　　反對三張嘴一同在堅持？

專橫的小大王立刻頒發
　　她的法令說："現在開始吧。"
二大王比較溫和地說話，
　　她希望"故事要亂墜天花！"
三大王一分鐘裏可不止一次
　　打斷這故事，要人家作答。

過不久，忽然顯得好安靜，
　　她們出神入迷地追隨
夢中的孩子在一個奇境
　　穿過怪異和新奇的地方，
同小鳥或野獸友好地談心——
　　此人聽得幾乎信以為真。

每次在故事把想像的源泉
　　　漸漸消耗得不剩一點，
疲憊的講故事的人軟綿綿，
　　　設法把故事放在一邊，
"下回分解吧——""這正是下一回！"
　　　快樂的嗓音嚷成了一片。

奇境的故事就這樣發展，
　　　一段接一段就這樣慢慢講。
虛構了種種事希奇又古怪——
　　　現在這故事已經說完，
於是全體船員把舵掌，
　　　夕陽下我們愉快地返航。

愛麗絲！請接受這孩童的故事，
　　　並且請用溫柔的手把它
放在那裏：童年的夢已織進
　　　回憶的不可思議的飄帶，
就像朝聖者枯萎的花環，
　　　那些花從遙遠的國度採來。

第一章

掉下兔子洞

愛麗絲挨着她的姐姐坐在河邊，由於無事可做，開始覺得沒意思。她剛才對姐姐正在閱讀的書本瞧了一兩眼，可是書上既沒有圖畫，也沒有對話；愛麗絲覺得："一本書既沒有圖畫，又沒有對話，那有甚麼用處呢？"

因此她在自己心裏琢磨着（她盡可能這麼做，因為這炎熱的天氣把她弄得昏昏欲睡，呆頭呆腦），編一個雛菊花環的樂趣，是不是值得她不怕麻煩，爬起身來，去一朵一朵地採摘雛菊。這時候，突然有一隻粉紅眼睛的大白兔跑到她跟前來。

這件事並不令人非常驚訝；愛麗絲聽見大白兔自言自語地說："哦，天哪！哦，天哪！我要遲到啦！"她也不覺得很奇怪。（她事後再想想，才覺得自己對這件事本來應該感到特別，但是當時這一切都似乎非常自然。）不過，大白兔這時候竟然從牠的背心口袋裏掏出一隻錶來，瞧瞧時間，然後匆匆跑掉；愛麗絲便馬上站了起來，因為她心中忽然閃過一個念頭：自己過去從來也沒有看見過一隻兔子有背心口袋，也沒有看見過從那口袋裏會掏出一隻錶來，她感到奇怪得不得了，便跟蹤追擊，跑過田野，正好及時趕到，看見牠一下子跳進籬笆下面一個大兔子洞裏去。

一轉眼工夫，愛麗絲便跟着牠跳了進去，卻想都沒想一下，自己究竟怎樣才能夠再跑出來。

兔子洞像一條隧道那樣筆直向前，走過了一段路以後，卻忽然向下傾斜，斜得那麼突然，愛麗絲根本來不及想到停住腳步，便發現自己好像正在一口非常深的井裏往下掉。

那口井如果不是非常深的話，那就是愛麗絲掉下去的速度非常慢，因為她一面往下掉，一面還有足夠的時間東張西望，並且猜想下一分鐘會發生甚麼事。起初，她打算往下看，想弄清楚自己要落在哪裏，但是下面太黑了，甚麼也看不見。然後，她打量了一下四面井壁，只見四周全都是碗櫥和書架：她看到束一處西一處的掛釘上掛着地圖或者圖畫。她身子經過的時候，順手從一個書架上取下一隻瓶子，上面貼着標籤："柑橘醬"，可是叫她十分失望的是，那是隻空瓶。她不想把空瓶扔下去，怕這樣會把下面的甚麼人砸死，因此，在她往下掉又經過一個碗櫥的時候，她設法把空瓶放到碗櫥裏面了。

"好呀！"愛麗絲心裏想。"經過這樣一次往下掉，以後從樓梯上翻滾下去就能不當一回事了！家裏的人全都會覺得我是多麼勇敢呀！哼，即使我從屋頂上掉下來，對於這件事我決不說一個字！"（這一點很可能是真的。）

往下，往下，往下掉。會不會掉個沒完沒了呢？"我不知道此時我往下掉了幾英里啦？"她大聲說道。"我一定正在接近地心的甚麼地方了。讓我想想看：我想可能往下掉了四千英里啦

——”（你瞧，這是因為愛麗絲在教室裏唸書的時候，一知半解地學到了這一類學問，雖然此刻並非顯示她的知識的大好時機，因為現在沒有人在聽她講，雖然如此，把它説出來依然是很好的實習嘛。）“—— 不錯，大概正是這樣一段路程 —— 不過，我卻要問問，我已經到達甚麼經緯度啦？”（愛麗絲一點都不懂甚麼是緯度，也不懂甚麼是經度，但是她覺得説得出這兩個詞真了不起。）

過了一會，她又説道：“我不知道自己是否要跌下去，一直穿過地球哇！這樣一來，似乎要掉在那些頭朝下邊行走着的人群當中了，這該多麼有趣呀！我想，那些是討厭傢伙 ——”（她這回很高興沒人在聽她説話，因為聽起來完全用詞不當。）“—— 不過，你明白的，我將不得不向他們打聽那個國家叫甚麼名字。夫人，請問這裏是不是新西蘭？或者是不是澳大利亞？”（她一面説，一面就打算行個屈膝禮 —— 想想看吧，你是在半空中往下掉的時候行屈膝禮呀！你想你辦得到嗎？）“我這麼一問，她會覺得我是一個十分無知的小女孩了！不，決計不能問，也許我會看見國名在甚麼地方寫明的。”

往下，往下，往下掉。現在沒有甚麼事情可做，因此愛麗絲立刻又説起話來。“我能肯定，今天夜裏戴娜要想死我了！”（戴娜是那隻貓的名字。）“我但願他們會記得在吃茶點的時候給她一碟牛奶。戴娜，我的寶貝！我真希望你在這裏跟我一起往下掉！我想這裏半空中是沒有老鼠的，但是你可能抓住一隻蝙蝠，你知道牠很像一隻老鼠。不過貓吃不吃蝙蝠呢？我不知道。”説到這裏，愛麗絲開始感到困倦了，用一種睡夢昏憒的調子自言自語地繼續説着：“貓吃不吃蝙蝠呢？貓吃不吃蝙蝠呢？”有幾次卻説：

"蝙蝠吃不吃貓呢？"你瞧，由於這兩個問題她都答不上來，因此不管她怎麼問都沒有甚麼關係。她覺得自己在打瞌睡，開始夢見自己正跟戴娜手拉手在散步，正在一本正經地對她說："喂，戴娜，跟我說實話，你究竟吃過蝙蝠沒有啊？"忽然就在這時候，撲通！撲通！她掉到一堆枯枝敗葉上了，這次下降也就結束了。

愛麗絲一點也沒有傷着，她馬上一蹦就站了起來。她抬頭仰望，只見一片漆黑。在她面前的是另外一條長長的通道，她瞧見那隻大白兔正沿着那條通道急急跑去。一刻也不能耽擱啊，愛麗絲像一陣風一樣離去，正好趕上聽見大白兔轉彎時候說的話："哦，我的耳朵和硬鬍呀，現在多麼晚了呀！"愛麗絲轉過彎來那時刻是緊跟着大白兔的，可是此刻大白兔卻不見了；她發現自己待在一間長長的、低矮的廳堂裏，屋頂上掛着的一排燈正亮堂堂地照着這地方。

這間廳堂四面有許多扇門，不過都是鎖着的。愛麗絲從一邊一路走過去，又從另一邊一路走過來，每一扇門都試開過以後，垂頭喪氣地走到廳堂中央，不知道自己究竟如何再出去。

她忽然發現有一張三條腿的小桌子，全部用厚實的玻璃做成，上面甚麼也沒有，只放着一把小小的金鑰匙。她的第一個想法是，這把鑰匙可能是開廳堂裏哪一扇門的。可是，天哪！不是門鎖太大，就是鑰匙太小，不論哪一扇門，她用盡辦法都打不開。不過，在她走第二圈的時候，她偶然發現剛才沒有注意到的一幅矮矮的幕布，幕布遮掩着一扇大約十五英寸高的小門。她用那把小金鑰匙插進鎖孔試試，倒是正好，她真高興得不得了！

愛麗絲打開那扇門，只見一條小小的通道，小得不比老鼠大多少。她跪了下來，望着通道那一頭一個從未見過的最可愛的花園。她多麼希望能走出這間黑暗的廳堂，走到那些長着美麗鮮花的花壇中和那些清涼的噴泉邊，在那中間走來走去，可是她連把頭伸過門口都辦不到。"即使我的頭真能鑽過去，"可憐的愛麗絲想道："我的肩膀鑽不過去，也沒有甚麼用處啊。哦，我多麼希望自己能夠像一副望遠鏡那樣縮攏！我想，只要我知道如何開始，我就能縮攏。"你瞧，正是因為這一陣子發生了那麼多異乎尋常的事情，所以愛麗絲開始覺得，的確很少有甚麼事情是真正不可能的。

呆等在小門邊上看來是沒有用的，因此她走回到那張桌子跟前，不怎麼有把握地希望能在桌子上找到另外一把鑰匙，或者至少找到一本書，裏邊講如何把人像望遠鏡那樣縮攏的法則。不過這一次她在桌子上發現了一個小瓶子，(愛麗絲說："剛才桌子上肯定沒有這東西。")瓶頸上縛着一張紙標籤，標籤上用大字精美地印着這樣的話："喝我呀"。

說"喝我呀"這話倒是好極了，可是聰明的小愛麗絲卻不忙於照此辦理。"不，我得先瞧瞧，"她說，"看看有沒有標明'毒品'字樣。"這是因為她曾經讀過幾篇挺不錯的小故事，講的是一些碰到晦氣事情的孩子，他們有的被燒痛，有的被野獸吃了，還有的碰到一些不幸，這全都因為他們把朋友們教他們的簡單道理忘在腦後。比如說：一把燒得通紅的撥火棍，你如果拿得時間太長就要炙痛你的手；如果你用一把刀子割手指割得太深，通常就要出血；還有她曾經牢記在心的一點：如果你把標明"毒品"字樣的瓶子裏的東西喝得太多，幾乎可以肯定你遲早要遭殃。

不過不管怎麼說，這個瓶子並沒有標明"毒品"，所以愛麗絲斗膽嚐了一口，並且發現味道挺不錯，(事實上，瓶子裏的東西含有一種車厘子撻、吉士、菠蘿、烤火雞、拖肥糖，以及牛油多士一起混合起來的風味。)於是她咕嘟咕嘟一下子全喝光了。

"多麼奇怪的感覺啊！"愛麗絲說。"我想必正在像一副望遠鏡那樣縮攏起來了！"

事情真是如此：她現在只有十英寸高了，想到自己此刻身高已經可以鑽過那扇小門，走到那座可愛的花園裏去，她真是容光煥發。不過，她先得等幾分鐘，看看自己是不是還在縮下去，她對此感到有點不安。"因為，你知道，"愛麗絲自言自語，"我這樣徹底小下去，可能像一支蠟燭那樣完結的。我不知道那時候自己會是甚麼樣子。"她於是盡量想像，在蠟燭被吹滅以後，蠟燭火是甚麼樣子的，因為她不記得曾經看見過這樣的東西。

過了一會，她看出不會再發生甚麼事情了，便決定立刻走到花園裏去。可是，可憐的愛麗絲，真糟糕！她走到門口的時候，發覺忘記帶那把小金鑰匙了，等到她走回到桌子那裏去拿鑰匙的時候，又發現自己用手無法夠到它了。透過玻璃桌面，她可以很清楚地看見它，便使出渾身解數去攀爬桌子的腿，可是太滑溜了。可憐的小東西爬呀爬的，累得精疲力竭了，只得坐下來號啕大哭。

"別哭啦，哭成這個樣子也沒有用！"愛麗絲相當尖銳地批評自己。"我勸你馬上停住！"她通常自己給自己非常好的忠告(雖然很少實行)，而且有時候把自己罵得那麼厲害，連眼淚都要淌出來了。她還記得有一次真想掌自己的嘴，那一次，她自己跟自己玩槌球遊戲的時候騙了自己。這位奇怪的孩子非常喜歡一人扮成兩人。"可是現在扮演兩個人是沒有用的了！"可憐的愛麗絲心中想道。"是啊，我剩下這麼一點，都不夠成為一個受人尊敬的人啦！"

過了一會，她的目光落在桌子下面放着的一個玻璃盒子上面。打開來一看，只見裏面放着一塊一點點大的蛋糕，上面用葡萄乾拼綴出漂亮的字體："吃我呀"。"好吧，我就把它吃下去，"愛麗絲說，"要是它能使我變大，我就可以拿得到那把鑰匙；要是它使我變小，我就可以從門縫下面爬過去。所以不管怎麼樣我都能到花園裏去，所以不管發生哪一種情況我都不放在心上！"

她咬了一小口蛋糕，好生心急地問自己："哪一種情況呢？哪一種情況呢？"同時把手放在頭頂上，摸摸它朝哪一種情況變化。叫她很驚訝的是，她發現自己依然那麼大小。當然啦，吃蛋糕，一般來說都不會發生甚麼事情的。但是愛麗絲已經那麼習慣於期待發生甚麼異乎尋常的事情，因此要是日子那麼平平常常地過下去，就似乎太枯燥乏味了。

於是她大吃起來，不一會就把那塊蛋糕全部吃完了。

第二章

涙水池

"**越**是越奇怪，越是越奇怪了！"愛麗絲嚷嚷着説，（她驚訝得了不得，以至於此刻她把如何説好英語忘得一乾二淨了。）"我現在正在像一副世界上最大的望遠鏡那樣伸展開來！再見吧，我的雙腳啊！"（因為她朝下望望自己的雙腳，雙腳似乎看都看不見了，它們變得那麼遙遠。）"哦，我的可憐的一雙小腳啊，親愛的，我不知道現在誰會來替你們穿上你們的襪子、鞋子呀？我肯定地説，我是不可能辦到了！我將會變得極其遙遠，遠得都不能為你們操心了。你們必須好自為之，盡力而為——不過，我也必須好好對待它們，"愛麗絲轉念一想，"否則的話，它們也許就不肯走我要走的道路了！讓我想想看吧。我打算在每個聖誕節都送給它們一雙新的長筒靴子。"

於是她繼續在心裏籌劃如何辦理這事。"必須由送貨人來辦，"她這樣想，"不過給自己的一雙腳送禮，這似乎多麼滑稽啊！收件人的姓名地址看來又是多麼彆扭啊！

愛麗絲的右足先生台收

壁爐前地毯，

壁爐圍欄附近。

（愛麗絲敬贈）

哦，天哪，我在亂講甚麼話呀！"

正在這時候，她的頭撞到了這間廳堂的屋頂。此刻她實際上已經長到不止九英尺高了，她立刻拿起桌子上的那把小金鑰匙，急急忙忙跑到花園門前。

可憐的愛麗絲呀！她現在所能做的只是側身臥倒，用一隻眼睛從門縫裏張望那座花園，要想鑽過去，可就難上加難，毫無希望了。於是她又坐下來放聲大哭。

"你應該為你自己感到可恥，"愛麗絲說，"像你這樣一個大女孩子，（她倒是說得不錯）卻這副樣子哭呀哭的！立刻停止，我告訴你！"可是她仍然哭個不停，一加侖一加侖的淚水從眼中流出來，把她的四周變成了一個大水池子，約有四英寸深，漫掉了半個廳堂。

一會之後，她聽見遠處傳來一陣小小的腳步聲，啪嗒啪嗒響，她趕緊擦乾眼淚，看看是誰來了。原來是大白兔回來了，穿着好生氣派，一隻手拿了一副白色的小山羊皮手套，另一隻手拿了一把大扇子。牠一路非常匆忙，跳跳蹦蹦地跑過來，嘴裏還自言自語地咕嚕着："哦！公爵夫人啊！公爵夫人啊！哦！要是我讓她這麼久等，她豈不會大發雷霆嗎！"愛麗絲感到身陷絕境，一籌莫展，隨時都願意向任何人求救，所以在大白兔跑近她的時候，她用一種膽怯的聲音低聲懇求說：“先生，對不起——”大白兔給嚇了一大跳，連忙丟下地那副小山羊皮手套和那把扇子，唰溜一下，拚命跑到黑暗之中去了。

愛麗絲拾起扇子和手套，她一面說着話，一面不停地用扇子對自己扇風，因為廳堂裏太熱了。“天哪，天哪！今天每件事情都這麼奇怪呀！昨天事情還正像平常那樣進行。我不知道自己是否在昨天夜裏變了樣？讓我想想看：今天早晨我醒來的時候是不是老樣子呢？我差不多覺得自己能夠記得是感到有點不一樣。不過，如果我已經不是老樣子了，那麼下一個問題是：‘我究竟是誰呢？’啊，這可叫人大惑不解了！”於是她開始把她認識的同年齡的孩子全部都想遍，看看自己是否已經變成他們中間的任何一個人。

“我敢肯定我不是艾達，”她說，“因為她的頭髮捲成那麼長的鬈髮，我的頭髮卻完全沒有捲成鬈髮。我也敢肯定我不可能是梅寶，因為我甚麼事情都知道，她呢，哦，知道的事情只那麼一點點！而且，她就是她，而我就是我，而且——哦，天哪，這一切多麼叫人莫名其妙啊！我要試試看，我過去知道的事情現在是不是全都知道。讓我算算看：四乘以五是十二，四乘以六是十三，四乘以七是——哦，天哪！照這樣算下去，我將怎麼也算不到二十呀！不過，乘法表並不重要，讓我們試試地理吧。倫敦是巴黎的首都，巴黎是羅馬的首都，羅馬——不對，這全部亂了，我斷定是這樣！我一定已經變成梅寶了！我來試試背誦《那條小小的——》，”她交叉雙手，放在腿上，彷彿正在背書那樣，開始背起來。然而她的嗓子聽來啞了，陌生了，唸出聲的字也不像過去常唸的那樣：

> 那條小小的鱷魚怎麼樣
> 　使牠發亮的尾巴更發亮，
> 還把尼羅河的水澆身上，
> 　洗得每塊鱗片都金光閃！
> 喜滋滋的樣子看來多動人，
> 　張牙舞爪的動作多輕靈，
> 那兩顎一開大口笑迎賓，
> 　小小的魚請進，都請進！

"我敢肯定原文不是這樣子的，"可憐的愛麗絲說，她接着說下去的時候，眼睛裏還噙着淚水，"到頭來，我一定還是梅寶，我將不得不住在那座狹小的房屋裏，幾乎沒有玩具玩，並且，哦，還一直有那麼多的功課要做！不行，對此我已經下了決心：如果我是梅寶我就要在這地底下等下去！他們要是伸長脖子對着下面喊：'再爬上來吧，乖乖！'也沒有用處。我就只是往上面瞧一眼，回答說：'那麼，我是誰呢？先把這一點跟我說清楚，然後，要是我願意做那一位，我就會爬上來，否則的話，我就要在這地底下等着，直到我成為另外一個人'——不過，哦，天哪！"愛麗絲大聲叫道，同時淚水一下子流了出來，"我實在希望他們會伸長脖子朝下看呀！我孤孤單單一個人留在這裏真是太叫人厭倦了呀！"她一面說，一面看看自己兩隻手，忽然驚奇地發現自己在說話的時候已經把大白兔的一隻白色小山羊皮小手套戴上了。"我怎麼竟然能夠戴上這隻手套！"她心裏想。"我一定是又在變小了。"她站起來，走到那張桌子邊，用桌子來量量自己的身材，結果發現事實幾乎跟她猜想的一樣，她現在大約兩英尺高，並且正在迅速地縮小。她立刻發覺這是由於手上拿着的那把扇子的緣故，於是急忙扔掉了它，正好及時挽救了自己，沒有縮到無影無蹤。

“這真是死裹逃生啊！”愛麗絲說，對於這突然的變化驚嚇不已，不過由於發現自己仍然存在而十分慶幸。“這會該到花園裹去啦！”於是她便箭也似的奔回那扇小門前；可是，哎呀！那扇小門又關上了，那把小金鑰匙像過去那樣躺在那張玻璃桌子上。“事情從來沒有這麼糟糕，”這個可憐的孩子想道，“因為我過去從來沒有像這樣矮小，從來沒有呀！我聲明此事太糟糕，一點都不假！”

就在她說這些話的時候，她的一隻腳滑了一下，接着只聽見撲通一聲，她掉到水裹去了，鹹鹹的水沒到了她的下巴！她首先想到的是自己不知怎麼會一下掉到大海裹來了，“如果是這樣的話，我就能夠坐火車回家了，”她這樣自言自語。（愛麗絲這輩子只到海濱去過一次，並且總結出一條經驗，即你到英國海岸的任何地方去，都能發現海灘上停放着許多更衣車，一些孩子用木鏟挖掘海灘上的沙子，再過去是一排出租房舍，房舍後面便是火車站。）不過，她馬上弄清楚了，原來自己是掉進了淚水池，這是她九英尺高的時候哭出來的。

“我真希望自己沒有哭得那麼厲害呀！”愛麗絲說，她游來游去，想找一個出口。“我想，現在我要為此受到懲罰，淹死在我自己的眼淚裹了！毫無疑問，這肯定是一件稀罕的事！不過，今天甚麼事都是稀罕的呢。”

就在這時候，她聽見有甚麼東西在這個小池子裏稍遠的地方潑啦潑啦地划水，便游近一些去看看到底是甚麼。她開始認為那必定是一頭海象，要不就是一頭河馬，不過她接着便想起自己現在是多麼渺小，於是立刻明白那不過是一隻老鼠罷了，那隻老鼠像她自己一樣，也是失足滑到池子裏來的。

　　"這會，要是跟這隻老鼠談談，"愛麗絲心想，"會不會有甚麼用處呢？在這下面，一切事情都是如此特裏特別的，因此，我應該想到這隻老鼠很可能會說話。不管怎麼說，試一試總沒有害處吧。"於是她開口説："哦，老鼠，你可知道這個池子的出口在哪裏？哦，老鼠啊，我在這裏游來游去已經非常厭倦了！"（愛麗絲覺得這一定是跟老鼠説話的正確途徑。她過去從來沒有做過這樣的事，不過她記得曾經在她哥哥的《拉丁語法》書上看到過："一隻老鼠 —— 關於一隻老鼠的 —— 屬於一隻老鼠的 —— 一隻老鼠 —— 哦，老鼠！"）那隻老鼠帶着頗為生疑的目光瞧着她，她覺得那隻老鼠似乎還着一隻小眼睛，但是牠甚麼也沒有説。

　　"也許牠不懂英語，"愛麗絲這樣想。"我敢説牠是一隻法國老鼠，是跟征服者威廉一起到英國來的。"（因為愛麗絲的歷史知識儘管有一些，但是對於一件事情發生在多久以前卻沒有很清楚的概念。）因此她又開始説道："Où est ma chatte？"這是她的《法語》教科書中的頭一句。那隻老鼠突然一下子從水裏跳出來，同時似乎嚇得全身抖個不停。"哦，請你原諒！"愛麗絲急忙大聲説，唯恐自己傷了這個可憐的動物的感情。"我的確忘了你不喜歡貓。"

　　"不喜歡貓！"那隻老鼠情緒激動地尖聲叫嚷起來。"如果你是我的話，你會喜歡貓嗎？"

"嗯，也許不會，"愛麗絲用一種撫慰的聲調說；"你別為這事發火吧。然而我還是希望能把我們的貓戴娜給你瞧瞧。只要你能瞧她一眼，我想你會喜歡貓的。她可是一個非常可愛的不吵不鬧的東西，"愛麗絲繼續說，半是對她自己說的，她還一面在池子裏懶懶地划着水，"她坐在壁爐邊，那麼美妙地喵喵叫着，還舔着爪子，洗着臉 —— 她是那麼一個乖乖的、讓人愛撫時感到柔軟的東西 —— 她又是個能手，抓起老鼠來 —— 哦，請您原諒！"愛麗絲再一次叫起來，因為這次那隻老鼠全身的鼠毛都豎了起來，她確確實實地感到牠一定是真的惱火了。"如果你不想聽，那麼咱們以後就決不再談她了吧。"

"我們，你還好說！"那隻老鼠叫道，牠從頭到尾都顫抖着。"彷彿是我要談這樣一個題目似的！我們這個家族從來都恨透了貓們，這些個令人作嘔的、低級的、下賤的東西呀！別再叫我聽見這個名字！"

"我真的不說了！"愛麗絲說，迫不及待地改變談話內容。"那麼你 —— 你可喜歡 —— 那些 —— 那些狗嗎？"那隻老鼠不吭聲，於是愛麗絲急切地繼續說道："在我家附近有一隻那麼漂亮的小狗，我真願意讓你看看！跟你說，那是一隻眼睛亮亮的小獵犬，哦，牠身上棕色的鬈毛是那麼長啊！你把東西扔出去，牠會銜回來，牠還會坐在地上討飯吃，還會許多許多事情 —— 我連一半都想不起來 —— 跟你說，牠的主人是一位農夫，他說牠是那麼有用，值一百英鎊呢！他說牠看見老鼠就咬死，而且 —— 哦，天哪！"愛麗絲悲哀地喊道。"我怕自己又冒犯牠啦！"因為那隻老鼠正在用盡全身力氣划水，從她那裏游開去，弄得池子裏水花四濺。

於是她低聲下氣地對牠喊道："親愛的老鼠啊！你再游回來吧，要是你不喜歡貓啊，狗啊，我們就不談牠們了吧！"那隻老鼠聽見這句話以後，就轉過身子，慢慢地向她游回來。牠臉色蒼白（愛麗絲覺得這是氣極了的緣故），用顫抖的壓低的聲音說道："讓我們游到岸邊去，然後我會把我的身世跟你說，你就會明白我為甚麼憎恨那些貓和狗。"

現在正是離開的時候，因為已經有許多鳥和獸落到了水池子裏，擠擠插插的。有一隻母鴨、一隻渡渡鳥、一隻吸蜜小鸚鵡、一隻小鷹，以及其他幾種珍奇動物。愛麗絲在前面領路，全班人馬跟着她向岸邊游去。

第三章

競選指導委員會的競賽
和一個長篇故事

這一大幫人馬聚集在岸上，看上去的確是稀奇古怪——飛禽們身上羽毛下垂，走獸們身上的毛變成一綹綹的緊貼着皮，大家都是水淋淋的的，好不難受哇。

首要的問題當然是如何恢復乾燥。對此，牠們作了一番商量。幾分鐘以後，事情看來是自然而然的，愛麗絲發現自己已經跟牠們親切地談起了話，彷彿她生下來就認識牠們似的。確實，她跟吸蜜小鸚鵡辯論了相當長的時間，那隻鸚鵡到最後變得很不高興，只想說："我比你年紀大，肯定知道得多。"愛麗絲不知道牠究竟多大歲數，不肯承認這一點。由於這隻鸚鵡一口拒絕說出牠的年齡，這就沒有甚麼好多說的了。

那隻老鼠看來在牠們之中具有某種權威，牠最後喊道："你們大家全都給我坐下來，聽我說話！我馬上能使你們身上變乾燥！"於是牠們全都坐下來，圍成一個大圓圈，把那隻老鼠圍在中間。愛麗絲的眼睛直愣愣地盯着牠瞧，心中焦急不安，因為她感覺到自己要是不非常快地把身上弄乾燥的話，她肯定要得重感冒。

"嗯哼！"那隻老鼠威風凜凜地哼了一聲。"你們都準備好了嗎？就我所知，要説乾，沒有甚麼比這件事更乾巴巴的。全體肅靜，勞駕啦！'征服者威廉的目標得到教宗的支援，不久便使英國服從他，英國需要一些領導者，近來又很習慣於篡奪權位和遭到征服這類事。梅爾西亞伯爵艾德溫和諾森伯利亞伯爵穆爾卡——'"

"哎唷！"吸蜜小鸚鵡渾身打寒顫，叫起來。

"對不起！"老鼠皺着眉頭説，但還是彬彬有禮。"你説話了嗎？"

"我沒説！"吸蜜小鸚鵡慌慌張張地説。

"我覺得你説過的，"老鼠説。"我接下去談。'梅爾西亞伯爵艾德溫和諾森伯利亞伯爵穆爾卡聲明擁護他，甚至那位熱愛祖國的坎特伯雷大主教斯梯幹德也發現那個是適當的——'"

"發現甚麼呀？"母鴨説。

"發現那個，"老鼠頗為不快地回答。"你當然明白'那個'是甚麼意思。"

"'那個'是甚麼意思，我是夠清楚的，我要是發現一個甚麼東西的時候，"母鴨説道，"一般來説，那是一隻青蛙，或者一條毛毛蟲。現在的問題是，那位大主教究竟發現了甚麼？"

老鼠沒有注意這個問題，而是急急忙忙地講下去："'——發現那個是適當的，即與埃德加·艾塞林一同去會見威廉，把王冠奉獻給他。威廉的舉止起初是有分寸的。但是他的諾曼第人的狂妄自大——'親愛的，你現在覺得怎麼樣？"老鼠繼續講，在牠説話的時候，轉過頭來問愛麗絲。

"身上跟原來一樣濕，"愛麗絲用悶悶不樂的聲調説。"這種辦法似乎一點也不能使我身上變得乾燥。"

"既然是這樣，"渡渡鳥站起身來，鄭重其事地説，"我提議休會，以便立即採用更為充滿活力的補救辦法——"

"請説英語！"小鷹説道。"這麼長的字句，我連一半的意思都弄不懂，而且，尤有甚者，我不相信你自己能懂！"於是小鷹低下頭來，不讓人家看見牠在笑。可是卻能聽見其他一些禽鳥在暗暗竊笑。

"我想要説的是，"渡渡鳥用一種快快不樂的聲調説，"使我們乾燥的最好東西應該是一次競選指導委員會的競賽。"

"競選指導委員會的競賽是甚麼東西呀？"愛麗絲問道。這並不是因為她很想知道，而是因為渡渡鳥剛才突然停下不説，彷彿牠認為應該有哪一位來發話，但是卻沒有人打算發言。

"嗯，"渡渡鳥説道，"解釋這個詞語的最好辦法就是做出來看。"（因為你可能願意在某一個冬日親身一試，所以我將告訴你渡渡鳥如何做出來。）

首先，牠畫出一條跑道，是一種圓圈的形狀，（"確切的形狀關係不大，"牠這樣説。）然後，全體成員都被安排在跑道旁，這裏一個，那裏一個。沒有"一，二，三，起步！"的口令，而是牠們誰喜歡跑就跑，誰喜歡離開就離開，以至於競賽甚麼時候結束，是不容易看出來的。不過，牠們跑了大約半個小時左右，身上都恢復到相當乾燥的時候，渡渡鳥突然喊道："競賽結束！"於是大家全都圍着牠站住，氣喘吁吁地問道："不過，誰贏了呢？"

這個問題渡渡鳥無法回答，牠得先好好想一想，因此牠用一隻手指抵着前額，站立了好久（這一姿勢你平常可以在畫莎士比亞的畫像上看到），此時，別人都靜靜地等候着。最後，渡渡鳥說道：＂大家都贏了，每一位都必須得獎。＂

＂可是由誰拿出獎品來呢？＂差不多是眾口一詞地問道。

＂不用說，當然是她，＂渡渡鳥用一根手指頭指着愛麗絲說。於是全體動物立刻把她團團圍困起來，鬧鬧嚷嚷地亂叫喚：＂獎品！獎品！＂

愛麗絲不知道如何是好，無法可想之中，她把手伸進自己的衣袋裏，掏出一盒糖果來（幸運的是鹹水沒有滲進盒子裏），她把糖果向牠們遞了一圈，作為獎品。一圈兜下來，正正好好每位各得一塊。

＂不過，你們知道，她自己也應該得到一個獎品，＂老鼠說。

＂那當然，＂渡渡鳥非常嚴肅地回答。＂你的口袋裏還有別的甚麼東西嗎？＂牠又轉過身來衝着愛麗絲問道。

＂只有一隻頂針箍，＂愛麗絲傷心地說。

＂把它交到這裏來，＂渡渡鳥說。

於是牠們又一次圍着她擠在一起，渡渡鳥則莊重地向她贈送那個頂針箍，同時說道：＂我們請求你笑納這個雅致的頂針箍，＂牠簡短的致詞完畢以後，全體歡呼。

愛麗絲覺得這整個事情真夠荒唐，但是看來大家都那麼嚴肅，她便不敢笑出聲來，而且由於她想不出任何話來說，便僅僅鞠了一躬，收下了頂針箍，盡可能擺出一臉莊重的樣子。

接下來的事情是吃糖果。這引起了一些吵鬧和混亂：大鳥們抱怨說牠們無法品嚐糖果的滋味；小鳥們則梗塞在喉嚨口，必須在背上拍兩下才行。不過，事情終於過去，牠們又在地上坐成一圈，請求老鼠再跟牠們說些甚麼。

"你知道，你答應過把你的歷史告訴我，"愛麗絲說，"以及你為甚麼憎恨——喵喵和汪汪，"她悄沒聲地加上這一句，有些害怕說明白了又會冒犯牠。

"我的故事很慘，說來話長！"老鼠轉過頭來對愛麗絲說，還歎了一口氣。

"當然啦，尾巴很長，"愛麗絲說，驚奇地朝下看着老鼠的尾巴。"可是你為甚麼說他是很慘的呢？"在老鼠滔滔不絕地講述的時候，愛麗絲對此一直迷惑不解，因此她對於這段故事的印象有點像這個樣子：

```
         一隻野狗，名叫虎子，
            來到屋子，遇到
               一隻
                老鼠，
               牠說：
               "我們
                 一起
                  上法庭
                   我要
                    控告
                     你。——
                      來吧，我
                      不許你
                      頑抗；
                      我們必須
                    對簿
                   公堂。
                   因為
                  確實
                 今天
                早上，
```

```
                          我沒
                           事
                        好做。”
                        老鼠
                      對野狗
                    說道：
                  “先生，
               如此
                  官司，
                     沒有
                       陪審團
                         和法官，
                          將會是
                           白費
                             唇舌的事。”
                           “我會當
                           法官
                         我會當
                         陪審團。”
                    狡猾的
                    虎子
                      說道。
                      “我會審訊
                             這整個
                            案情，
                          並且
                       把你
                       判
                       處
                       死刑。”
```

　　“你沒有注意聽啊！”老鼠嚴厲地對愛麗絲說。“你在想甚麼呀？”

　　“對不起，”愛麗絲非常謙恭地說；“我想你已經轉了五個彎了吧？”

　　“我沒做這一切！”老鼠非常生氣地尖聲喊叫起來。

　　“你打了一個結！”愛麗絲說，她老是隨時準備出力，所以心急地四處找甚麼。"哦，讓我一定幫你解開這個結！"

"我怎麼也不讓你做這種事，"老鼠說着站起身來走掉了。"你說如此無聊的話來侮辱我！"

"我並沒有這個意思呀！"可憐的愛麗絲辯解着說。"可是，你知道，你太容易多心了呀！"

老鼠不回答，只是喉嚨裏咕嚕咕嚕的。

"請你回來吧，把故事講完吧！"愛麗絲對着牠的後背喊道。其餘各位也都參加了大合唱："對啦，請回來講吧！"然而老鼠只是不耐煩地搖搖頭，步子邁得更快了些。

"多麼可惜，牠不肯待一會！"就在牠快要從眼前消失的時候，吸蜜小鸚鵡歎口氣說。一隻老螃蟹趁此機會對自己的女兒說道："啊，我的寶貝！你可以從這個事情裏吸取教訓，決不要發脾氣！""媽，閉嘴！"年輕的螃蟹有點心情煩躁地說道。"你真可以挑動一隻蠔的耐心了！"

"我真希望自己把我們的戴娜帶了來呀！我知道自己真是這樣想的呀！"愛麗絲大聲嚷嚷着，倒不是專門對哪一位說的。"她會馬上把老鼠抓回來的！"

"假如我可以冒昧地提個問題的話，能問問誰是戴娜嗎？"吸蜜小鸚鵡說。

愛麗絲迫不及待地作了回答，因為她總是十分高興談談她的寵物："戴娜是我們的貓咪。她抓起老鼠來真是沒得說的，你想都想不到！而且，哦，我真希望你能看到她如何抓鳥！哎呀，她一看見一隻小鳥就能一口把牠吃下去！"

這段演說在全體聽眾之間引起了一陣不小的騷動。有一些禽鳥立刻匆忙溜掉了。有一隻老喜鵲開始非常小心地把牠自己包攏起來，說道：“我真的必須回家去了，夜間的寒氣對我的喉嚨不好！”一隻金絲雀用顫抖的聲音對牠的孩子們高喊道：“走吧，我的寶貝！現在正是你們都該上牀的時候啦！”全體人員都以各種各樣的藉口走開了，愛麗絲立刻陷入孤獨的境地。

　　“我真希望自己沒有談到戴娜才好啊！”愛麗絲用一種憂鬱傷感的聲調自言自語道。“看來在這一帶地方誰都不喜歡她，而我敢肯定她是世界上最好的貓咪！哦，我的親愛的戴娜呀！我不知道自己是否還會再看到你一眼啊！”說到這裏，可憐的愛麗絲又開始哭起來，因為她覺得非常孤單，精神疲憊。不過，隔了一會，她又聽見輕微的腳步聲啪噠啪噠地從遠處傳來，便抬起頭，急切地張望着，心中帶着希望，但願那隻老鼠已經改變了主意，正在走回來，打算講完牠的故事。

第四章

大白兔派來一位小壁兒

來者原來是那位大白兔，牠搖搖擺擺地慢步走了回來，一面走，一面憂心忡忡地東張西望，彷彿掉了甚麼東西似的。愛麗絲還聽見牠自言自語地咕噥着說：“那位公爵夫人！那位公爵夫人！哦，我的親愛的腳爪呀，哦，我的毛皮和鬍子呀！她會處決我的，這事就像白鼬就是白鼬一樣肯定！我真不明白，我會在哪裏丟了那些東西呢？”愛麗絲一下子就猜到了，大白兔是在找那把扇子和那副小山羊皮白手套，她便非常和善地到處尋找起來，可是哪裏也找不到——從她在那池子裏游泳以來，好像一切都已經改變了。那座大廳、那張玻璃桌子和那扇小門都消失得無影無蹤了。

愛麗絲在到處尋找的時候，大白兔很快看見了她，牠用氣呼呼的腔調大聲對她嚷着：“喂，瑪麗·安恩，你在這外邊做甚麼呀？立時立刻就給我跑回家去，把我那副手套和一把扇子拿來！快些，馬上！”愛麗絲嚇得不得了，立即照着牠指的方向奔去，根本不打算解釋一下牠弄錯的事情。

"牠把我當作牠的女僕人了，"她一面跑，一面對自己説。"等到牠發現我究竟是誰的時候，牠將會如何驚訝啊！不過，我還是把牠的扇子和手套拿來為好——這是説，如果我找得到的話。"她一説完這句話，就忽然看見一所精巧的小房子，門口釘着一塊鋥亮的銅牌，上面鐫刻着"大白兔"的名字。她不敲門就走了進去，匆匆登上樓梯，心裏怕極了，唯恐碰上真正的瑪麗·安恩，那樣的話，她還沒有找到那把扇子和那副手套，就要被趕出家門了。

"看來多麼奇怪啊，"愛麗絲自言自語地説，"竟然給一隻兔子當差！我猜想下一次戴娜也要吩咐我了！"她開始想像會發生的這樣的事情："'愛麗絲小姐！立刻到這裏來，你得準備去散步了！''保姆，我一會就來！不過，我必須守着這個老鼠洞，直到戴娜回來；我得看着，不讓老鼠跑出來。'不過，我覺得，"她往下想，"要是戴娜開始像這樣吩咐別人的話，他們不會讓她待在屋裏的！"

這時候，她已經找到一條路，走進一間小小的整潔的房間，那裏靠窗放着一張桌子，桌子上（正如她曾經希望的那樣）有一把扇子，兩三副白色小山羊皮做的小手套。她拿了一把扇子，一副手套，正要離開房間的時候，她的視線忽然落在那梳妝鏡子旁的一隻小玻璃瓶上。這一次，瓶子上可沒有印上"喝我呀"字樣的標籤，然而她還是拔開瓶塞，對着嘴巴喝起來。"我一吃或者一喝甚麼東西的時候，"她對自己説，"我知道，就一定會發生甚麼有趣的事情。所以，我就要看看這瓶東西會有甚麼作用。我真希望它能使我重新長大，因為對於變成這樣矮小，我確實厭倦極啦！"

她期望的倒是真的成了事實，而且比她預期的快得多；她還沒有喝掉半瓶，就發現自己的頭已經頂着天花板，於是不得不彎下身子，以免把脖子折斷了。她急忙放下瓶子，對自己說道：“這已經足夠了 —— 我希望自己決不要再長了 —— 即使現在這樣，我都無法從門口出去 —— 我真希望自己剛才沒有喝掉那麼多！”

可惜呀！希望如此已經太晚啦！她繼續生長、生長，她不久便必須跪在地板上。只過了一會，連這樣跪着都跪不下了，於是她躺了下來，用一隻手臂抵住門，另一隻手臂抱着頭，看看效果如何。可是她仍然繼續生長，作為最後一招，她只得把一隻手臂伸到窗戶外面去，把一隻腳放到煙囱上，同時對自己說：“不管再發生甚麼情況，現在我是已經無計可施啦。我究竟會變成甚麼樣子呢？”

愛麗絲很幸運，那隻小小的魔術瓶這會藥效已經發揮完了，她因而不再生長。不過，她還是很不舒服，並且看來她一點也沒有機會再走出這個房間，難怪她感到不開心，這也是怪不得她的。

“留在家裏，我可是愉快得多，”可憐的愛麗絲想道，“那時候，我們並不老是一會長大，一會縮小，也並不被老鼠和兔子差來差去的。我幾乎希望自己沒有掉進那個兔子洞才好 —— 可是呀 —— 可是呀 —— 你知道，這種樣子的生活倒是相當少見的呀！我真不明白，究竟有甚麼事情會發生在我身上！我過去經常閱讀童話故事的時候，我猜想這類事情從來沒有發生過，可是此時此地，我卻處在一個童話中間！應該有一本寫我的書，是應該有一本！等到我長大了，我要寫一本 —— 不過我現在已經長大了呀，”她用一種悲傷的調子加上一句，“至少在這裏已經沒有一點地方再容我長大了呀。”

"不過，應該這樣說，"愛麗絲心裏想，"我永遠也不會比現在更長大一點嗎？一方面，這也是個安慰——永遠也不會成為一個老太婆了——不過，話要這樣說——卻一直要學習功課呢！哦，我怎麼也不喜歡這種事！"

"哦，你這個愚蠢的愛麗絲呀！"她回答自己的想法說。"你怎麼能在這裏學習功課呢？瞧，這裏簡直沒有地方容納你了，更沒有一點地方容納任何課本！"

她就這樣往下想，先是從這一面想，然後從另一面想，而且把這件事可說是整個編成了一場對話。不過，幾分鐘之後，她聽見外面有聲音，便不再往下想，靜靜地聽着。

"瑪麗·安恩！瑪麗·安恩！"這是那聲音。"立刻把我的手套拿來！"接着傳來腳在樓梯上行走的輕微的啪嗒啪嗒聲。愛麗絲明白這是大白兔跑來找她了，她嚇得渾身顫抖，弄得屋子都搖晃起來，差不多忘記自己現在已經比大白兔大了一千倍，根本沒有理由怕牠。

大白兔轉眼就跑到了門口，試着開門；但是，門是朝裏開的，愛麗絲的手臂緊緊地抵在那裏，大白兔的努力結果是徒勞無功。愛麗絲聽見牠自言自語地說："那麼我要兜過去從窗戶裏跳進去。"

"你可辦不到這個！"愛麗絲心裏想，她等待着，在猜想自己聽見大白兔來到窗戶的正下方之後，便突然伸開了五指，亂抓一通。她甚麼也沒有抓到，但是聽見一聲細小的尖叫，一陣摔跌，以及玻璃被打碎的聲音，愛麗絲從這聲音推斷大白兔很可能掉進一個青瓜棚或者這一類東西裏面去了。

接着傳來憤怒的喊聲 —— 是大白兔在喊 ——"佩特！佩特！你在哪裏呀？"接着響起愛麗絲從來沒有聽見過的嗓音："我當然是在這裏嘛！正在挖掘蘋果哪，大人！"

"正在挖掘蘋果，你還好説！"大白兔怒氣沖沖地説。"到這裏來！幫我從這東西中脱身！"（傳來更多的碎玻璃聲。）

"現在跟我説，佩特，窗戶上究竟是甚麼東西？"

"沒錯，大人，那是一隻手臂！"（牠讀作"加巴"。）

"一隻手臂，你這個笨鵝！誰瞧見過這樣大尺寸的手臂？嘿，牠把整個窗戶都塞滿啦！"

"沒錯，是那樣，大人；不過，雖然如此，它還是一隻手臂。"

"好吧，不管怎麼樣，牠都沒有理由塞在那裏。你去把它挪開！"

這句話説完以後，接着是一段長時間的沉默。愛麗絲只能時不時地聽到幾聲悄悄話，例如："沒錯，大人，我不喜歡那個東西，根本不喜歡，根本不喜歡！""照我吩咐的去做，你這個膽小鬼！"她終於又伸開五指，再空抓了一回。這一次，響起了兩聲細小的尖叫，更多的玻璃破碎聲。"那裏一定有很多青瓜棚！"愛麗絲心裏想。"我不知道牠們下一步要做甚麼！至於把我挖到窗外去，我是多麼希望牠們辦得到！我肯定我本人決不要在這裏多待一會！"

她等待了一會，卻聽不見再有甚麼動靜。最後，響起一輛小手推車的車輪滾動聲，同時傳來七嘴八舌嘰嘰喳喳的談話聲。她聽出了這些話："另外一架梯子在哪裏？ —— 嗨，我剛才只能搬一架來。壁兒拿了另一架 —— 壁兒！把它拿到這裏來，老弟！ ——

拿到這裏來，在這個角落裏豎起來 —— 不對，先得把兩架接起來綁好 —— 它們還不夠高，一半都不夠 —— 哦，這就夠了。不要愛挑剔 —— 喂，壁兒！抓住這根繩子 —— 屋頂承受得了嗎？ —— 小心那一塊鬆動的石板瓦 —— 哦，它掉下來啦！下面的頭都躲開！"(哐噹一聲巨響) —— "嗨，這是誰做的事？ —— 是壁兒吧，我猜 —— 誰從煙囱裏爬下去呢？ —— 不，我才不做呢！要做就你做！ —— 那麼，我也不做那種事！ —— 這非壁兒下去不可 —— 喂，壁兒！主人説一定要你爬到煙囱裏去！"

"哦，那麼壁兒一定要從這煙囱裏爬下來啦，是不是呀？"愛麗絲自言自語。"天啊，牠們似乎把甚麼事情都推到壁兒身上！給我多少好處我也不願處在壁兒的地位。沒錯，這個壁爐很狹窄，不過我覺得我能夠稍稍踢那麼一下！"

她把一隻腳放下來，盡可能攔在煙囱那裏，然後等待，直到聽見一隻小動物（她猜不出那是甚麼動物）在抓着，爬着，就在她上面的煙囱裏。於是，她一面對自己説："這是壁兒，"一面狠狠地踢了一腳，等着瞧接着會發生甚麼事情。

她聽見的第一件事情是一陣異口同聲的歡呼："壁兒上天哪！"接着是大白兔自己的聲音 —— "你們待在籬笆旁邊的，接住牠！"然後是一陣沉默，跟着是又一陣亂七八糟的嚷嚷聲 —— "把牠的頭抬高 —— 快些拿白蘭地 —— 別嗆着牠 —— 那是怎麼回事啊，老弟？你碰到了甚麼啦？把一切都講給我們聽呀！"

最後傳來一陣微弱的嘰嘰吱吱的聲音。（愛麗絲想："那是壁兒。"）"嗯，我簡直不明白 —— 不喝了，謝謝你。我這會好些了 —— 不過，我現在心裏很亂，沒法和你們講 —— 我僅僅知道，有個甚麼東西碰着我，像是一個彈簧玩偶那樣，我便像一個冲天焰火似的飛上來了！"

"是這樣，老弟！"其他的伙伴一同説。

"我們必須把這所房屋燒掉！"説這話的是大白兔的聲音。於是愛麗絲拚命高聲喊道："你要是這樣做，我就叫戴娜來咬你！"

一下子變得鴉雀無聲了，愛麗絲自己在心裏琢磨："我不知道牠們下一步將會做甚麼！如果牠們有一點頭腦的話，牠們會把屋頂掀掉的。"過了一兩分鐘，牠們又開始走來走去了，愛麗絲聽見大白兔説："起先，兩輛手推車裝一車就行了。"

"一車甚麼呀？"愛麗絲心想。然而她無需疑惑多長時間，因為跟着而來的是一陣雨點般的小卵石打了過來，劈劈啪啪地打在窗戶上，有幾塊打中了她的臉。"我可要制止這種事，"她對自己説，然後大聲嚷着："你們還是別再做這種事為好！"這一聲導致了又一陣鴉雀無聲。

愛麗絲不無驚訝地察覺到，那些小卵石掉到地板上的時候，全都變成了小餅餅，她的頭腦裏便閃過一個聰明的想法。"我要是吃了一個這種餅餅，"她心裏想，"肯定會使我的身材發生某種變化。由於不可能使我變得更大了，那麼必然會使我變得小一些，我猜想。"

於是她吞下了一個餅餅，然後高興地發現自己立刻開始縮小。縮呀縮的，直到縮小到可以跨出門框框，她立即就跑，跑出了這所屋子，迎面看見一大群小野獸和禽鳥等候在外面。那隻可憐的小蜥蜴壁兒躺在中間，由兩隻豚鼠托着頭，正在拿一隻瓶子裏的甚麼藥水餵牠喝。愛麗絲一出現在牠們面前，牠們便都猛攻過來，但是她拚命奔逃，一直逃到一座密林裏，發現後面沒有追兵了。

"我必須做的第一件事，"愛麗絲對自己說，這時她在樹林子裏漫無目標地亂走，"就是重新長到我本來的高矮胖瘦。第二件呢，就是找到走進那座可愛的花園裏去的路。我覺得這將是最好的計劃。"

毫無疑問，這個計劃聽起來是再好不過的，安排得乾淨俐落，簡單明瞭。不過唯一的困難是，如何着手去實行，她卻連一點想法都沒有。而且，就在她在樹林子裏焦慮不安地東張西望的時候，只聽得頭頂上方響起又低又尖的犬吠聲，她急忙抬頭看。

一隻非常巨大的幼犬睜大圓圓的眼睛朝下對她瞧着，同時溫和地伸出一隻腳爪，打算碰碰她。"可憐的小東西啊！"愛麗絲用哄孩子的聲調說，她用力地想對牠吹一聲口哨，可是這時候她嚇得不得了，因為她猜想這隻幼犬也許正餓着肚子，這樣的話，就很可能一口把她吃掉，不管她怎麼哄牠也不行。

愛麗絲不知道自己怎麼一來，就拾起了一根小樹枝，對着那隻幼犬伸過去。於是，幼犬立即四腳騰空，跳了起來，同時開心地叫着，撲向那根樹枝，假裝要亂咬的樣子。愛麗絲連忙閃避到一棵高大的大薊後面躲起來，以免被幼犬壓在身上。她剛從大薊的另一邊探出頭來的時候，幼犬又向那根樹枝猛衝，在急急忙忙要咬住它的時候，卻翻了一個大筋斗。愛麗絲覺得這太像跟一匹拉車的高頭大馬做遊戲了，每時每刻都有可能被牠踩在鐵蹄下面，於是，她又繞着大薊轉圈子。這隻幼犬便開始了一系列對於樹枝的短暫攻擊。牠每一次向前奔跑很短的一段路，卻後退長長的一段路，並且一刻不停地聲音沙啞地吠叫，直到最後，牠在相當一段距離外坐了下來，氣喘吁吁，舌頭下垂到嘴巴外面，眼睛則半開半閉着。

在愛麗絲看來，這可是一個極好的逃跑時機，她便立刻撒腿跑開了，跑得她精疲力竭，跑得她上氣不接下氣，直到那隻幼犬的吠聲在遠處響得很輕微。

"然而那隻小幼犬多麼可愛呀！"愛麗絲說道，這時她靠着一株毛茛屬植物喘息，並且拿着一片葉子對自己扇風。"我本來應該很喜歡教牠玩些把戲的，要是——要是我恢復了原來的身材來教牠的話！哦，天哪！我幾乎忘記了自己必須再長大！讓我想想看——怎麼辦才好呢？我想我應該吃點或者喝點甚麼東西。不過最大的問題是'甚麼東西？'。"

最大的問題當然是"甚麼東西？"。愛麗絲環顧四周，看了看花呀、青草葉呀甚麼的，但是在目前情況之下，她看不出有甚麼東西看上去正是她應該吃或者喝的。有一隻巨大的蘑菇就長在她的身旁，差不多跟她本人一樣高。不過，她在蘑菇下面瞧看，在它兩邊瞧看，在它後面瞧看，這時候，她忽然想起自己或許也該瞧看一眼在蘑菇頂上有甚麼東西。

她踮起腳尖，伸長脖子，從蘑菇邊上窺視過去，她的眼睛立刻瞧見了一條那種青色的大毛毛蟲，牠正坐在頂上，雙臂抱在胸前，不聲不響地抽着一個很長的水煙筒，根本不注意愛麗絲或者任何其他的東西，一點都不。

第五章

毛毛蟲的忠告

毛毛蟲和愛麗絲彼此對視着，默不作聲。後來毛毛蟲終於從嘴巴上取下了水煙筒，用一種懶洋洋的、昏昏欲睡聲音同她寒喧。

"你是誰呀？"毛毛蟲問道。

這可不是讓人高興開腔對話的開始語。愛麗絲相當存戒心地回答說："我 —— 先生，我不大清楚，就目前來說 —— 至少我明白今天早晨我起牀的時候我是誰，然而，從那以後，我覺得自己一定已經被改變了好幾次啦。"

"你這是甚麼話？"毛毛蟲嚴厲地說。"你自己解釋一下吧！"

"先生，我怕我自己無法解釋，"愛麗絲說，"因為你看，我不是我自己。"

"我看不出來，"毛毛蟲說。

"我怕我無法把這事講得更清楚了，"愛麗絲彬彬有禮地回答，"首先，因為我自己也搞不懂；而且，一天之內變了那麼多大小不同的身材，這是叫人非常困惑不解的事。"

"並非如此，"毛毛蟲説。

"嗯，也許你到現在為止還沒有感覺到這一點，"愛麗絲説。"等你不得不變成一條蝴蝶的蛹蟲的時候 —— 你心裏明白，有一天你會變的 —— 然後，你變成了一隻蝴蝶，我想你會覺得這事有點怪，是不是呢？"

"一點也不會，"毛毛蟲説。

"嗯，也許你的感覺可能不同一些，"愛麗絲説。"我所知道的只不過是：這事對於我，會感到非常怪。"

"對於你！"毛毛蟲用不屑一顧的口氣説。"你是甚麼人？"

這句話把他們重新帶回到這場談話的開頭。愛麗絲對於毛毛蟲老是作如此簡短的評語，感到有點惱火，於是她挺直身子，非常嚴蕭地説道："我覺得首先你應該告訴我，你是誰。"

"為甚麼？"毛毛蟲説。

這裏是另外一個令人困惑的問題。由於愛麗絲想不出任何美妙的理由來，而且看樣子毛毛蟲心裏不愉快得很，她便轉身走開了。

"回來！"毛毛蟲在她的背後大喊。"我有要緊的話跟你説！"

的的確確，這句話聽起來是有商量的。愛麗絲便轉過身來，再走回去。

"不要發火，"毛毛蟲説。

"就是這句話嗎？"愛麗絲説，她盡了最大的努力把怒氣嚥下去。

"不是，"毛毛蟲説。

愛麗絲覺得自己既然沒有別的辦法，她還是等待的好，也許牠終究會對她講一些值得一聽的事情。有好幾分鐘，牠一言不發，只顧吞雲吐霧。但是到最後，牠交叉着手臂，把水煙筒又從嘴巴上取下來，說道："那麼你覺得自己被別人改變了，是嗎？"

"先生，我怕自己是這樣想，"愛麗絲說。"我想不起來我過去經常記住的東西——同時我無法把同樣的身材保持十分鐘！"

"你想不起甚麼事情呢？"毛毛蟲說。

"嗯，我曾經想背誦《那隻忙碌的小蜜蜂怎麼樣了》，但是背出來全都變樣了！"愛麗絲用非常悲傷的聲音回答。

"背背《你老了，威廉爸爸》，"毛毛蟲說。

愛麗絲把兩隻手疊在一起，背了起來：

> 那個青年說："你老了，威廉爸爸；
> 　　很白很白呀，你的頭髮。
> 可是你一刻不停地豎蜻蜓，興高采烈啊——
> 　　你年事已高，這麼玩行不行？"

> 威廉爸爸回答他的兒子說：
> 　　"年輕時，只怕腦子會傷着；
> 可現在我完全肯定自己沒腦子，
> 　　所以我一玩再玩也沒事。"

> 那個青年說："我剛才說過，你老了，
> 　　而且胖得天下都難找；
> 可是在門口，你一個後滾翻，進了屋裏——
> 　　請說說，這麼做竟是何道理？"

> 這胖胖長者搔搔他雪白的頭髮，
> 　　說道："年輕時，我的四肢柔又滑，

就因為用了這油膏 —— 一盒售一先令 ——
可允許我來賣給你兩盒？"

那個青年説："你老了，牙齒沒用，
比板油硬點的，你就嚼不動；
然而你卻把鵝連骨帶喙都吃光 ——
請説説，你究竟如何往肚裏裝？"

爸爸説："年輕時，我學的是法律，
老婆跟我辯論每一件案例；
因此體力強，肌肉健，下顎堅，
這叫我享用一直到晚年。"

那個青年説："你老了，難以設想
你的目光會像從前一樣強；
然而你把鰻魚用鼻尖直着頂 ——
甚麼使你如此驚人地機靈？"

爸爸説："我已經回答了三個問題，
你不要一直這樣盛氣凌人！
你以為我能夠整天聽你這樣胡謅？
去吧，否則我要把你踢下樓！"

"你背得不對，"毛毛蟲説。

"不十分對，我怕是，"愛麗絲膽小地説，"有些字已經改動
過了。"

"從頭到尾都錯了，"毛毛蟲不容置疑地説。接着有幾分鐘的
沉默。

還是毛毛蟲先開腔説話。

"你要的是甚麼樣的身材呢？"牠問道。

"哦，對於身材嘛，我並不挑剔，"愛麗絲慌忙回答説；"只不過不喜歡這樣常常變樣子，你知道的。"

"我不知道，"毛毛蟲説。

愛麗絲不説話了。她這一輩子從來沒有被人如此駁斥過，因而她覺得自己快要忍不住發脾氣了。

"你現在滿意嗎？"毛毛蟲問。

"嗯，我但願再大一點，先生，假如你不在意的話，"愛麗絲説。"三英寸是如此可憐的高度啊。"

"這確實是非常好的高度啊！"毛毛蟲怒氣沖沖地説，一邊把自己的身子直豎起來。（正好三英寸高，不多不少。）

"可是我不習慣這麼點高呀！"可憐的愛麗絲傷心地用懇求的聲音説。然後她心裏在想："我希望這些生物不那麼容易不高興！"

"你遲早會習慣這個身高的，"毛毛蟲説，牠把水煙筒放到嘴巴裏，重新抽起煙來。

這一次，愛麗絲耐心地等待着，直到毛毛蟲重新打算説話。過了一兩分鐘，毛毛蟲取下嘴上的水煙筒，打呵欠打了一兩次，抖了抖自己的身子。然後，牠從那隻大蘑菇上爬下來，緩緩地爬到草叢裏，爬走的時候，僅僅丟了一句話："這一邊會使你長得高些；另一邊會使你變得矮些。"

"甚麼的這一邊呢？甚麼的另一邊呢？"愛麗絲自己心裏琢磨着。

"這隻蘑菇的兩邊，"毛毛蟲說，就像是愛麗絲出聲問過牠似的。一轉眼工夫，毛毛蟲便不見了影蹤。

愛麗絲留在那裏，對那隻蘑菇左思右想地打量了一會，要想弄清楚它的兩邊在哪裏。可是，它怎麼看都是圓圓的，因此她發現這是個非常困難的問題。不過，她終於把兩隻手臂盡量伸長，抱住這隻大蘑菇，左右兩隻手各扯下一小塊蘑菇的邊皮。

"那麼現在哪一塊是哪一邊的呢？"她自言自語，並且把右手上的一小塊咬了一小口，想看看結果如何。只一下子工夫，她就覺得自己的下巴底下猛烈地捱了一擊：原來下巴撞到了自己的腳啦！

對於這一非常突然的變化，她真是嚇得不輕；但是她覺得沒有時間多想，因為自己正在飛速地縮小。於是她立刻動手把另外一小塊吃一口。她的下巴如此緊密地貼着她的腳，以致她很難張開口。但是她終於做到了這一點，並且設法吞嚥了一口左手上的那一小塊。

"好啊，我的頭終於自由啦！"愛麗絲用欣喜的聲調說，接下來這聲調卻變成了驚慌失措的叫喊，因為她發現自己的肩膀找不到了。她往下看的時候，只見一根長得不得了的脖子，就好像是從很低很低的下面的一大片綠葉裏豎起的一根花莖。

"那一大片綠色的東西會是甚麼呢？"愛麗絲說。"我的肩膀又落到哪裏去啦？哦，我的可憐的雙手啊，我怎麼看不見你們呢？"她說話的時候，把自己的雙手動來動去，然而似乎沒有甚麼作用，只不過遠遠的綠樹葉叢裏邊有一點擺動。

看來她沒有希望把雙手放到自己的頭上了，因此她打算把頭低下來邁就雙手，這時她高興地發現自己的脖子就像一條大蛇似的，能夠輕而易舉地朝任何方向彎下來。她剛剛成功地彎下脖子，形成一個優美的 Z 字形，並且正要插入那片綠葉叢，她發現那片綠葉不是別的，而是她曾經在那下面行走的樹林的樹冠。就在這時候，一聲尖銳的噓聲使她慌慌張張地縮回脖子。一隻巨大的鴿子飛到她的臉上來，用翅膀猛烈地撲打着她。

"大蛇！"鴿子尖聲叫道。

"我不是一條大蛇！"愛麗絲惱怒地說。"不要碰我！"

"我再說一遍：大蛇！"鴿子重複說，但是用一種比較溫和的聲調，接着又帶着抽泣的聲音繼續說："我想盡了種種辦法，可是看來沒有甚麼東西能適合牠們！"

"你在說甚麼呀，我一點都聽不懂，"愛麗絲說。

"我曾經試過樹根；我曾經試過河岸；我曾經試過籬笆，"鴿子不理睬她的話，只顧自己說下去，"可是那些大蛇呀！沒有甚麼能討好牠們！"

愛麗絲越來越弄不懂了，但是她覺得在鴿子把話說完以前，她不管說甚麼也沒有用處。

"就好像孵蛋的事還不夠麻煩似的，"鴿子說，"可是我還必須日日夜夜提防着大蛇！咳，整整三個星期我都沒合一下眼皮！"

"剛才驚擾了你，我非常抱歉，"愛麗絲說，她已經開始明白牠話中的意思了。

"我在樹林子裏剛剛住到這株最高的樹上的時候，"鴿子把聲音提得又高又尖，繼續往下說，"就在我剛剛覺得自己終於擺脫了牠們的時候，牠們卻一定要從天上歪歪扭扭地扭下來！哎唷，大蛇！”

“不過我跟你説，我不是一條大蛇！”愛麗絲説。“我是一個
—— 我是一個 ——”

“好哇！那麼你是甚麼東西呢？”鴿子説。“我看得出，你在
打算編造些甚麼話！”

“我 —— 我是一個小女孩，”愛麗絲説，説得疑疑惑惑的，因
為她記起這一天自己所經歷的許多次變化。

“説得好像是真的一樣！”鴿子用最鄙夷不屑的聲調説。“在
我的一生中曾經見到過好多好多小女孩，可是從來沒有一個長着
像你這樣的脖子！不對，不對！你是一條大蛇，要不承認也沒有
用。我猜想，你下一句打算跟我説，你從來也沒有嚐過蛋的味道
了吧！”

“我當然嚐過蛋的味道啦，”愛麗絲説。她是一個非常誠實的
孩子。“不過，你知道，小女孩吃蛋往往就跟大蛇吃蛋一個樣。”

“我才不信呢，”鴿子説。“不過，如果她們真是那樣，那麼
她們就是一種大蛇。我只能這麼説。”

這種想法對於愛麗絲來説真是聞所未聞，這使她不言不語足
足有一兩分鐘，而這就給了鴿子説下去的機會：“你是來找蛋的，
對此我一清二楚。至於你究竟是一個小女孩還是一條大蛇，這點
跟我有甚麼關係？”

“這點跟我的關係可大呢，”愛麗絲急忙説道。“然而我偏偏
不是來找蛋的。而且，如果我來找蛋，我也決不要你的蛋。我可
不喜歡吃生蛋。”

“好吧，那麼你走吧！”鴿子用一種悶悶不樂的聲調説，一面

又在牠的窩巢裏安頓下來。愛麗絲在樹叢中間盡量設法蹲下來，因為她的脖子老是在枝杈中間給纏住，時不時地，她得停下不動，轉動脖子避開那些樹枝。過了一會，她記起自己手上仍然拿着蘑菇的碎片，於是她非常小心地開始工作，先咬一口這隻手上的，然後咬一口那隻手上的，一下子長得高一些，一下子又縮得矮一些，直到她成功地使自己降低到原來的高度。

經過那麼漫長的時間，她才成為一種接近正確身材的某種東西，開頭，她對它覺得相當陌生。但是幾分鐘之後，她卻對它習慣了，並且像平常那樣對自己說話：“好啦，現在我的計劃完成一半啦！這些變化叫人多麼迷惑不解！我怎麼也不能肯定自己從這一分鐘到下一分鐘將變成甚麼樣子！不過，我總算已經回到自己原來的身材了。下一步呢，是到那座美麗的花園裏 —— 我不知道，如何辦到這件事。”她正在如此這般說着的時候，忽然就到了一個空曠的地方，那裏有一幢小房屋，大約四英尺高。“不管是誰住在那裏，”愛麗絲心裏想，“以我這樣的身材碰見他們是萬萬不行的。咳，我一定會把他們嚇得驚慌失措的！”因此，她再咬一小口右手上的蘑菇碎片，直到她把自己降到九英寸高的時候，才敢走近那幢房屋。

第六章

豬娃和胡椒

她站在那裏對那幢房屋瞧了一兩分鐘，不知道下一步該怎麼辦，這時候，一位穿着制服的男僕從樹林子裏奔了出來，（她猜想他是位男僕，因為他穿着制服。否則的話，單單從他的臉來推測，她可能會把他喚做魚。）他用手指關節響亮地敲門。門由另外一位穿制服的男僕打開了，他的臉圓圓的，眼睛大大的，像青蛙一樣。愛麗絲注意到這兩位男僕都在滿頭鬢髮上撒了香粉。她感到自己好奇心很大，想知道這是怎麼回事，便從樹林子裏悄悄走出來一點，側耳靜聽。

那位魚臉男僕首先從手臂下面拿出一個很大的信封，幾乎跟他本人一樣大，他把信封遞交給了另外一位，用一種一本正經的聲調說道："致公爵夫人。王后邀請參加槌球遊戲的請柬。"那位蛙臉男僕用同樣一本正經的聲調重複他的話，只不過稍稍改動了詞句的先後次序："王后來函。邀請公爵夫人參加槌球遊戲的請柬。"

於是他們兩人相對鞠躬，以致兩人的鬢髮糾纏到一起去了。

對此，愛麗絲笑得那麼厲害，以致她不得不跑回樹林裏去，以免被他們聽見。在她再一次探出身子望望的時候，那位魚臉男僕已經走了，另外那位正坐在門旁的地上，傻頭傻腦地眼望青天。

愛麗絲膽戰心驚地走到門口，舉手敲門。

"敲門是沒有甚麼用處的事情，"那位男僕說，"有兩個理由。第一，因為我跟你同樣是在門的外邊；第二，因為他們在裏邊吵得鬧哄哄的，聲音太大，沒有誰能夠聽見你敲門。"果然不錯，裏邊是有一陣極不平常的鬧聲在響着 —— 一陣繼續不斷的吼叫聲和打噴嚏的聲音，時不時地夾雜着砰的一下碎裂聲，彷彿一隻碟子或者水壺被人摔得粉碎。

"那麼，請教，"愛麗絲說，"我怎麼樣才能進去呢？"

"要是我們兩個之間隔着那扇門的話，你篤篤敲門可能有些道理。"那位男僕對她不加理睬，只顧繼續說下去。"比方說，如果你在門裏邊，你也許篤篤敲門，你知道，我就能讓你走出來。"他說話的整個時候都眼望青天，愛麗絲覺得這是明白無誤地缺乏教養。"不過，也許他是身不由己，"她自言自語地說，"他的眼睛長得這個樣，太接近他的頭頂心了。不過，無論如何，他應該回答問題呀。—— 我怎麼樣才能進去呢？"她提高聲音，重複這句話。

"我要一直坐在這裏，"那位男僕說，"坐到明天 ——"

這時候，這幢房屋的門打開了，有一隻大盤子平飄着飛了出來，筆直地向那位男僕的頭上飛去，剛剛好擦過他的鼻子，撞到他身子後邊的一棵樹上，撞得粉碎。

"—— 或者，也許再下一天，"那位男僕用原來的聲調繼續說下去，完完全全像是甚麼事情也沒有發生過。

"我怎麼樣才能進去呢？"愛麗絲把聲音提得更高，又問他。

"你究竟是不是要進去呢？"那位男僕問道。"你知道，這是首要的問題。"

毫無疑問，是這樣的。只不過愛麗絲不喜歡人家對她這樣說話。"這些動物跟人爭辯全都是這個樣，"她喃喃自語地說，"真正可怕，足以把人給逼瘋了！"

那位男僕似乎覺得這是個好機會，能變着法重複自己的話。"我要坐在這裏，"他說，"時不時地坐在這裏，一天又一天，一天又一天。"

"可是讓我做甚麼呢？"愛麗絲問道。

"你喜歡做甚麼就做甚麼，"那位男僕說完就開始吹起口哨來。

"哦，跟他談話等於白說，"愛麗絲說，覺得絕望了，"他是一個十足的傻瓜！"於是她打開那扇門徑自走了進去。

一進門就看見一間大廚房，裏面從這頭到那頭滿是煙霧。那位公爵夫人坐在廚房中央的一隻三條腿的凳子上，懷裏抱了個嬰兒。那個廚師正在火爐旁，俯身攪拌一隻大鐵鍋裏的東西，那看來是滿滿一鍋子湯。

"那鍋湯裏肯定放了太多的胡椒！"愛麗絲阿嚏阿嚏的連連打着噴嚏，同時又對自己說。確實，空氣裏的胡椒味太濃了。即使那位公爵夫人也有時來一個噴嚏。至於那個嬰兒呢，又噴嚏，又是號哭，兩者輪流發作，一刻也不停。廚房裏只有兩個傢伙不打噴嚏，就是那位廚師和一隻大花貓，牠正躺在爐竈旁，嘴巴咧開，從這邊耳朵咧到那邊耳朵，笑着。

"可以請你告訴我嗎？"愛麗絲有點心虛膽怯地問，因為她不大能肯定，自己先開口是不是有禮貌，"為甚麼你的貓這樣齜牙咧嘴地笑呢？"

"這是一隻柴郡貓，"公爵夫人説，"這就是為甚麼牠這個樣子笑。豬娃！"

她這後面一聲喊是那麼突然，那麼聲色俱厲，愛麗絲嚇得跳起來。不過她馬上發現那是衝着那個嬰兒喊的，不是衝着她，於是她鼓起勇氣，再説下去：

"我不知道柴郡貓總是露齒而笑的；事實上，我不知道貓們會露齒而笑。"

"牠們全都會，"公爵夫人説，"牠們大多露齒而笑。"

"我可不知道有哪一隻貓會笑，"愛麗絲非常有禮貌地説，覺得已經開展對話，很是高興。

"你並不知道多少事，"公爵夫人説，"這是一個事實。"

愛麗絲一點也不喜歡對方説這句話的腔調，她覺得還是換個甚麼別的話題來談為好。就在她打算決定一個話題的時候，那位廚師把那一大鍋湯從火上端了起來，立刻便着手把凡她夠得到的東西大扔特扔，扔向那位公爵夫人和那個嬰兒 —— 首先是火鉗、鐵鏟、撥火棒之類的東西飛了過來；然後又下了一陣蒸煮鍋、燉鍋、盤子、盆子、碟子的雨。那位公爵夫人竟然毫不在意，即使那些東西打中了她也一樣。那個嬰兒呢，因為一直號哭得那麼厲害，所以不大可能説明白究竟那些東西是不是傷了他。

"喂，請你注意自己在做些甚麼！"愛麗絲高聲嚷着，她驚恐萬狀地上蹦下跳。"哦，他的珍貴的鼻子可要完了！"這時候，一個異乎尋常的大蒸煮鍋飛臨那個嬰兒的鼻子近端，幾幾乎就要把它削掉。

"要是人人都不管別人的閒事，"公爵夫人用一種沙啞的怒吼聲說道，"這個地球就會比它現在轉動得快得多。"

"這可不會有甚麼好處呀，"愛麗絲說，她能得到機會炫耀自己一點知識，心裏非常高興。"只要想一想，這將使得白天和黑夜變得怎麼樣啊！你瞧，地球二十四小時繞着它的軸自轉弗止——"

"提起了斧子，"公爵夫人說道，"把她的腦袋砍掉！"

愛麗絲相當惶恐不安地瞟了那位廚師一眼，看看她是否打算實施這一暗示；但是那位廚師正在忙於攪拌大鍋湯，不像是在聽甚麼，因此她再繼續說下去："我想是二十四小時；否則，是不是十二小時呢？我——"

"哦，不要叫我心煩！"那位公爵夫人說。"我一點都受不了數目字！"說着，她重新開始哄她的嬰兒，一面哄一面對嬰兒唱一種催眠曲，在每一句的最後一個音，把嬰兒突然地搖撼一下：

> 對你的小孩說話要粗暴，
> 　要是他打噴嚏就打他別輕饒。
> 他打噴嚏只為了使人惱，
> 　因為戲弄人的事他知道。

合唱

（廚師和嬰兒加入其中）：

喔嗚！喔嗚！喔嗚！

那位公爵夫人唱這首歌曲的第二段歌詞的時候，也一直把那個嬰兒猛烈地往上拋往下甩，那個可憐的小東西號哭得那麼厲害，以至於愛麗絲難以聽清楚歌詞：

　　　　　　對孩子説話我沒有好腔調，
　　　　　　　他打噴嚏我打他很公道；
　　　　　　因為只要他喜歡聞胡椒，
　　　　　　　就能夠隨心所欲聞個飽！

合唱

喔嗚！喔嗚！喔嗚！

　　"喂！要是你願意的話，你可以抱抱他！"那位公爵夫人對愛麗絲説，一面説一面就把那個嬰兒拋給了她。"我必須走了，要準備去跟王后玩槌球遊戲了，"於是她就匆匆忙忙地走出廚房。那位廚師把一隻煎鍋扔過去追趕她，但是只差一點，沒打中。

　　愛麗絲好不容易才接住了那個嬰兒，因為他是一個形狀特異的小怪物，他的四肢都直直地伸開，"就像一隻海星，"愛麗絲心中這樣想。在她接住那個可憐的小東西的時候，他正在像蒸汽機那樣呼哧呼哧地噴鼻息，同時不停地一會把身體弓起來，一會又把身體挺得直直的，凡此種種，使她在頭一兩分鐘的時候，盡了最大的能力才抱住了他。

　　她終於弄明白抱這個嬰兒的正確方法，（那就是把他擰成一個像是繩結那樣的東西，然後牢牢地抓住他的右耳朵和左腳，以免他自己恢復原狀。）這時候，她把他抱到露天裏來。"假如我不把這個孩子帶走的話，"愛麗絲心裏想，"一兩天之內，他們肯定會把他殺死的。把他扔在那裏不理，不就等於是謀殺嗎？"後面這句話她是高聲説出來的，那個小東西則嘴巴裏咕嚕咕嚕響着作為回答（這一次他已經停止打噴嚏了）。"不要咕嚕咕嚕叫，"愛麗絲説，"這完全不是表達你自己的想法的正確方法。"

那個嬰兒卻又咕嚕咕嚕叫了，愛麗絲非常焦急地看着他的臉蛋，要明白他究竟是怎麼樣的。毫無疑問，他長着一個非常上翹的鼻子，很像一個豬鼻子，不太像一個人的鼻子。他的眼睛對於一個嬰兒説來也是過份小了。整體看來，愛麗絲一點也不喜歡這個傢伙的長相。"不過，或許他只不過是在嚶嚶啜泣吧，"她心裏想，並且再一次看着他的眼睛，想知道他的眼睛裏是否有淚水。

沒有，不見淚水呀。"我親愛的，假如你正在變成一頭豬娃的話，"愛麗絲嚴肅地説，"我就跟你再也沒有甚麼關係了。你可要小心點！"那個可憐的小東西又啜泣起來，（或者説咕嚕咕嚕叫，你不可能分清到底是哪一樣。）接着他們有一段時間大家不聲不響。

愛麗絲心裏想："現在我要是把這個小生物帶回家去，該怎麼辦哪！"就在這時候，那個嬰兒又咕嚕咕嚕直叫了，叫得那麼厲害，使得她有點驚慌失措，眼睛朝下直盯着他的臉瞧。這一次，不可能有任何錯誤了：不多不少，牠正好是一隻豬娃，因此她覺得自己要是再抱着牠走下去就未免太滑稽了。

於是，她把這個小生物放下來，眼看牠安安靜靜地邁着小快步走到樹林子去，覺得鬆了一口氣。"如果牠長大，"她自言自語地説，"牠會變成一個醜八怪的小孩子。不過，我覺得牠已經成為一個相當漂亮的豬娃了。"接着她開始思量她認識的其他孩子們，要是成為一些豬娃的話，誰可能有很不錯的樣子。就在她對自己說："如果誰真的知道把他們變一變的正確方法的話——"這時候，她忽然瞧見離她幾碼遠的一根粗樹枝上蹲着那隻柴郡貓，不免有點吃驚。

那隻貓看見愛麗絲的時候，只是露齒而笑。她覺得牠看來脾氣不壞。然而貓爪子非常長，又有許多許多牙齒，所以她覺得要恭恭敬敬地對待牠才是。

"柴郡咪咪，"她戰戰兢兢地開口說，因為她完全不知道牠是不是喜歡這個名字。然而，牠只是露齒而笑，嘴巴咧得更闊些。"好哇，牠聽了那麼高興，"愛麗絲心想，於是她繼續說。"能不能請你告訴我，從這裏走，我該走哪條路？"

"這在很多方面取決於你想到哪裏去，"那隻貓說。

"我不太在意到哪裏去——"愛麗絲說。

"那麼，你走哪條路就沒有甚麼關係了，"那隻貓說。

"——只要我能走到某個地方就行，"愛麗絲補上這句話作為一種解釋。

"哦，只要你走得夠遠的，"那隻貓說，"你肯定會達到這個目的。"

愛麗絲覺得這一點無可否認，因此她試着問另一個問題。"這一帶都住着哪一些人啊？"

"在那一邊，"那隻貓把牠的右腳爪舞了一圈，"住着一位製帽匠。而在那一邊，"牠舞着另一隻腳爪，"住着一位三月裏的野兔。隨便你喜歡訪問哪一位吧，他們兩個都瘋了。"

"但是我可不要走到瘋子堆裏去，"愛麗絲說道。

"哦，這你就無可奈何了，"那隻貓說，"這裏，我們大家全都瘋了。我瘋了；你也瘋了。"

"你怎麼知道我瘋了呢？"愛麗絲問道。

"你一定是瘋了，"那隻貓說，"否則你就不會到這裏來。"

愛麗絲全然不認為這件事能夠作為證明；不過，她繼續問道："你又怎麼知道你自己瘋了呢？"

"首先，"那隻貓說，"一隻狗沒有瘋，你承認這一點嗎？"

"我想可以，"愛麗絲說道。

"好，那麼，"那隻貓繼續說，"你知道的，一隻狗發怒的時候汪汪吠叫；高興的時候則大搖尾巴。而我呢，我高興的時候卻嗚嗚吼叫；發怒的時候則大搖尾巴。因此，我已經瘋了。"

"不過，我不稱之為吼叫，我稱之為喵嗚喵嗚叫，"愛麗絲說道。

"隨便你怎麼稱之為吧，"那隻貓說。"今天你跟那位王后玩槌球遊戲嗎？"

"我非常願意跟她玩，"愛麗絲說道，"但是我到現在還沒有得到邀請。"

"你將會在那裏見到我的，"那隻貓說完就無影無蹤了。

對此，愛麗絲並不覺得很驚訝，因為她對於接連發生的許多怪事已經漸漸習以為常。就在她依然對着那隻貓消失的地方凝望的時候，牠忽然又出現了。

"順便問問，那個嬰兒的情況怎麼樣？"那隻貓問道。"我幾乎忘記問了。"

"他變成了一隻豬娃，"愛麗絲非常平靜地回答，彷彿這隻貓重新出現是很自然的事。

"我料想他會這樣的，"那隻貓説，説完又不見了。

愛麗絲等了一會，有點希望再看見牠，然而牠不再出現。又過了一兩分鐘，她朝着人家説是三月裏的野兔住處的方向走過去。"我以前看見過一些製帽匠，"她自言自語。三月裏的野兔則會是最最有趣的，由於現在是五月，也許牠不會瘋得無法無天——至少不會像牠在三月裏那樣瘋。"她説這句話的時候，眼睛朝上一望，只見那隻貓又在那裏，坐在一根粗樹枝上。

"你剛才説的是'豬娃'還是'無花果'？"那隻貓問道。

"我是説'豬娃'，"愛麗絲回答説。"我希望你不要老是那麼突然地一下子出現，一下子消失。你弄得我頭昏腦脹啦！"

"行啊，"那隻貓説，這一次牠相當緩慢地消失，先從尾巴的末端開始，到露齒而笑結束，那張咧開的嘴在其餘部分都無影無蹤以後還停留了一會。

"很好！我過去常常看見沒有露齒而笑的貓，"愛麗絲心裏想，"但是，沒有貓的露齒而笑哇！我這一輩子還從來沒有見過如此奇怪的事情！"

她沒有走多遠就看見了那隻三月裏的野兔的房子。她認為那所房屋一定錯不了，因為那兩個煙囪的樣子像兩隻耳朵，屋頂上則是用毛皮蓋的。那所房屋很大，她不願意走近些，後來，她又咬了一些左手上的蘑菇碎片，使自己長高到兩英尺左右。即使如此，她還是膽戰心驚地向房子走去，一面對自己説："如果到頭來牠竟然瘋得無法無天呢！我差不多希望自己沒有來這裏，而是去看了那位製帽匠才好！"

第七章

瘋狂的午茶會

那所房屋前面有一棵樹，樹下放着一張擺好茶點的桌子，那隻三月裏的野兔和那位製帽匠正在那裏用午茶，他們兩個之間則坐着一隻榛睡鼠，睡得正酣，那兩位就把牠當作一個靠墊使用，各把一隻胳臂肘放在牠身上，越過牠的頭頂彼此交談。"這對於那隻榛睡鼠一定非常不舒服，"愛麗絲想道。"只不過牠睡着，我猜想牠就不在意了。"

那是一張大桌子，但是那三位卻擠坐在一角。"沒有地方了！沒有地方了！"他們看見愛麗絲走來的時候，嚷嚷着説。"地方有的是！"愛麗絲惱怒地説，然後在桌子一端的一張大扶手椅上坐下來。

"喝點酒吧，"三月裏的野兔用一種鼓勵的聲調説。

愛麗絲對桌子打量了一圈，發現桌子上除了茶以外，甚麼也沒有。"我可沒瞧見有甚麼酒哇，"她説。

"是沒有甚麼酒，"三月裏的野兔説。

"那麼你勸我喝酒就不是很有禮貌的事，"愛麗絲生氣地説。

"你沒有受到邀請便坐下來，也不是很有禮貌的事，"三月裏的野兔回敬了她一句。

"我並不知道這是你們的桌子，"愛麗絲說。"桌子上擺的東西遠遠超過供你們三位用的。"

"你的頭髮該剪了，"那位製帽匠說。他懷着極大的好奇心望着愛麗絲，望了好久，才第一次開口說話。

"你應該知道不要干涉人家私人的事情，"愛麗絲帶點嚴厲的神態說。"這是非常無禮的。"

那位製帽匠聽了這句話，把眼睛睜得大大的，然而他卻只說了一句："為甚麼渡鴉像一張書桌呀？"

"好哇，我們現在要做些遊戲了！"愛麗絲心裏想。"我很高興牠們已經開始叫人猜謎語啦——我相信我猜得出來，"她接着說出這句話來。

"你難道認為自己能夠猜出這個謎語嗎？"三月裏的野兔問道。

"完全正確，"愛麗絲說。

"那麼你應該說出你想說的話，"三月裏的野兔繼續說。

"我是這樣的，"愛麗絲急忙回答。"至少——我所說的就是我想說的——這是一回事，你知道的。"

"一點也不是一回事！"製帽匠說。"這樣一來，你也就可以說：'我看見我所吃的'跟'我吃我所看見的'是一回事了！"

"你也就可以說，"三月裏的野兔加上一句，"'我喜歡我所得到的東西'跟'我得到我所喜歡的東西'是一回事了！"

"你也就可以說，"那隻榛睡鼠加了一句，牠似乎在牠的睡夢中談話，"'我睡覺的時候呼吸'跟'我呼吸的時候睡覺'是一回事了！"

"這對於你正是一回事，"那位製帽匠說，到這裏，對話中止了，大家靜靜地坐了一分鐘，這時，愛麗絲把自己記得起來的關於那些大渡鴉和書桌的一切都想了一遍，卻想不出很多。

那位製帽匠首先打破了沉默。"今天是這個月的幾號呀？"他問道，轉過頭來對着愛麗絲。他已經從口袋裏掏出了一隻錶，這時他正局促不安地看錶，時不時地搖兩下，又放在耳朵邊聽聽。

愛麗絲推算了一會，然後說道："四號。"

"錯了兩天啦！"那位製帽匠歎着氣說。"我跟你說過，牛油是不適合塗鐘錶機件的！"他怒氣沖沖地瞅着三月裏的野兔，加上這句話。

"那可是最上等的牛油啊，"三月裏的野兔低聲下氣地回答。

"不錯，可是一些麵包屑肯定也摻進去啦，"那位製帽匠甕聲甕氣地抱怨說。"你真不該用切麵包的刀去給錶加油。"

三月裏的野兔把錶拿過來，悶悶不樂地對它瞧着；然後把錶放在一杯茶裏浸一下，再對它瞧着。可是牠想不出比牠剛才說過的更好的話來，只是說："那可是最上等的牛油啊，你知道的。"

愛麗絲已經帶點好奇心地從牠的肩頭望了一眼。"多麼滑稽的錶呀！"她說。"只表明一個月的幾號，卻不表明現在是幾點鐘！"

"為甚麼要表明這個呢？"那位製帽匠咕嚕着說。"你的錶是不是告訴你今年是哪一年呢？"

"當然不啦，"愛麗絲脫口而出地回答。"不過那是因為同一年要連續那麼長久的時間呀。"

"這也正是我的錶的情況，"那位製帽匠說。

愛麗絲覺得迷惑得不得了。那位製帽匠的話在她聽來簡直一點意義也沒有，然而那確實是英語。"我聽不大懂你的話，"她盡可能有禮貌地說。

"那隻榛睡鼠又睡着了，"那位製帽匠說，接着把一點熱茶倒在牠的鼻子上。

那隻榛睡鼠不耐煩地搖搖頭，眼睛也不睜，說道："當然啦，當然啦，我自己正是打算這麼說。"

"你猜出那個謎語了嗎？"那位製帽匠又轉過頭來對愛麗絲說。

"沒有，我不想猜啦，"愛麗絲回答說。"謎底是甚麼呢？"

"我真正一點都不知道，"那位製帽匠說。

"我也不知道，"三月裏的野兔說。

愛麗絲有氣無力地歎了一聲。"我覺得你可以把時間用在更好的事情上，"她說，"而不要把它浪費在問一些沒有謎底的謎語上。"

"如果你像我一樣對時間很熟的話，"那位製帽匠說，"你就不會說甚麼把它浪費了。該說他才是。"

"我不知道你這是甚麼意思，"愛麗絲說。

"你當然不知道啦！"那位製帽匠說着輕蔑地把頭一甩。"我敢說你甚至從來都不曾跟時間談過話！"

"也許是吧，"愛麗絲小心翼翼地說。"但是我知道我學音樂的時候不得不打拍子。"

"啊，原來如此！"那位製帽匠說。"他不會忍受拍打的。瞧，你只要跟他保持良好的關係，他就會在時鐘上做幾乎你所喜歡的任何事情。比如說，假定現在是上午九點鐘，正是要開始上課的時間；那你只要對時間悄聲暗示一下，只一眨眼工夫，時針就會轉動！轉到一點半，午飯的時間到啦！"

（"我就是希望如此呀，"三月裏的野兔壓低聲音對自己說。）

"當然啦，那是棒極了，"愛麗絲若有所思地說。"不過，這樣的話——你知道，我肚子卻不餓，不想吃午飯呢。"

"開頭，也許如此，"那位製帽匠說。"不過，你可以把時間停留在一點半，你喜歡停多久便停多久。"

"你自己就是採用這個辦法的嗎？"愛麗絲問道。

那位製帽匠悲哀地搖搖頭。"我沒有！"他回答說。"你知道，就在他發瘋之前，（他用茶匙指指三月裏的野兔）在今年三月裏，我們吵了一場——那是在紅心皇后舉辦的盛大音樂會上，我不得不演唱那首歌的時候，我唱：

　　　　閃爍，閃爍，小小的蝙蝠，
　　　　我不知道，你忙些甚麼！　　　　·

或許，你知道這首歌吧？"

"我曾經聽到過像這樣的歌，"愛麗絲說。

"接下去，你知道，"那位製帽匠繼續說，"這首歌是這樣唱的：

　　　　在世界之上你飛呀飛，
　　　　像天空裏一隻茶盤打來回。
　　　　　閃爍，閃爍——"

這時候，那隻榛睡鼠搖動着身子，開始在睡夢裏唱道："閃爍，閃爍，閃爍，閃爍——"唱了很久，以至於他們非得擰牠使聲音停止不可。

"嗯，我剛剛唱完第一段歌詞，"那位製帽匠説，"那位皇后就大喊大叫地説：'他在謀殺時間啦！把他的頭砍下來！'"

"多麼殘酷野蠻呀！"愛麗絲驚叫着説。

"那次以後，"那位製帽匠用一種悲哀的語調繼續説道，"我所要求的事情，他就一件都不做！現在就一直是六點鐘。"

愛麗絲恍然大悟起來。"是否這就是為甚麼如此之多的茶具擺放在這裏，是吧？"她問道。

"是的，正是這樣，"那位製帽匠歎了一口氣，説道。"現在始終是喝午茶的時間，我們都沒有兩次之間的時間來洗洗東西了。"

"所以你們一直兜圈子挪動座位，是不是？"愛麗絲説。

"完全正確，"那位製帽匠説；"在東西用過了的時候。"

"不過，你們又挪到開頭的地方該怎麼辦呢？"愛麗絲不怕冒犯地問道。

"我們換個話題談談怎麼樣，"三月裏的野兔打着呵欠，插進來説。"我對此已經厭倦了。我提議請這位小姐講個故事給我們聽。"

"我怕自己一個故事都沒有，"愛麗絲説，她對這個提議相當緊張。

"那麼請榛睡鼠講吧！"那兩位喊道。"該醒啦，榛睡鼠！"那兩位同時在兩邊擰牠。

榛睡鼠慢慢地睜開眼睛。"我沒有睡着，"牠用一種沙啞的細聲細氣的嗓子說，"我聽得見你們這幫傢伙剛才說的每一個字。"

"講個故事給我們聽！"三月裏的野兔說。

"對啦，請你講吧！"愛麗絲懇求說。

"而且要快些講，"那位製帽匠加上一句，"否則你還沒有講完就要睡着了。"

"從前，有三個小女孩，她們是親姊妹，"榛睡鼠迫不及待地連聲起個頭；"她們的名字是艾爾西、萊西和蒂莉；她們住在一口井的裏邊 ——"

"她們靠吃甚麼過日子呢？"愛麗絲問道，她對於吃喝問題一直懷有極大的興趣。

"她們靠吃糖漿過日子，"那隻榛睡鼠想了一兩分鐘以後說。

"你知道，她們不能那麼辦，"愛麗絲溫和地指出。"那樣她們要生病的。"

"她們是病了，"榛睡鼠說，"病得厲害呢。"

愛麗絲做了一點努力，讓自己想像一下，這種不同尋常的生活方式會是甚麼樣子的，但是怎麼也想像不出，因此愛麗絲接着問道："但是，她們為甚麼住在井底呢？"

"再多喝點茶吧，"三月裏的野兔非常莊重地對愛麗絲說。

"我到現在甚麼都沒有喝過，"愛麗絲用生氣的口吻回答說，"所以我就不能再多喝點。"

"你是說不能再少喝點，"那位製帽匠說。"比起甚麼都沒有喝過，再多是非常容易的啦。"

"沒有人徵求過你的意見，"愛麗絲説。

"現在是誰在評論起個人啦？"那位製帽匠洋洋得意地問道。

愛麗絲對這個問題不大清楚該説些甚麼好；於是她喝了點茶，吃了點塗牛油的麵包，然後轉向那隻榛睡鼠，重複她的問話："她們為甚麼要住在井底啊？"

那隻榛睡鼠又想了一兩分鐘，然後説道："那是一口糖漿井呀。"

"沒有這種東西！"愛麗絲開始非常憤怒了，但是那位製帽匠和三月裏的野兔"唏！唏！"地發出聲音，同時那隻榛睡鼠則不高興地繃着臉説道："假如你不能彬彬有禮的話，你最好還是自己編完這個故事吧。"

"不行，請你講下去！"愛麗絲非常謙恭地説。"我將不再打斷你啦。我敢説可能是有那麼一口井。"

"是啊，有一口啊！"那隻榛睡鼠怒氣沖沖地説。不過，牠答應講下去。"於是，這小小的三姐妹 —— 你知道，她們正在學着汲取 ——"

"她們汲取甚麼呀？"愛麗絲完全忘記了自己的諾言，問道。

"糖漿呀，"那隻榛睡鼠説，這次一點都不假思索。

"我需要一隻清潔的杯子，"那位製帽匠插進來説，"讓我們大夥都往前挪一挪。"

他一面説一面就挪了個座位，那隻榛睡鼠跟着挪。三月裏的野兔挪到那隻榛睡鼠的座位，愛麗絲相當不情願地坐在三月裏的野兔的位子上。唯獨製帽匠一個，從這次挪動中得到好處；愛麗絲則比先前糟糕得多，因為三月裏的野兔剛才把牛奶罐打翻在他自己的盤子裏了。

愛麗絲不想再冒犯那隻榛睡鼠，因此她非常小心地開口問道：“但是我不懂。她們打哪裏汲取糖漿呢？”

“你能夠從水井裏汲取清水，”那位製帽匠説，“因此，我想你就可以從一口糖漿井裏汲取糖漿吧——哎，笨不笨？”

“然而她們是待在井裏邊啊，”愛麗絲對榛睡鼠説，並不打算去注意剛才最後那句話。

“她們當然如此啦，”榛睡鼠説，“靠緊裏邊。”

這個回答使得可憐的愛麗絲簡直莫名其妙，她只好讓那隻榛睡鼠繼續説一陣子，不去打斷牠。

“她們正在學着汲取，”那隻榛睡鼠一面往下説，一面打着呵欠，揉着眼睛，因為牠正在變得非常困倦了。“她們汲取了各式各樣的東西——每一樣東西都是 M 打頭的——”

“為甚麼是 M 打頭的呢？”愛麗絲問道。

“為甚麼不是呢？”三月裏的野兔説。愛麗絲不説話了。

這時候，那隻榛睡鼠已經閉上了眼睛，正在迷迷糊糊地進入半睡眠狀態。不過，牠被那位製帽匠擰了一下，不禁輕輕尖叫了一聲，便又醒來，繼續講下去：“——都是 M 打頭的，比如捕鼠夾啦、月亮啦，還有記性啦，還有大量啦。你知道，你説這些東西都是‘半斤八兩’，你到底看見過有哪一件汲取來的東西是大量的？”

“的確不錯，現在你既然問我，”愛麗絲説，她感到非常困惑，“我覺得是沒有——”

“那麼你就免開尊口，”那位製帽匠説。

這一句魯莽的話，愛麗絲承受不了，因此她極為厭惡地站起身來，立即就走開了。那隻榛睡鼠馬上進入了夢鄉，另外兩個誰都不注意她走開，一點都不，雖然她回頭望了一兩次，有點希望他們叫住自己。她最後瞧瞧他們的時候，只見他們正在設法把那隻榛睡鼠塞到那隻茶壺裏去。

「無論如何我都決不願意再到那裏去了！」愛麗絲説，這時，她正擇路穿過那片樹林。「我這一輩子，從來也沒有參加過如此愚蠢無聊的午茶會！」

就在她説這句話的時候，她看見有一根樹幹上開着一扇門，通到樹身裏。「多麼奇怪的事情啊！」她心裏想。「不過今天每一件事情都奇怪。我想我還是立刻走進去為好。」於是她走了進去。

她又一次發現自己留在那間長長的廳堂裏，靠近那張小小的玻璃桌子。「嗯，這一次我可要做得好一些了，」她自言自語地説，便着手拿起那把小小的花園門鑰匙，打開那扇通往花園的門。然後，開始工作，把那片蘑菇（她曾經把一小塊蘑菇藏在口袋裏）放在嘴巴裏咬，直到自己身高縮到一英尺左右。然後，她沿着那條小小的過道走去。然後 —— 她發現自己終於走到一座美麗的花園裏，四周是五彩繽紛的花壇和清涼沁人的噴水池。

王后的槌球場

近花園的入口處長着一棵高大的玫瑰樹，樹上長着白色的玫瑰花，但是卻有三個園丁正在那裏忙着把花塗成紅色。愛麗絲覺得這是一件非常奇怪的事情，便走近一些打量他們，就在她走到他們旁邊時，她聽見其中一個說："喂，小心點，黑桃五！不要像這樣子把顏料濺到我身上來！"

"我沒有辦法呀，"黑桃五用不高興的聲調說。"黑桃七碰了我的手臂啦。"

對此，黑桃七抬起頭來望了望說道："好呀，黑桃五！老是把壞事推在別人身上！"

"你呀還是別說話的好！"黑桃五說。"我就在昨天聽見王后說，該把你的頭砍掉。"

"為甚麼？"頭一個開口說話的那個說。

"黑桃二，這不關你的事！"黑桃七說。

"不錯，這是他的事！"黑桃五說。"我來告訴他吧 —— 這是因為他把鬱金香的球根給了廚師，而不是把洋葱給了他。"

黑桃七扔下手中的顏料刷，剛開始說：「嗯，天下所有不公正的事情之中——」這時候，他的眼光偶然落在愛麗絲身上，愛麗絲則站在那裏盯着他們瞧，他便突然住口不說下去了。另外兩個也回過頭來看，於是他們全都低低地彎下身子。

　　「能不能請你們告訴我，」愛麗絲有點膽怯地問道，「你們為甚麼要塗那些玫瑰呢？」

　　黑桃五和黑桃七不說話，只是看着黑桃二。黑桃二壓低嗓音開始說：「嗯，小姐，你瞧，事實是，這地方本該種一棵紅的玫瑰樹，可是我們弄錯了，把一棵白玫瑰栽了進去。這樣，你知道，要是王后發現這件事，我們全都要人頭落地。所以，小姐，你瞧，在她大駕光臨之前，我們正在竭盡全力，把——」就在此刻，一直在焦急不安地注視花園那一頭的黑桃五大聲喊叫：「王后來啦！王后來啦！」於是這三個園丁立刻臉面朝下，直挺挺地趴在地上。這時響起了許多腳步的聲音，愛麗絲環顧四周，急於見見那位王后。

　　最先來到的是十個扛着棍棒的士兵，他們的樣子全都跟那三位園丁相像：扁平的長方形，雙手和雙腳長在四隻角上。其次是十個侍臣，他們全身上下都用鑽石裝飾起來，像那十個士兵一樣兩個兩個地並肩行走。跟着來到的則是王室的孩子們，共有十個，小寶貝們一對一對，手拉着手，跳跳蹦蹦、歡歡喜喜地走來，他們全都用紅心作為裝飾。接着來的是賓客，大多數是國王們和王后們，愛麗絲在其中認出了那位大白兔，牠正在說着話，一副急急忙忙、緊張興奮的樣子，對人家講的每件事都報以微笑，走過去的時候並沒有注意到愛麗絲。跟在後面的是那位紅心傑克，手裏托着放在一塊深紅色絲絨墊子上的一頂王冠。在這浩浩盪盪的行列走完之後，出現的是：紅心國王和紅心王后。

愛麗絲相當猶疑不決，不知自己該不該像那三個園丁一樣，臉面朝下趴在地上，不過她想不起來有哪一次曾聽到過對於行列有這種規矩。"而且，"她想，"如果人們全都必須臉面朝下躺倒，因此而看不見行列的話，這個行列又有甚麼用處呢？"所以，她就站立原地不動，等候在那裏。

行列來到愛麗絲的對面的時候，他們全體立定，對她瞧着，那位王后聲色俱厲地問道："這個人是誰？"她是衝着紅心傑克發問的，紅心傑克不停地鞠躬和微笑，以此作為回答。

"白癡！"王后斥責說，一面不耐煩地把頭一甩，然後轉身衝着愛麗絲說道："小孩子，你叫甚麼名字？"

"敬向陛下回話，我的名字是愛麗絲，"愛麗絲非常有禮貌地說。不過她在心裏暗暗加上說："怎麼啦，他們說到底只不過是一副撲克牌罷了。我不用害怕他們！"

"這幾個又是甚麼人啊？"王后指着趴在玫瑰樹周圍的三個園丁問道。因為，你瞧，他們三個都臉面朝下臥倒，他們背上的花樣跟一副牌的其他各張一模一樣，王后便認不出他們到底是園丁呢，還是士兵呢，還是侍臣或是她自己的三個孩子。

"我怎麼知道哇？"愛麗絲說，對於自己的勇氣不禁感到驚訝。"這可不是我的事情呀。"

那位王后憤怒得臉脹得通紅，睜大眼睛瞪着她看了一會，像一頭野獸似的，然後，尖聲大叫起來："把她的頭砍掉！砍掉——"

"胡説八道！"愛麗絲非常堅定地大聲一喊，那位王后便默不作聲了。那位國王把手按在她的手臂上，小心翼翼地説："親愛的，三思而行，她只不過是個孩子呀！"

王后怒氣沖天地轉身離開國王，對傑克下命令説："把他們翻過來！"

傑克用一隻腳非常小心地照辦了。

"站起來！"王后用又尖又響的嗓音叫道。那三個園丁便立刻蹦起來，並且對國王、王后、王室的孩子們以及其他每一個人鞠躬。

"別這樣！"王后用刺耳的尖叫聲説。"你們使我頭昏腦脹啦！"然後，她又轉向那棵玫瑰樹，繼續説道："你們剛才在這裏做甚麼呀？"

"但願陛下不要見怪，"黑桃二單腿下跪，用非常謙卑的聲調説道，"我們剛才正打算 ——"

"我弄清楚啦！"王后説，她此時已經查看過玫瑰花。"把他們的頭砍下來！"行列便向前移動，其中三個士兵留在後面來處死這三個園丁，三個園丁奔向愛麗絲尋求保護。

"你們決不會被砍頭的！"愛麗絲説着把他們插進旁邊一隻大花盆裏邊。那三個士兵徘徊了一兩分鐘，對他們瞧瞧，然後悄悄地跟在行列後面開步走了。

"他們的頭都砍掉了嗎？"王后高聲嚷道。

"願陛下滿意，他們的頭都沒了！"三個士兵喊着回答。

"很好！"王后也喊道。"你會玩槌球嗎？"

三個士兵不作聲，眼睛對愛麗絲看着，因為這個問題顯然是問她的。

"會的！"愛麗絲喊道。

"那麼，來吧！"那位王后吼着説，愛麗絲便加入了行列，心裏好生疑惑，下一步不知道會發生甚麼事。

"今天 —— 今天天氣真正好！"愛麗絲身邊響起膽怯的聲音。她是跟那位大白兔並排行走，大白兔正在焦慮不安地望着她的臉。

"真正好，"愛麗絲説。"那位公爵夫人在哪裏呀？"

"噓！別聲張！"大白兔説話的聲音又低又急。他一面説，一面回頭惶惶不安地打量，然後踮起足尖，嘴巴湊近她的耳朵，低聲細語地説："她被判處了死刑。"

"甚麼罪名？"愛麗絲問道。

"你剛才是説'多麼遺憾！'嗎？"大白兔問道。

"不，我沒有這樣説，"愛麗絲説。"我不認為這事情有甚麼遺憾之處。我説的是：'甚麼罪名？'"

"她掌了王后的嘴 —— "大白兔開了個頭。

愛麗絲卻尖聲笑了一下。"哦，噓！"大白兔膽戰心驚地壓低聲音説。"王后要聽見你的笑聲了！你瞧，她來得稍晚，那位王后説過 —— "

"各就各位！"王后大聲叫喊，響得如雷鳴一般，所有的人便開始奔向四面八方，彼此互相碰撞，亂成一團。不過，過了一兩分鐘，他們就都平靜下來，槌球遊戲就此開始。

愛麗絲覺得自己這輩子從來也沒有看見過如此奇怪的槌球場。場地到處都是溝溝坎坎的，活的刺蝟作槌球，活的火烈鳥作球棍，那些士兵們則必須彎下身子，手腳着地，作為一個個門。

最初，愛麗絲發現主要的困難在於控制好她的火烈鳥。她成功地用她的手臂把牠的身體服服帖帖地夾起來，讓牠的兩條腿垂下來，但是，就在她讓牠的脖頸像模像樣地伸直，打算用牠的頭照準刺蝟擊去的時候，牠通常總要把自己扭轉過來，仰望她的臉，帶着如此迷惑不解的表情，使她情不自禁地放聲大笑。這時，她要是把牠的頭按下去，打算重新來一遍的話，就會非常煩惱地發現那隻刺蝟已經把蜷起來的身體伸直，正在一步一步地爬走。除了這一切以外，不論她要把刺蝟送到哪裏去，一般總有一道溝阻礙着。同時，由於那些彎身站着的士兵們老是要直起腰來，走到槌球場的另外的地方去，愛麗絲不久便得出結論，認定這的確是一種非常不容易玩的球戲。

參加玩槌球的人們都一起玩起來，完全不管輪到沒輪到，而且一刻不停地爭吵，打架，為那些刺蝟你搶我奪。在非常短的時間裏，王后便勃然大怒了，她走來走去，踩腳吼叫："砍掉那個男的頭！"或者："砍掉那個女的頭！"大概一分鐘叫一次。

愛麗絲開始感到很不好受，當然，直到目前為止，她還沒跟這位王后有過任何爭論，不過，她心裏明白這種事情隨時都可能發生，"而那個時候，"她想，"我將會怎麼樣呢？這地方，他們駭人聽聞地喜歡砍掉別人的頭，奇怪的事情莫過於還讓人活着！"

她東張西望，想找條能逃走的路，同時又疑惑自己是否能夠逃走而不被人發覺，就在這時候，她看見空中出現一個奇怪的形象。一開始，這叫她非常迷惑，但是在盯着牠瞧了一兩分鐘之後，她弄明白這原來是個齜牙咧嘴的笑容，於是她對自己說："那是柴郡貓呀，現在我可以有個朋友談談話了。"

"你過得怎麼樣啊？"那隻貓在現出了足夠用來說話的嘴的時候這樣問道。

愛麗絲等到牠的眼睛出現時點了點頭。"對牠說話沒有用，"她想，"除非牠的耳朵出來了，或者至少有了一隻耳朵。"她剛這樣想，那邊整個的頭就出現了，於是愛麗絲把她抱着的火烈鳥放下來，開始報告這場槌球遊戲，心中覺得非常高興，終於有個朋友聽她說話了。那隻貓彷彿認為自己此刻讓人看到的形象已經足夠了，於是沒有更多的部分顯現出來。

"我覺得他們玩球完全不公平，"愛麗絲用相當抱怨的聲調開始說，"他們大家都那麼兇狠地爭吵，一個人根本聽不見自己說些甚麼 —— 而且他們似乎沒有甚麼特定的遊戲規則。至少是，如果有的話，沒有誰遵守規則 —— 而且由於所有的用具都是活的，你不知道那有多麼混亂。比方說吧，我要把球打過去的下一個球門，牠卻在球場的另外一頭走來走去 —— 還有，我本該在這時槌打那位王后的刺蝟的，可是牠一看見我的刺蝟來了，牠就逃走了！"

"你喜歡那位王后嗎？"那隻貓壓低嗓子問道。

"一點也不喜歡，"愛麗絲說。"她是那麼極其 —— "就在此時，她看見那位王后走近她的身後偷聽，於是她改口說下去 " —— 有可能會贏，因而簡直沒有必要打完這場槌球戲了。"

那位王后微微一笑，從她身邊走了過去。

"你是在跟誰說話呀？"國王走來問愛麗絲，同時瞧着那隻貓頭，奇怪得不得了。

“牠是我的一個朋友——一隻柴郡貓，”愛麗絲説，“請允許我把牠介紹給你。”

“我一點也不喜歡牠那副模樣，”國王説道。“不過，牠可以吻我的手，要是牠想這麼做的話。”

“我寧願不這麼做，”那隻貓發表意見説。

“休得無禮，”國王説道，“也不得如此這般對我瞧着！”他一面説一面站到愛麗絲背後去。

“一隻貓是可以瞧着一位國王的，”愛麗絲説。“我曾經在一本書上讀到過這句話，不過我記不起來是在哪一本上讀到的。”

“嗯，一定要把那隻貓弄掉，”國王非常堅決地説道，同時叫唤此時正走過去的王后説：“親愛的！我希望你能把那隻貓弄掉！”

那位王后解決所有困難問題時，不論問題大小，辦法只有一個。“砍掉牠的頭！”她連看都不回頭看，便如此吩咐。

“我親自去把劊子手找來，”國王很起勁地説，便急急忙忙地走開了。

愛麗絲覺得不妨也走回去看看槌球遊戲進行得怎樣了，因為她聽見王后在遠處暴跳如雷地尖聲叫喊。她已經聽見她判處了三個玩槌球的人死刑，因為他們在輪到打球的時候不上陣，而且她徹底討厭這種種情況，因為這場球戲竟然如此混亂，她完全不清楚是不是輪到自己了。於是她走開，去尋找自己的那隻刺蝟。

那隻刺蝟正在忙於跟另外一隻刺蝟打架，看來對於愛麗絲這是一次極好的機會，可以用其中一隻刺蝟去撞擊另外一隻。唯一的困難是，她的火烈鳥已經跑到花園的那一頭去了，愛麗絲能看見牠正在用一種徒勞無益的方法,想要飛到一棵樹上去。

在她逮住了她的火烈鳥,把牠抱回來的時候,可惜打架已經結束,那兩隻刺蝟已經無影無蹤了。"不過這沒有多大關係,"愛麗絲心裏想,"因為所有的球門都已經從球場的這一邊走掉了。"於是她把她的火烈鳥夾在手臂下面,這樣牠便不會再逃跑了。她往回走去,要跟她那位朋友再談一會。

等到她回到那隻柴郡貓那裏的時候,她吃驚不小,只見有好大一幫子人聚集在牠四周。那個劊子手,以及國王和王后之間正在展開一場爭論,三方面同時開腔,其餘的人一言不發,靜得很,卻顯出非常不自在的樣子。

愛麗絲一來到現場,那三方面就都請求她來解決這個問題,他們對她重複自己的論點,然而,因為他們同時各說各的,愛麗絲發現很難弄清楚他們究竟說些甚麼。

劊子手的論點是,除非那個頭有一個身體,否則你就無法把它從甚麼地方砍下來,他過去從來也沒有非得幹這樣的事情不可,在他一生的如此時刻,他也不打算開始幹。

那位國王的論點是,凡是有一顆頭的任何東西都可以砍頭,你休得胡說八道。

那位王后的論點是,如果不立時立刻辦好那件事,她就要砍掉每一個人的頭,一個不留。(就是這最後一句話使得整個人群顯得那麼神情嚴肅和惶惶不安。)

愛麗絲想不出別的話來說,只是說:"那隻貓是公爵夫人的,你們最好還是問問她該怎麼辦吧。"

"她在牢房裏,"那位王后對那個劊子手說,"把她帶到這裏來。"劊子手便箭一般地跑掉了。

　　就在他跑得不見人影的時候，那隻貓的頭影開始淡下去了，而在他把公爵夫人帶回來的時候，貓頭已經完完全全消失不見了。於是那位國王和那個劊子手發瘋似的奔來奔去搜尋牠，而此時，其餘的人都回去繼續玩槌球遊戲了。

第九章

假海龜的故事

"你這個親愛的老夥伴啊，你不知道我重新看見你有多麼高興啊！"公爵夫人一面說，一面親親熱熱地挽着愛麗絲的手臂，一同走開。

愛麗絲非常高興地看到她心情如此愉快，不免暗自猜想，她們那次在廚房裏相見的時候，也許僅僅是胡椒使她變得那麼野蠻。

"等到我是一個公爵夫人的時候，"愛麗絲對自己說（不過語調並不非常樂觀），"我就全然不會讓我的廚房裏有一點胡椒。湯做得非常好，而不放 —— 也許從來都是胡椒使得人們脾氣暴躁，"她繼續自言自語，非常高興自己發現了一種新的規則，"而酸醋使得人們酸溜溜的 —— 而黃春菊使得人們滿腹牢騷 —— 而 —— 而大麥棒糖以及諸如此類的東西則使得孩子們又乖又甜。我真正希望人們明白這一點，那麼他們就不至於在給孩子吃糖方面那麼小氣了，你知道 ——"

這時候，她已經把公爵夫人忘得一乾二淨了，一聽見公爵夫人的聲音近在耳邊，她不禁有點驚嚇。"親愛的，你在想甚麼心事，這使得你忘記談話啦。現在我還不能告訴你這件事的教訓到底是甚麼，不過，我一會工夫就會想起來的。”

“也許其中並沒有甚麼教訓吧，”愛麗絲斗膽發表意見。

“噓，噓，孩子！”公爵夫人斥責説。“任何事情裏都包含教訓，只要你能夠發現它。”她説話的時候，把身子向愛麗絲更挨近一些。

愛麗絲可不怎麼喜歡她如此近地靠攏自己，首先是因為這位公爵夫人模樣非常醜；其次，因為她的個子不高不矮正好把她的下巴放在愛麗絲的肩膀上，而那個下巴尖得讓人不舒服。不過，愛麗絲不願意待人粗暴，因此她盡可能地忍受着她的下巴。

“那場槌球遊戲現在進行得比較順利了，”她説，用意在於把談話稍稍維持一下。

“果然如此，”公爵夫人説。“而其中的教訓是 ——‘哦，是愛，是愛，使這個世界運行不衰！’”

“有人卻説，”愛麗絲喃喃低語説，“那是每個人做好自己的事才能這樣的！”

“啊，不錯！意思幾乎是一樣的，”公爵夫人説，同時把她的小小的尖下巴戳進愛麗絲的肩膀，加上一句説：“這裏的教訓是：‘意義小心照顧，聲音不費工夫’。”

“她多麼喜歡在事情裏面找出教訓來啊！”愛麗絲心中暗想。

“我敢説，你正在奇怪我為甚麼不把手臂摟着你的腰，”在停頓片刻之後，公爵夫人説。“其原因是，我不知道你的火烈鳥的脾氣。我來試驗一下好不好？”

“牠會咬人的，”愛麗絲謹小慎微地説，她一點也不感到要急於做這個試驗。

"非常對，"公爵夫人說。"火烈鳥和芥末兩者都會咬人的。其中的教訓是——'羽毛一樣，鳥聚一起'。"

"只不過芥末可不是鳥啊，"愛麗絲評論說。

"跟剛才一樣，你說得不錯，"公爵夫人說。"你分辨事情是多麼清楚明白！"

"我覺得，芥末是一種礦物質，"愛麗絲說。

"當然是的啦，"公爵夫人說，她似乎隨時準備同意愛麗絲所說的每一件事情。"這裏附近有一個很大的芥末礦。其中的教訓是——'我的東西越多，你的東西越少'。"

"哦，我明白啦！"愛麗絲高聲喊道，她並沒有留心在意地聽那最後的一段話。"它是一種蔬菜。它不像蔬菜，然而是蔬菜。"

"我十分同意你的說法，"公爵夫人說道。"其中的教訓則是'就成為你看上去的那個樣子'，或者，你喜歡把它說得簡單一些，那就是'決不要想像自己不是別人可能覺得的樣子，那就是你過去不是，或者可能曾經不是那種你曾經可能被別人感覺到的樣子'。"

"要是你曾經把這一句寫下來的話，"愛麗絲非常有禮貌地說，"我想我一定會理解得好一些。可是你嘴巴上說，我就很難跟得上了。"

"對於我說話的能耐來說，要是我想說，這句話可算不了甚麼，"公爵夫人用洋洋得意的聲調作答。

"求你不要不怕麻煩再說比這更長的話吧，"愛麗絲說。

"哦，不要說甚麼麻煩不麻煩！"公爵夫人說。"到現在為止，我說過的每一句話都是我給你的一件禮物。”

“一種廉價的禮物罷了！”愛麗絲心裏想。“我很高興人們可不像這樣送生日禮物！”不過她沒有大膽到說出聲來。

“又在想甚麼嗎？”公爵夫人用她的尖下巴再戳了一下，問道。

“我有想的權利，”愛麗絲不客氣地說，因為她已經開始感到有點不耐煩了。

“就像豬有權利飛那樣，”公爵夫人說，“其教——”

可是說到這裏，叫愛麗絲大為驚奇的是，那位公爵夫人的聲音忽然消失了，即使這時她剛把她最喜愛的字眼“教訓”只說了一半，而她挽住愛麗絲的手臂的那隻手開始顫抖起來。愛麗絲抬頭一看，原來是王后站在她們跟前，她抱着雙臂，像雷雨欲來那樣緊皺雙眉。

“王后陛下！天氣很好，”公爵夫人用一種微弱的低聲開口說。

“聽着，我毫不含糊地警告你，”王后一面用腳跺地，一面大聲嚷道，“要麼是你、要麼是你的頭離開，而且立時立刻實行！你選擇吧！”

公爵夫人作了選擇，她馬上就走了。

“讓我們繼續進行球賽，”王后對愛麗絲說。愛麗絲卻嚇得一句話也說不出來，但還是慢慢地跟隨她回到槌球場去了。

其他的客人們利用王后離開一會的機會，正在樹陰下休息。不過，他們一看見王后，便急急忙忙趕回去打球；王后只是說了一句，誰耽誤一下子就要誰的命。

他們玩球的整個時候，王后始終沒有放棄跟其他的球員們吵鬧，並且大聲嚷嚷：“砍掉他的腦袋！”或者：“砍掉她的腦袋！”

被她判決的那些人都由士兵們看管起來，士兵們當然只得不再當拱門而去做這件事，因此，大約一個半小時以後，就沒有拱門再剩下來，除了國王、王后和愛麗絲以外，所有的球員都被看管，並且被判了極刑。

這時，王后離場了，累得氣喘吁吁，對愛麗絲說："你可曾看見過假海龜呀？"

"沒有，"愛麗絲說。"我甚至連甚麼是假海龜也不知道。"

"假海龜就是用來做假海龜湯的東西呀，"王后說。

"我從來沒有看見過，也從沒有聽說過，"愛麗絲說。

"那麼，來吧，"王后說，"牠會把牠的生平告訴你。"

她們一起走開的時候，愛麗絲聽見國王用低低的聲音對所有的隨從人員說："你們全都被赦免了。""好哇，這可是件好事情！"她對自己說道，因為她對於王后命令把那麼多的人判處死刑感到很不開心。

他們不一會便遇見一個格里芬，牠正躺在陽光裏酣睡。"起來，懶傢伙！"王后喊道，"把這位小姐帶去看看假海龜，聽聽他講自己的經歷。我必須趕回去照看我命令執行死刑的一些情況。"她走開了，把愛麗絲獨自留着跟格里芬在一起。愛麗絲不大喜歡這個怪獸的樣子，不過，她覺得，跟牠在一起，比跟隨那個野蠻的王后走，大體上來說安全程度差不多是一樣的，因此她就等待着。

那個格里芬坐了起來，揉揉眼睛，然後望着走去的王后，直到望不見為止，然後吃吃地笑。"多麼有趣啊！"格里芬說，一半是對自己，一半是對愛麗絲。

"甚麼東西有趣呀？"愛麗絲問。

"嗯，她呀，"格里芬説。"那完全是她的幻想罷了。你知道，他們從來也不殺死一個人的。來吧！"

"這裏大家都説'來吧！'"愛麗絲慢吞吞地跟隨牠走的時候，心裏想。"我從來也沒有這樣被人家牽着鼻子走，這一輩子也沒有哇！"

他們沒有走多遠便看見了那個假海龜，牠在遠處，孤孤單單，傷心地坐在一塊小礁石上，他們走得更近的時候，愛麗絲能聽見牠唉聲歎氣，彷彿心要碎了。她深深地可憐牠。"牠為甚麼悲傷呀？"她問那個格里芬，格里芬的回答幾乎跟剛才説的話一樣："你知道，那完全是牠的幻想罷了。牠根本沒有甚麼悲傷。來吧！"

於是他們來到那個假海龜跟前，假海龜用眼淚汪汪的大眼望着他們，卻一聲不吭。

"這裏的這位小姐，"格里芬説，"她想要知道你的經歷，她確實這樣想。"

"我可以告訴她，"那個假海龜用低沉的嗡嗡聲説道。"坐下來，兩位都坐下來，我把話説完之前，你們可不要插一個字啊。"

他們便坐了下來，有好幾分鐘誰也沒説話。愛麗絲心裏想："要是牠不開口説話，那麼牠究竟怎麼能説完呢。"不過她還是耐心地等待着。

"從前，"假海龜深深歎了一口氣，終於説開了，"我是一個真海龜。"

這句話的後面是一陣很長時間的沉默，只是被那個格里芬偶然發出的"嘿喀！"的叫喊聲，以及那個假海龜一刻不停的重重的抽咽聲所打破。愛麗絲真想立刻站起身來，説一句：“先生，謝謝你説了有趣的故事，”不過她還是禁不住想必定有更多的話會聽到，所以她靜靜地坐在那裏，一言不發。

“我們幼小的時候，”假海龜終於繼續説下去，牠比較冷靜些了，雖然時不時地還是有點抽抽搭搭，“我們到海裏的學校上學。老師是一位老海龜 —— 我們卻老是叫牠陸龜 —— ”

“假如牠不是一個陸龜，你們為甚麼叫牠陸龜呢？”愛麗絲問道。

“因為牠教我們校規，所以我們叫牠陸龜，”假海龜氣呼呼地説。“你真是太不聰明了！”

“你竟然問出如此簡單的問題，真該為自己感到慚愧！”格里芬加上一句。於是牠們兩個靜靜地坐在那裏，瞧着那個可憐的愛麗絲，她立刻感到甘願鑽到地底下去。最後，格里芬對假海龜説道：“接下去説，老友！不要一整天盡説這個！”於是牠繼續説了下面這些話：

“對啦，我們到海裏的學校去上學，儘管你可能不相信這事 —— ”

“我從來沒有説過不相信啊！”愛麗絲打斷牠的話。

“你説過，”假海龜説。

“不要多嘴多舌的！”格里芬在愛麗絲還沒有再説話之前，插上這一句。假海龜便繼續往下説。

“我們受到過最好的教育 —— 事實上，我們每天都去上學 —— ”

“我也曾經在私立走讀學校讀書，”愛麗絲説。“你大可不必驕傲得這副樣子。"

"有額外的東西嗎？"假海龜有點焦急地問道。

"有，"愛麗絲説，"我們還學法語和音樂。"

"還有洗衣服嗎？"假海龜問道。

"當然沒有啦！"愛麗絲不高興地説。

"啊！那麼你們的學校可不是一所真正的好學校，"假海龜用一種大大鬆了一口氣的腔調説。

"瞧，在我們的學校裏，在賬單的最後面，他們寫着：'法語，音樂，以及洗衣服——額外收費。'"

"你們不可能十分需要洗衣服，"愛麗絲説，"你們生活在海底下呀。"

"我可負擔不起學這種事，"假海龜歎了一口氣，説道。"我只選修正規的課程。"

"甚麼是正規的課程呢？"愛麗絲問道。

"當然啦，一開頭學的是打轉轉和扭來扭去，"假海龜回答説；"然後是各個不同門類的算術——比如雄心啊，消遣啊，醜化啊，嘲笑啊。"

"我從來也沒有聽見過'醜化'這個詞，"愛麗絲冒昧地説。"那是甚麼意思？"

格里芬驚訝地舉起牠的兩隻腳爪。"從來也沒有聽説過醜化呀！"牠大聲嚷道。"我想，你總該知道甚麼叫做美化吧？"

"不錯，"愛麗絲疑疑惑惑地説；"它的意思是——把——任何東西——弄得——漂亮一些。"

"那麼，好，"格里芬繼續説，"假如你不知道甚麼是醜化的話，你就是一個傻瓜。”

愛麗絲感到人家並不歡迎她再問關於這一類的問題，因此她轉而對假海龜問道：“那麼，你們還得學甚麼別的東西呢？”

“嗯，還有神秘事，”假海龜回答說，同時用牠的闊鰭拍打着，逐項數出課目來——“神秘事，古代的跟現代的，以及海學。還有嘛拖話——拖話老師是一位老康吉鰻，經常是每星期來一次，他教我們拖話、伸展肢體，以及昏厥成圈圈 9 。”

“那是甚麼樣子的啊？”愛麗絲問。

“嗯，我本人無法表演給你看，”假海龜說，“我太僵硬了。而格里芬從來也沒有學過。”

“我可沒有時間學，”格里芬說。“不過，我常常到古典文學老師那裏去上課。牠是一位老螃蟹，牠正是這樣一位。”

“我可從來不上牠的課，”假海龜歎了一口氣說。“牠們老是說牠教的是哈哈笑和傷心事。”

“是這麼回事，是這麼回事，”格里芬說，這回輪到牠歎氣了。這兩個生物於是都用爪子摀着臉。

“你們一天有多少小時的功課呢？”愛麗絲問道，她心中急於轉換那個話題。

“第一天是十個小時，”假海龜說。“第二天是九個小時，依此類推。”

“多麼奇怪的方案啊！”愛麗絲喊道。

“這就是為甚麼它們稱之為‘功課’呀，”格里芬發表意見說。“因為它們一天比一天剋扣下去。”

對於愛麗絲說來，這個說法好新鮮，她對此想了一會，然後再開口問。"這麼説來，第十一天一定是放假的日子啦？"

"當然是放假的日子，"假海龜説。

"那麼到第十二天你們做甚麼呢？"愛麗絲急切地繼續追問。

"關於功課嘛，這就足夠啦，"格里芬用一種非常決斷的聲調插進來説。"現在跟她説説比賽的事情吧。"

第十章

龍蝦四對方陣舞

假海龜深深地歎了一口氣，舉起一隻闊鰭，用鰭背抹抹自己的兩隻眼睛。牠看看愛麗絲，欲言又止，抽抽搭搭一兩分鐘，說不出話來。"就像有一根骨頭卡了喉嚨似的，"格里芬說，同時開始起勁地搖晃牠，捏起拳頭猛敲牠的背。假海龜終於恢復過來，能說話了，牠滿臉淚水漣漣，繼續說道：

"你也許不大住在海底下，"（"我沒有在那住過，"愛麗絲說。）"也許你從來也沒有讓人介紹給一位龍蝦吧 ——"（愛麗絲剛開口說"我有一次嚐過 ——"自己就連忙停住了，改口說："沒有，從來也沒有。"）"—— 那麼你就無法想像龍蝦四對方陣舞是一件多麼開心的事情啦！"

"是的，的確如此，"愛麗絲說。"這是一種甚麼樣的舞蹈呢？"

"是這樣，"格里芬說，"你們先沿着海灘排成一行一行 ——"

"排成兩行！"假海龜喊道。"海豹哇、海龜哇、大馬哈魚哇，以及其他等等。然後，你們就把所有的海蜇都清除掉 ——"

"這件事嘛，一般都需要些時間，"格里芬插話説。

"—— 你們往前進兩次 ——"

"每一次有一個龍蝦作舞伴！"格里芬喊道。

"當然啦，"假海龜説。"往前進兩次，然後與舞伴相對而舞 ——"

"—— 交換龍蝦，再按照同樣順序後退，"格里芬繼續説。

"然後，你們知道，"假海龜接着説，"你甩開那些 ——"

"那些龍蝦！"格里芬大聲嚷嚷，同時蹦到半空中。

"—— 甩到海裏去，越遠越好 ——"

"游過去追趕牠們！"格芬尖聲叫喊起來。

"在大海裏邊翻一個筋斗！"假海龜喊着説，牠歡蹦亂跳，興奮得不得了。

"再一次交換龍蝦！"格里芬聲嘶力竭地狂叫。

"再回到陸地上來，而 —— 這就是第一節的全部花式了，"假海龜突然之間放低聲音説。那兩個生物剛才還像發瘋的傢伙一樣，一下不停地滿場子蹦蹦跳跳，這時卻非常悲傷地重新靜靜地坐下來，望着愛麗絲。

"那一定是非常好看的舞蹈吧，"愛麗絲膽怯地説。

"你想看一會嗎？"假海龜問道。

"真的非常想看，"愛麗絲説。

"來吧，我們跳第一節花式看看！"假海龜對格里芬説。"沒有龍蝦我們也能跳的，你知道。誰來唱呢？"

"哦，你唱呀，"格里芬説。"我已經忘記歌詞了。"

牠們便開始一本正經地跳起舞來，繞着愛麗絲一圈一圈地轉，在離她太近的時候，時不時地踩着她的腳趾頭；在假海龜用非常遲緩和悲傷的聲音唱下面一首歌的時候，牠們倆舞動着前爪打拍子。

> 牙鱈對蝸牛這樣説："你能走得快些嗎？
> 有一隻海豚緊隨在後，踩到了我的尾巴，
> 那些龍蝦和海龜齊往前，瞧有多急啊！
> 牠們等候在海濱砂石上 —— 舞蹈你可願来参加？
> 　　舞蹈你願、不願、你願、不願啊来参加？
> 　　舞蹈你願、不願、你願、不願啊来参加？

> "你真的無法知曉這究竟有多麽美妙：
> 當牠們把我們同龍蝦一起向大海拋！"
> 那蝸牛卻答道："太遠了，太遠了！"眼睛一瞟 ——
> 牠説由衷地感謝牙鱈，但不願参加這舞蹈。
> 　　牠不願、不能、不願、不能啊参加這舞蹈。
> 　　牠不願、不能、不願、不能啊参加這舞蹈。

> "拋得多遠有何妨？"有鱗的朋友回答牠。
> "離英國越是遠，離法國就越是近些啦。
> 你知道，另有個海灘在那邊的藍天下。
> 親愛的蝸牛啊，不要臉發白，来参加舞蹈吧。
> 　　舞蹈你願、不願、你願、不願啊来参加？
> 　　舞蹈你願、不願、你願、不願啊来参加？"

　　"謝謝你，看這種舞蹈是非常有趣的事，"愛麗絲説，這時舞終於跳完了，她心中為此感到非常欣慰。"而且我真的很喜歡聽

這首關於牙鱈的奇怪的歌曲！"

"哦，至於牙鱈嘛，"假海龜説，"牠們 —— 當然，你從前看見過牠們吧？"

"不錯，"愛麗絲説，"我從前常常看見牠們在飯 —— "她急忙把話縮了回去。

"我不知道飯可能在哪裏，"假海龜説，"不過，假如你從前經常看見牠們的話，你當然知道牠們是甚麼樣子啦？"

"我相信是這樣的，"愛麗絲一面想一面回答。"牠們的嘴巴裏長着尾巴 —— 而且牠們全身都裹着麵包粉。"

"關於麵包粉你可説錯了，"假海龜説。"麵包粉在海裏都會給沖洗掉的。不過牠們的尾巴是長在嘴巴裏，其原因是 —— "假海龜説到這裏不禁打了個呵欠，閉上了眼睛。"把原因等等都原原本本地告訴她吧，"牠對格里芬説。

"原因是，"格里芬説，"牠們要和龍蝦一起去參加舞蹈。所以牠們給拋到海裏去了。所以牠們必須跌得很遠。所以牠們的尾巴牢牢地長在嘴巴裏。所以牠們就無法再把牠們拔出來。如此而已。"

"謝謝你，"愛麗絲説，"這事情非常有趣。關於牙鱈，我過去從來也沒知道得這麼多。"

"要是你高興聽的話，我還能説得更多呢，"格里芬説。"你可知道牠為甚麼被叫做牙鱈嗎？"

"我從來也沒有想到這一點，"愛麗絲説。"究竟為甚麼呢？"

"牠可以用來擦長筒靴和皮鞋，"格里芬非常嚴肅地回答。

愛麗絲給完全搞糊塗了。"用來擦長筒靴和皮鞋！"她用一種聽不明白的口吻重複那句話。

「怎麼啦，你的皮鞋是用甚麼東西擦的呢？」格里芬説。「我的意思是，甚麼東西使你的皮鞋這樣光亮呢？」

愛麗絲低頭望望皮鞋，考慮了一下，然後作出回答。「我相信，那是用黑鞋油擦的。」

「在海底下，長筒靴和皮鞋，」格里芬用一種低沉的嗓音繼續説道，「是用牙鱈來擦的。現在你知道了吧。」

「長筒靴和皮鞋是用甚麼東西做成的呢？」愛麗絲用一種極其好奇的聲調問道。

「當然啦，是用鯧魚和鰻魚做成的啦，」格里芬很不耐煩地回答説。「不管哪一隻小蝦都能跟你説明白的。」

「假如我曾經是牙鱈的話，」愛麗絲説，她的腦子依然在想着那支歌，「我就會對那個海豚説：'喂，離我遠點！我們可不要你跟我們在一起！'」

「牠們卻非要牠跟牠們在一起不可哇，」假海龜説。「沒有一種聰明的魚到甚麼地方去的時候不帶着一個海豚。」

「都帶着？是真的嗎？」愛麗絲用驚訝得不得了的聲調問。

「當然啦，」假海龜説。「怎麼樣，假如一條魚向我游來，跟我説牠打算去旅行，我就一定會問道：'帶甚麼海豚呀？'」

「你的意思是'目的'吧？」愛麗絲問道。

「我所説的就是我的意思，」假海龜用生氣的聲調回答説。於是格里芬添加一句説：「好啦，讓我們聽聽你的一些冒險故事吧。」

「我可以把我的冒險故事講給你們聽 —— 從今天早晨的事説

起，”愛麗絲有點膽怯地説。“不過，回頭説到昨天的事就沒有益處了，因為我那時是跟現在不同的人。”

“把這一切都解釋清楚！”假海龜説。

“不，不！先講講冒險故事，”格里芬用一種忍耐不住的聲調説。“解釋清楚需要一長段討厭的時間。”

因此，愛麗絲開始對牠們講她的冒險故事，從她第一次看見那隻大白兔講起。她剛開始講的時候，看到那兩個生物挨得那麼近，兩雙眼睛和兩隻嘴巴張得那麼大，她不免有點緊張；但是她繼續講下去便產生了勇氣。她的聽眾鴉雀無聲地聽着，直到她講到她對那隻毛毛蟲背誦《你老了，威廉爸爸》那一段字句全部背錯了的時候，假海龜長長地倒抽一口冷氣，説道：“這可是非常奇怪呀！”

“全篇都奇怪到極點！”格里芬説。

“全篇都背錯了呀！”假海龜若有所思地重複着説。“我倒是很想讓她現在試試看，聽聽她好背誦些甚麼。叫她開始吧。”牠瞧着格里芬，彷彿覺得牠對於愛麗絲具有某種權威似的。

“站起來，背誦‘這是懶人的聲音’，”格里芬説道。

“這兩個生物多麼會支配人家，還叫人家背誦功課呢！”愛麗絲想着。“我倒不如立刻回到學校裏去的好。”雖然如此，她還是站了起來，開始背誦，不過她滿腦子裏都是那龍蝦四對方陣舞，以致她簡直不知道自己在背些甚麼，而她背的字句也確實是非常稀奇古怪的。

這是龍蝦的聲音，我聽見牠發話：
"你把我烤得太焦啦，我的髮鬚得用糖灑。"
就像鴨子用眼瞼，牠卻用鼻子
整褲帶和鈕子，把腳翻成外八字。
沙灘完全曬乾時，牠像雲雀樂陶陶，
談起鯊魚來，牠用鄙夷不屑的腔調。
可是，浪潮起，鯊魚遍處出現的時候，
牠的聲音戰戰兢兢，顫顫抖抖。

"這跟我還是個孩子的時候常常背誦的那首不一樣啊，"格里芬說。

"嗯，我以前也從來沒有聽見過這首詩，"假海龜說。"不過它聽來不是一般的莫名其妙。"

愛麗絲閉口不言語，她已經坐了下來，雙手捂着臉，心裏琢磨着，不知道一切事情究竟會不會再正常起來。

"我很願意這事情能解釋一下，"假海龜說。

"她無法解釋，"格里芬連忙說。"繼續背下一首詩吧。"

"不過關於牠的腳趾頭怎麼啦？"假海龜盯着問。"牠怎麼能夠用牠的鼻子把腳弄成外八字，你說說看？"

"那是舞蹈裏的第一個足部基本位置，"愛麗絲說。不過她已經被這整個事情弄得暈頭轉向，狼狽不堪了，她渴望換個題目談談。

"繼續背下一首詩吧，"格里芬重複說道。"開頭一句是：'我經過他的花園。'"

愛麗絲不敢不服從，雖然她覺得自己一定會全部都背錯的，因此她用顫抖的聲音繼續背誦：

我經過他的花園，用我的一隻眼睛
瞥見貓頭鷹和豹子在分享一隻批。
豹子吞下了批，連皮帶滷汁和肉餡，
貓頭鷹只得到空盤子，作為牠那一份。
批全都吃完了，貓頭鷹才得到允許
將匙羹放在口袋裏，作為恩賜的獎品。
這時候，豹子大吼一聲，拿了刀和叉，
這頓宴會就這樣終止——

"假如你背下去的時候不加解釋，你背這一大堆亂七八糟的東西有甚麼用處呢？"假海龜打斷她，說道。"顯然，在我聽到過的東西中，以此為最最叫人莫名其妙的了！"

"不錯，我覺得你還是別再背了吧，"格里芬說，而愛麗絲對此真是求之不得。

"咱們試試龍蝦四對方陣舞的另一種花式怎麼樣？"格里芬繼續說道。"或者，你可喜歡聽聽假海龜給你再唱一支歌呢？"

"哦，一支歌呀，請吧，要是假海龜能好心唱一支，"愛麗絲回答說，她說得那麼急切，以致格里芬用相當不快的音調說道："哼！蘿蔔青菜，各人各愛！給她唱那首《海龜湯》吧，怎麼樣，老伙計？"

假海龜深深地歎了一口氣，開始用一種抽抽搭搭、斷斷續續的聲音這樣唱道：

可口的湯啊，味濃有營養，顏色綠汪汪，
待在大湯蓋碗裏，熱氣騰騰等人嚐！
見到如此美味誰能不彎腰讚歎？

今晚的湯啊，可口的湯啊！
今晚的湯啊，可口的湯啊！
　　可—口的—湯啊！
　　可—口的—湯啊！
　　——湯啊，今——嗯——嗯今晚的，
　　可口的、可口的湯啊！

可口的湯啊！誰還稀罕甚麼魚啊、
野味啊，或者任何別的菜？
誰還會不盡其所有來買這兩個
便士的，只要這點錢的可口的湯啊？
便士，只要這點錢的可口的湯啊？
　　可——口的——湯啊！
　　可——口的——湯啊！
　　——湯啊，今——嗯——嗯今晚的，
　　可口的、可——口的湯啊！

　"合唱部分再來一遍！"格里芬喊道。假海龜剛剛開口重複那部分，不料只聽得遠處傳來一聲高喊："審判開始！"

　"趕快！"格里芬大喊一聲，一下抓住愛麗絲的手，慌慌張張地跑走，也不等那支歌唱完。

　"那是甚麼審判呀？"愛麗絲邊跑邊喘着氣說。但是格里芬只回答說："趕快！"而且跑得更快了。這時候，微風跟在後面傳送越來越微弱的悶悶不樂的歌詞：

　　　——湯啊，今——嗯——嗯今晚的，
　　可口的、可口的湯啊！

第十一章
誰偷了水果撻

格里芬和愛麗絲到達的時候，紅心國王和紅心王后正雙雙坐在寶座上，四周簇擁着一大群動物——各種小鳥和野獸，以及一副完整的撲克牌。傑克站在他們面前，身上綁着鐵鏈，兩旁各有一個兵士押着。靠近國王的是那位大白兔，一隻手上拿着一個喇叭，另一隻手上拿着一捲羊皮紙。法庭的正中央放着一張桌子，桌子上放着用一隻大盤子盛的許多水果撻，水果撻是那麼讓逗人喜愛，愛麗絲看到它們就感到飢腸轆轆——"我真希望他們審判結束，"她心想，"把這些點心分派給大家！"可是看來這事沒有希望，因此，她開始對周圍的一切事物東瞅瞅，西瞧瞧，以此來消磨時間。

愛麗絲過去從來也沒有上過法庭，不過她曾經在書本上讀到過法庭的事，她很高興地發現自己說得出法庭裏幾乎所有的東西的名稱。"那是法官，"她自言自語地說，"因為他戴着他的大假髮。"

卻說那位法官正是國王本人，由於他把王冠戴在假髮的上面，他看來一點也不像舒服瀟灑的樣子，而且那樣子當然是不相稱的。

"那是陪審團席，"愛麗絲心想。"那十二位生物，"（你瞧，她不得不說"生物"，因為牠們有些是走獸，有些是飛禽。）"我猜想牠們就是陪審員了。"她把"陪審員"這幾個字在心裏反覆說了兩三遍，覺得很自豪。因為她想——而且也想得不錯——像她這樣的年齡的小女孩很少有幾個懂得"陪審員"究竟是甚麼意思。不過，把牠們叫做"陪審人"也是同樣可以的。

那十二位陪審員都非常忙碌地在各自的石板上寫字。"牠們在做甚麼呀？"愛麗絲悄悄地問格里芬。"在審判開始以前，牠們還不能寫下任何事情的呀。"

"牠們正在寫下自己的名字，"格里芬也悄悄地回答，"為的是害怕在審判結束以前就會忘記自己的名字。"

"都是些蠢貨！"愛麗絲用惱火的聲音說。不過她急忙停住了，因為那位大白兔喊道："法庭裏保持肅靜！"同時國王也戴上了眼鏡，惶惶不安地東張西望，要弄清楚是誰在講話。

愛麗絲彷彿站在牠們身後，從牠們的肩頭望過去似的，能夠看見這些陪審員全都在牠們的石板上寫下了："都是些蠢貨！"她甚至還能夠看出牠們之中的一個不知道怎麼寫"蠢"字，不得不請鄰座教教牠。"在審判完結之前，牠們的石板上一定會弄得亂七八糟！"愛麗絲心裏想。

其中一位陪審員的筆發出嘰嘰的聲音。愛麗絲當然受不了啦，她便在法庭裏繞着走過去，走到牠身後，馬上就找到一個機會把筆抽掉。她下手那麼迅速，那位可憐的小小陪審員（牠是蜥蝎壁兒）完全不清楚這是怎麼回事，因此，牠在到處找筆找了一陣之後，便不得不在這天餘下的時間裏用一隻手指頭寫字。可這一點用處都沒有，因為石板上甚麼印跡也沒留下。

"傳令官！宣讀罪狀！"國王下令。

大白兔一聽命令便拿起喇叭吹了三陣號聲，然後展開羊皮紙捲，宣讀如下：

> 紅心王后，她做了水果撻，
> 　正是在夏季裏的一天。
> 紅心傑克，他偷了水果撻，
> 　帶了那些撻逃跑！

"你們考慮怎麼判決？"國王問陪審團說。

"現在還不行，現在還不行！"大白兔急忙插嘴說。"在判決之前還有大量工作要做！"

"傳喚第一個證人，"國王說。大白兔便吹了三聲喇叭，然後大聲喊道："第一個證人！"

第一個證人是那位製帽匠。他一手拿着一杯茶，一手拿着一塊抹上牛油的麵包。"陛下，敬請原諒，"他開口說，"我把這些東西帶了來。不過，人家來傳喚我的時候，我還沒有全部用完茶點。"

"你應該早就用完了的，"國王說道。"你是甚麼時候開始的呢？"

製帽匠眼睛瞧着三月裏的野兔，牠是跟隨製帽匠，同榛睡鼠手臂挽着手臂，一起進來的。"我想那是三月十四號吧，"製帽匠説。

"十五號！"三月裏的野兔説道。

"十六號！"榛睡鼠説。

"把日期記下來，"國王對陪審團説，陪審員們便在各自的石板上急急地把這三個日期全都記下來，然後把三個數位加起來，再把答數換算成先令和便士。

"脱掉你的帽子！"國王對製帽匠説。

"這頂帽子不是我的，"製帽匠説。

"是偷來的！"國王高聲叫道，同時轉過頭來對着陪審員們，牠們立刻把這一事實記錄在案。

"我藏着帽子是賣的，"那個製帽匠接着作了解釋。"我自己一頂也沒有。我是一個製帽匠呀。"

這時，王后戴上她的眼鏡，開始目不轉睛地打量那個製帽匠，他變得面無血色，惶惶不安。

"説説你的證詞，"國王説，"不要緊張，否則我要把你就地正法。"

這句話看來一點也沒有起到鼓勵這個證人的作用，他不停地把身子的重心一會放在這隻腳上站站，一會又換另一隻腳站站，緊張地瞧着王后，慌亂中把他的茶杯咬掉一大塊，而不是去咬那塊抹上牛油的麵包。

就在此刻，愛麗絲忽然感到身上發生了一陣奇怪的變化，這使她很是迷惑不解，直到後來才弄明白這是怎麼搞的。原來她又在開始長大啦，於是她先是想自己還是立起身來，離開這個法庭為好；但是轉而一想，她決定留在原地，只要那裏容得下她就可以了。

"我希望你不要這樣擠過來，"榛睡鼠說，牠正緊挨在她的身邊坐着。"我簡直透不過氣來啦。"

"我毫無辦法，"愛麗絲非常溫順地說道。"我正在長大。"

"你可沒有權利在這裏長大，"榛睡鼠說道。

"不要胡說八道，"愛麗絲比較大膽地說。"你自己知道你也在長大呀。"

"不錯，然而我是以合情合理的速度長大的，"榛睡鼠說，"可不是你那種荒謬可笑的方式。"牠非常不高興地站起身來，走到法庭的另外一邊去。

在這整個時間裏，王后的眼睛一直沒有離開過那個製帽匠，而就在榛睡鼠穿過法庭走去的時候，王后對一個法庭官員說："把上一次音樂會裏的歌手名單給我拿上來！"那個可憐的製帽匠一聽到這句話，渾身顫抖得那麼厲害，以致把腳上的兩隻皮鞋都抖落了。

"說說你的證詞，"國王憤怒地重複說，"否則我就要你的命，不管你緊張不緊張。"

"陛下，我是一個可憐的人，"製帽匠開始說，聲音發抖，"那天我還沒有開始用茶 —— 頂多不超過一個星期左右 —— 一則因為那塊抹牛油的麵包弄得太薄了 —— 二則因為那個閃爍的茶 ——"

"閃爍的甚麼東西？"國王問道。

"那是從茶開始的，"製帽匠回答說。

"閃爍當然是從一個 T 開始的啦！"國王厲聲說道。"你是不是把我當作傻瓜蛋？説下去！"

"我是一個可憐的人，"製帽匠往下説道，"在那件事情以後，大多數的東西都閃爍 —— 只不過三月裏的野兔説過 —— "

"我沒有説過！"三月裏的野兔迫不及待地接口説。

"你説過！"製帽匠説道。

"我否認！"三月裏的野兔説。

"牠既然否認，"國王説道，"這一部分略去不記。"

"嗯，無論如何，那個榛睡鼠説過 —— "製帽匠繼續説，焦急地回過頭來望，看看牠是否也會否認。然而榛睡鼠甚麼都不否認，因為牠已經睡着了。

"在那件事情以後，"製帽匠接着説下去，"我又切下幾片抹牛油的麵包 —— "

"不過那個榛睡鼠説過些甚麼呢？"陪審團中的一員問道。

"這事情我可記不起來了，"製帽匠説道。

"你必須記起來！"國王指出，"否則我就要你的命。"

這個不幸的製帽匠手中的茶杯和抹牛油的麵包都掉了下來，他單腿下跪。"我是一個可憐的人，陛下，"他開始説道。

"你是一個非常可憐的笨口拙舌的人，"國王説道。

這時候，一些豚鼠中有一隻歡呼喝彩，立刻就被法院執達官們鎮壓了下去。(由於這個詞相當嚴重，我因而要對你們解釋解釋鎮壓如何實行。他們準備了一隻大帆布口袋，袋口用繩子紮起來。他們把那隻豚鼠頭朝下硬塞進去，然後坐在那上面。)

"我很高興自己親眼看見了這一幕，"愛麗絲心裏想。"我從報紙上讀到的可多啦，在審判結束的時候，'有些人企圖拍手叫好，立刻便招致法院執達官們的鎮壓'，而我卻從來也沒有搞清楚這是甚麼意思，到現在才懂啦。"

"如果關於此事你只知道這麼些，那你可以站下去了，"國王繼續說道。

"我無法站到更低的地方去呀，"製帽匠說。"按照實際情況來說，我已經站在地板上啦。"

"那麼，你可以坐下去了，"國王回答說。這時，另外一隻豚鼠喝起彩來，也被鎮壓了下去。

"哦，這一下豚鼠都完蛋啦！"愛麗絲心裏想。"這會我們的情況會好起來啦。"

"我寧願用完我的茶點，"製帽匠說，同時焦急不安地望着正在審閱歌唱者名單的王后。

"你可以走啦，"國王一說了這句話，製帽匠便來不及地離開了法庭，連稍等一下把鞋子穿上都沒有做。

"—— 就在外面砍掉他的腦袋，"王后接着對一個法庭執達官說；但是在執達官還沒有跑到門口的時候，製帽匠已經不見了蹤影。

"傳喚下一個證人！"國王命令說。

下一個證人是那位公爵夫人的廚師。她手裏拿着那隻胡椒瓶，靠近門外的一些人在她經過的時候都同時打起噴嚏來，所以在她甚至還沒有走進法庭時，愛麗絲便猜到此人是誰。

"說說你的證詞，"國王命令說。

"不可能，"那個廚師說。

國王焦急地望着那個大白兔，牠低聲說道："陛下必須盤問這個證人。"

"嗯,如果我必須做,我就一定做,"國王心情沉悶地説,他雙臂抱攏,雙眉緊鎖,雙眼眯得幾乎閉起來,直對着那個廚師,聲調低沉地説:"水果撻是用甚麼東西做成的?"

"胡椒,多半是胡椒,"那個廚師説。

"糖漿,"在廚師身後發出了一個睡意矇朧的聲音。

"揪出那隻榛睡鼠!"王后尖聲叫起來。"砍掉那隻榛睡鼠的頭!把那隻榛睡鼠押出法庭!鎮壓牠!掐牠!拔掉牠的鬍鬚!"

把那隻榛睡鼠押出去的時候,整個法庭有好幾分鐘一陣混亂,在他們重新安頓下來的時候,廚師已經無影無蹤了。

"別在意!"國王説,帶着一副大大鬆了一口氣的樣子。"傳喚下一個證人!"他接着壓低聲音對王后説道:"親愛的,説真的,必須由你來盤問下一個證人了。這事弄得我很頭痛!"

大白兔在名單上查找的時候,愛麗絲盯着牠瞧,感到非常好奇,想看看下一個證人會是甚麼樣子,"—— 因為他們到現在還沒有得到很多證據,"她自言自語。試想她是如何驚訝吧,那個大白兔用牠那細小尖鋭的嗓音喊到最高音,叫出來的名字是:"愛麗絲!"

第十二章

愛麗絲的證詞

"在！"愛麗絲大聲説道，在這個慌慌張張的片刻間，她完全忘記了在那最後的幾分鐘時間她已經長得多麼大了，因此，她那麼匆忙地一躍而起，以至於裙子的下襬把陪審團席帶倒了，把全體陪審員都打翻到下面旁邊群眾的頭上去了。牠們趴在那裏，到處都是，使她想起非常像自己在一星期前不小心打翻的那隻球形玻璃金魚缸。

"哦，對不起！"她用極為驚恐的聲調叫道，並且動手把牠們盡可能快地重新撿起來，因為那次金魚事件老是在她頭腦裏轉，使她產生一種模模糊糊的想法，覺得必須立刻把牠們收攏來，放回陪審團席，否則牠們就會死的。

"審判無法進行下去了，"國王用非常嚴肅的聲音說道，"除非所有的陪審員回到牠們應該在的位子上 —— 所有的！"他狠狠地加重語氣重複這幾個字，一面説，一面直愣愣地瞪視着愛麗絲。

愛麗絲看着陪審團席，看見自己竟然在忙亂中把那隻蜥蜴頭朝下倒放着，那隻可憐的小東西由於絲毫動不了，正在把尾巴甩來甩去，處境悲慘。愛麗絲立刻把牠重新提了出來，把牠擺正。"並非這樣做有多少重要性，"她自言自語。"我倒是覺得，不論牠哪一頭朝上，在審判裏面牠的作用都完全一樣。"

一等到陪審員們稍稍從翻倒的驚恐中恢復過來，石板和石筆都找到了，送回到牠們手裏以後，牠們就非常勤奮地開始工作，寫出這一偶然事件的歷史。牠們都在寫，只有那隻蜥蜴例外，牠似乎完全垮了下來，甚麼都做不了，只有張大嘴巴坐在那裏，張大眼睛呆望着法庭的屋頂。

"關於本案你知道些甚麼？"國王問愛麗絲。

"不知道，"愛麗絲說。

"不論甚麼都不知道嗎？"國王逼着問。

"不論甚麼都不知道，"愛麗絲說。

"這一點非常重要，"國王轉身對陪審團說道。就在陪審員們在石板上把這句寫下來的時候，大白兔卻插進來，"當然，陛下的意思是不重要，"牠用非常尊敬的口氣說，但是一面說，一面對國王擠眉弄眼做怪臉。

"當然，我的意思是不重要，"國王急忙說，然後又壓低着聲音自言自語地繼續說："重要 —— 不重要 —— 不重要 —— 重要 —— "彷彿是在掂量掂量哪一個詞好聽。

有幾位陪審員寫下："重要"，有幾位寫下："不重要"。愛麗絲看得見牠們寫的，因為她站在能看見牠們石板的近處。"可是這一點用處也沒有，"她心裏想。

國王已經在他的筆記簿上匆匆寫了一陣子，這時候，他大聲叫道："安靜！"於是照着他的筆記簿大聲唸起來："第四十二條法規。所有高於一英里的人都要離開法庭。”

一個個都朝愛麗絲望着。

“我沒有一英里高哇，”愛麗絲説。

“你有，”國王説。

“差不多兩英里高啦，”王后加一句。

“哼，不管怎麼樣，我就是不走，”愛麗絲説；“而且，那不是一種正規的法規，你剛剛才炮製出來的。”

“那可是書裏邊的最最古老的法規，”國王説。

“這樣説來，那應該是第一條啦，”愛麗絲説。

國王臉色變得蒼白，一下子合上筆記簿。“考慮你們的裁定，”他對着陪審團用一種低沉的、發抖的聲音説。

“啟稟陛下，還有證據尚待聽取，”大白兔急急忙忙跳起來説，“這張紙是剛剛撿到的。”

“上面寫些甚麼？”王后問道。

“我還沒有打開來，”大白兔説；“不過看上去像是一封信，一個囚犯寫給 —— 寫給甚麼人的。”

“必定如此，”國王説道，

“除非並不寫給甚麼人，你知道，一般可不這樣。”

“那是寫給誰的呢？”陪審團中的一位問道。

“完全沒有誰的姓名地址，”大白兔説。“事實上，外殼上甚麼也沒有寫。”牠邊説邊打開那張紙，然後又説：“這根本不是一封信。這是一組詩歌呢。”

“都是用囚犯的字體寫的嗎？”另一位陪審員問道。

“不，不是這樣，”大白兔説道，“關於此事，這一點是最最奇怪的事了。"（陪審員們全部露出迷惑不解的樣子。）

"他必定模仿了別的甚麼人的筆跡，"國王說道。（陪審員們全都重新精神煥發。）

"啟稟陛下，"傑克說，"不是我寫的，牠們無法證明我寫過，末尾沒有簽名。"

"假如你沒有簽過名的話，"國王說道，"這就只會把事情弄得更糟。你必定是故意要惡作劇，不然的話，你是會像個正人君子那樣簽上你的大名的。"

此話一出，響起了一片掌聲。這句話是這一天國王所說的真正聰明的話了。

"當然啦，此事證明了他的罪行，"王后說道，"因此，砍掉——"

"此事對這類事甚麼也證明不了！"愛麗絲說道。"怎麼啦，你們連那些詩歌講些甚麼都不知道呢！"

"唸出來，"國王說。

大白兔便戴上眼鏡。"啟稟陛下，從哪裏開始唸呢？"牠問道。

"從開始的地方開始，"國王非常嚴肅地說，"再一口氣唸到結束為止，然後停下來。"

法庭裏頓時鴉雀無聲，只聽見大白兔大聲唸出下面這些詩歌：

他們告訴我，你曾經去找她，
並且對他提起我這人。
她對我的評語很不差，
可是說我游泳卻不行。

他帶信給他們說我沒有走，
　　（此話是真我們都知道）
倘若她竟把事情細追究，
　　那麼你將如何辦是好？

我給了她一塊，他們給了他兩塊，
　　你給我們三塊或更多。
他們把給他的全給你還來，
　　雖然先前它們都屬於我。

倘若我或者她碰得不巧，
　　捲入這個事件裏頭，
他便委託你把他們都放掉，
　　就像我們過去一個樣。
過去我的看法是你一度
　　（她這次大發雷霆之前）
曾經是一個跑來的障礙物，
　　橫在他和我們和她之間。

不要讓他知道她最愛他們，
　　因為這情況永遠是秘密，
其他任何人都不得耳聞，
　　只有你和我二人知底細。

　　"這是迄今為止我們所聽到的最最重要的證詞，"國王搓着雙手說道。"所以現在讓陪審團——"

　　"假如牠們當中有任何一個能夠解釋這篇詩歌的話，"愛麗絲說道，（她在最近幾分鐘已經長得如此之大，以至於一點都不害怕打斷國王的話語了。）"我就給他六便士。我才不相信這裏邊有任何一點意思呢。"

陪審員們全部在石板上寫下來："她才不相信這裏邊有任何點意思呢"，但是牠們誰也不打算解釋這白紙黑字。

"假如這裏邊毫無意思，"國王說，"你知道，那麼就省掉許多許多的困難啦，因為如此我們便不必動腦筋找意思啦，"他繼續說着，同時把那篇詩歌在膝蓋上攤開來，用一隻眼睛瞄着。"我好像終於在這裏邊看出甚麼意思來啦。'—— 說我游泳卻不行——'你是不會游泳的，是嗎？"國王轉過頭衝着傑克加上這句話。

傑克傷心地搖搖頭。"我像會游泳的樣子嗎？"他問道。（他當然不像會游泳的樣子，他完完全全是薄紙板做的呀。）

"到目前為止，很好，"國王說道，接着他繼續嘟嘟噥噥地對自己唸着那些詩句："'此話是真我們都知道'—— 當然，這說的是陪審團——'倘若她竟把事情細追究'—— 這一定是說王后了——'那麼你將如何辦是好？'—— 甚麼話，的確不錯！——'我給了她一塊，他們給了他兩塊'—— 怎麼啦，你知道的，這一定是指他分配那些水果撻的事啊——"

"可是詩句接着說的是：'他們把給他的全給你還來'呀，"愛麗絲說道。

"可不是嘛，水果撻是在這裏呀！"國王指着桌上那些水果撻，洋洋得意地說。"再也沒有甚麼比這個更清楚的啦。再下面是——'她這次大發雷霆之前'—— 親愛的，我覺得，你從來也沒有過大發雷霆吧？"國王對王后說。

“從來也沒有哇！”王后説，她氣得不得了，一邊説一邊把一個墨水台對準那隻蜥蜴砸去。（那個不幸的小壁兒已經不再用一隻手指頭在地面前的石板上寫字，因為牠發覺手指頭寫不出字跡。不過牠現在急急忙忙地重新開始寫了，用的是墨水，這墨水滴滴答答地從牠的臉上滴下來，墨水滴多久，牠就寫多久。）

“那麼這些話並不適合你啦，”國王説，他微笑着環顧法庭一圈。法庭裏還是鴉雀無聲。

“這是一個雙關詼諧語！”國王用怒氣沖天的口吻接着説道，在場的每一位竟然都大笑起來。“叫陪審員們考慮作出他們的裁定，”國王説道，這大概是他今天説的第二十遍。

“不行，不行！”王后説。“先判決——後裁定。”

“多麼無聊的廢話！”愛麗絲大聲説道。“竟然想得出甚麼先判決！”

“閉上你的嘴！”王后喊道，她臉色發紫了。

“我不閉！”愛麗絲説。

“砍掉她的腦袋！”王后把嗓子提到最高點，大聲嚷道。可是沒有一個人移動腳步。

“誰把你們放在心上啊？”愛麗絲説道。（這時候，她已經長到她原來那般高了。）“你們甚麼也不是，不過是一副撲克牌罷了！”

此話一出，整副撲克牌便騰空而起，再紛紛飄落到她身上來。她發出短短一聲尖叫，半是驚恐，半是憤怒，同時試圖把那些撲克牌趕開，卻發現自己正睡在河岸邊，頭正枕在她的姐姐的腿上，她的姐姐正在把從樹上紛紛飄落的一些枯葉輕輕撣開。

"醒醒呀，親愛的愛麗絲！"她的姐姐説道。"哎呀，你睡了多麼長的時間啦！"

"哦，我做了一場多麼稀奇古怪的夢呀！"愛麗絲説。於是她盡自己記憶所及，把她那些奇妙的經歷全部都講給她的姐姐聽，那些經歷你剛才已經讀到了。等到她講完了，她的姐姐便吻了她，説道："親愛的，那確實是一場奇怪的夢。不過，現在該跑進屋裏去吃茶點啦，時候已經不早啦。"因此愛麗絲便站起身來跑開，一面跑，一面盡力想，剛才那場夢是多麼美妙的夢呀。

不過，愛麗絲離開以後，她的姐姐卻靜靜地坐在那裏，一隻手托着頭，凝望着西沉的太陽，想着小愛麗絲，以及她全部奇妙的經歷，直到她自己也開始恍恍惚惚地做起夢來，而她的夢是這樣的：

首先，她夢見了小愛麗絲本人，那雙小手又一次緊抱着一隻膝蓋，那雙明亮的渴望的眼睛正仰望着她的眼睛 —— 她能夠聽見完全是她的嗓音的聲調，也能夠看見她的頭那麼獨特地輕輕一甩，以便把那總老是會拂進她眼睛裏去的頭髮甩回去 —— 還有，在她傾聽着，或者似乎傾聽着的時候，她四周的地方整個都變得活躍起來：她的小妹妹的夢中的那些奇怪的生物都動起來了。

那隻大白兔在她身旁竄過去的時候，高高的野草在她的腳邊沙沙作響 —— 那隻心驚膽戰的老鼠正穿過附近的水池，一路濺起水花跑過去 —— 她能夠聽見三月裏的野兔跟牠的朋友們分享那頓永遠結束不了的茶點的時候，茶杯碰得咯嗒嗒嗒響，以及那個王后尖叫着勒令把她的不幸的客人們拖出去砍頭的聲音 —— 還有那隻豬娃在公爵夫人的膝蓋上再一次打噴嚏，同時那些盤子和碟子在牠周圍摔得粉碎——那個格里芬再一次發出的怪叫聲，那隻蜥蜴的石筆吱吱的響聲，以及那隻被鎮壓的豚鼠的哽咽聲，混雜着遠處那隻悲慘的假海龜的抽泣聲，一切都充塞在空中。

她閉着眼睛，仍然坐在那裏，差不多相信自己是身處在奇境中，雖然她明白自己只能不得不再睜開眼睛來，而一切都會變成乏味的現實——野草只會是在風中沙沙作響，搖曳的蘆葦使水池泛起陣陣漣漪——那些相碰的茶杯會變成叮鈴叮鈴的羊頸下的鈴鐺，那個王后的尖叫聲會變成牧童的呼喚——那個嬰兒的噴嚏，那個格里芬的怪叫，以及所有其他特別的吵吵鬧鬧的聲音，都會變成（她明白）那個忙碌的農場上的嘈雜的喧鬧聲——同時遠處牛群的哞哞聲會替代那隻假海龜的重濁的抽泣聲。

最後，她為自己描摹着一幅圖畫：她的這位小妹妹，在以後的歲月裏，自己會如何長成女人；在她整個成年時期裏，她會如何保持她這顆童年時代的單純的愛心；她又會如何把她的小孩子們聚攏在身邊，用許多奇妙的故事，也許甚至用好久以前的奇境中的夢來講給他們聽，使他們的眼睛發亮並着急；以及由於回憶起她自己的童年的生活，以及快樂的夏天的日子，她會如何同樣感受小孩子們所有的天真的憂愁，並且在他們所有的天真的快樂之中找到樂趣。

完

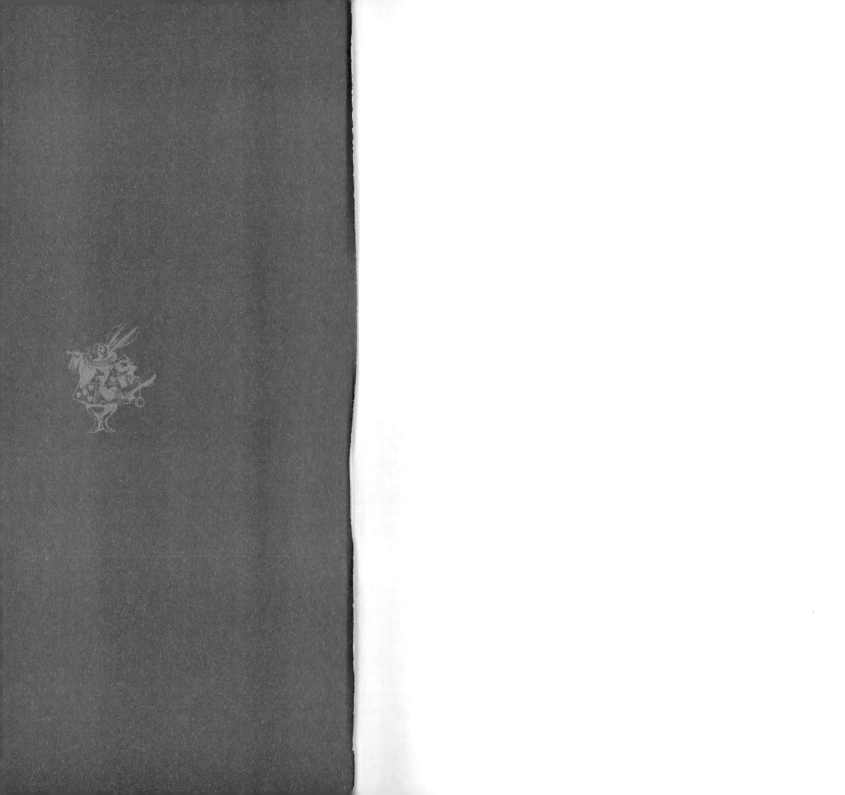